WETTER

WETTER

more true lesbian sex stories

EDITED BY
NICOLE FOSTER

alyson books
NEW YORK

Manufactured in the United States of America

Published by Alyson Books
245 West 17th Street, New York, NY 10011

Distribution in the United Kingdom
by Turnaround Publisher Services Ltd.
Unit 3, Olympia Trading Estate, Coburg Road, Wood Green
London N22 6TZ England

First Edition: May 2008

08 09 10 11 12 13 14 15 16 17 a 10 9 8 7 6 5 4 3 2 1

ISBN: 1-59350-053-X
ISBN-13: 978-1-59350-053-5

Library of Congress Cataloging-in-Publication data are on file.

Cover design by Victor Mingovits

Contents

Introduction

When I first proposed to the good folks at Alyson a sequel to *Wet,* they were greatly enthusiastic. After all, *Wet* is the book I hear about most often from my readers, and so it was inevitable that I should dream (or is that wet dream?) up a sequel. The question was what to call it. After all, *Wet 2* just didn't have the same sexy allure. We could have gone with a clever title like *2 Wet.* But in the end, *Wetter* was the ideal choice.

In the introduction to *Wet,* I stated that the book was called that for many reasons. Back then I wanted "something bold, something in-your-face." I wanted to "celebrate women's sensuality, their ability to get just as horny as the next guy." Sure, I'm repeating myself here, but that just makes *Wetter* all the better.

'Cause you know what? I think this collection *is* better. The sex is sexier, the women are hotter, their couplings . . . steamier. All of which (whether by the end of a particular story or by the end of this amazing collection) will leave you . . . wetter.

Enjoy, girls. And enjoy our girls. Who knows, perhaps we'll all regroup in a couple of years and explore just who among us got the wettest.

—Nicole Foster

Bloom

Yeva Wiest

The perfect whirl of the rose drew me into its dew-kissed sweetness. Its dusky red folds caressed one another tightly. The center of the rose lifted slightly—its inner fold peeling away to expose the firm red bud. I lifted the rose against my cheek and then pulled it lightly across my face to rest against my lips. Carefully, gently, I bit its outer fold. Hot, sweet, the aroma excited me and made me clinch inside. I named the rose Pamela.

Outside my kitchen window, roses grow in thick profusion. I could have my choice of flowers, but Pamela was a special bloom. She had perched long stemmed and eager above the rest. I wanted her. I picked her. I sheared her from the bush of other roses. With my store-sharpened scissors, I sliced her away from the rest. She was mine.

As recompense for my deed, I kissed her deeply, fully invading the soft whorls of her bud. My warm breath caused her to open—to blossom. I could feel her release.

Laughing at the torrid turn of my nonsensical thoughts, I quickly filled a vase with water, and plunged the rose into its tight mouth. Displaced water droplets splashed against my fingers, and I licked the cool moisture from them. Faintly, I could taste Pamela's sweetness. I left for work, running outside to catch my bus before I missed it and had to catch another.

From my window on the bus, I could see Pamela's silhouette shadowed against the stark whiteness of my kitchen cabinets. With a sigh, I leaned back and closed my eyes. The inside of my thighs were slightly damp. I knew why. Pamela had seduced me. The softness of her petals, the odor emanating from her center, the sharp prick of her thorns enticed me as no one had for such a long time. I smiled slightly and sighed again.

"Why the long sigh?" asked the woman from the seat in front of me.

"Excuse me?"

She turned around to face me. Her bright, cheery eyes greeted mine. A soft blush touched her cheeks. "I asked, why the long sigh?" She pointed out the window. "It's a glorious day."

I nodded. "Yes," I said. "Yes, it is. Thanks for reminding me."

"I don't mean to be presumptuous," she said, "but is that your cottage with all of the lovely roses?"

A smile, beaming, spontaneous, broke through me. "Yes. I love my roses."

"I can tell. Your eyes are shining." She smiled. "Would you introduce me to them sometime?"

Introduce. She understood. My roses were my people, my friends. Not many people understood my passion for roses. Sometimes, even I wondered at my lust for their gentle, rampant beauty.

Before I thought, I blurted out, "How about now? Today? I know this sounds crazy," I rushed on, "but I have one rose in particular that I would love for you to see. Her bloom is excellent this morning. I'm afraid that by this afternoon you'll miss the tight loveliness of her center."

Without a word, she gathered up her bag and reached for my hand. I looked questioningly at her.

"The bus has stopped. If we hurry, we can depart here," she said.

"Oh, right," I laughed.

Still holding hands, we ran the three blocks to my tiny house. Outside, she stopped to admire the proliferation of rose varieties edging the perimeters of my garden. Other flowers and ferns competed for space, but my roses were fragrant hussies who flaunted themselves into every available niche.

"They're beautiful," she breathed, and something in the way she spoke caused the tightness around the bud of my heart to unfurl.

I looked at her. She was small and roundly soft—like a rose just bloomed. Her skin was plump, yet tight. Ripe. She bent her head and reverently bowed to kiss an Alba. Its soft pink blossom was open to the sun. Inviting her with its burgeoning anther, the Alba lured her even closer.

"A true Belle Amour," she said.

"Yes," I said. I was breathless in the presence of such an exquisite rose aficionado.

"Would you like to come inside?" I asked. "I want you to see Pamela; she's from the Romanticas, a perfect hybrid tea rose. She's mine. I dreamed of her, and then I developed her."

Hand in hand, we ascended the rough-hewn steps into my cottage. My rose, my Pamela, was standing tall and proud in her vase. Even in such a short time, she had opened a bit more to the seductive warmth of the sun. We stood on either side of her.

"I would like for you to meet Pamela," I said.

She brought her hands together as though in prayer, bowed slightly, and said, "It is my pleasure, Pamela. I am Lilia. Lilia Rose."

Her voice was deep. Husky. Our eyes met.

"Hello, Lilia," I said and reached for her hand. I brought it up to my mouth to offer a kiss of introduction. It smelled of roses. I kissed the back of her hand, and then turned it over to kiss the palm. I buried my face in the palm of her hand as I had buried my face into the midst of Pamela.

Lilia pulled me close. She kissed me. Her fingers explored my face, my hair, the swirl of my ear. I kissed her back, tasting her, teasing her tongue with mine. I reached for Pamela, pulling her from her wet sanctuary into the sudden flowering of our passion. I teased Lilia with the bloom. I traced the soft petals against her throat, drawing them against the line of her chin.

I placed the bud between our lips and kissed her around it. We could taste the rose as well as each other. I led her down the hall to the back of my cottage. A small porch opens into the rear garden. It is surrounded by dense hedges of wild old roses of every color imaginable. Some of the blossoms are huge, seeming to burst from the dark green foliage. I have a long wicker chaise covered in cushions. It is like an old and comfortable friend. It welcomed us into its gnarled arms.

Lilia lay back on the lounger, savoring the floral fantasy around her. I stroked her face with the rose, and then with my fingers. Ever so lightly I began to kiss her again, teasing, sweet kisses that caused her lips to cling to mine. I opened the buttons, one by one, of her silky scarlet blouse. Its lace clung to my fingertips. Just like a rose unfurled, the dark blush uncovered her, revealing her perfect nakedness beneath.

She succumbed to my touch. I straddled her so that I could see all of her. Her breasts were full. Her nipples, bursting with wantonness, begged to be tasted. I complied. Rolling their tender tips with my tongue, nipping them with my teeth, and finally sucking them, taking turns between them. Trying to be fair, my fingers coached one perky peak, while my mouth devoured the other.

"Let me undress you," she said.

"Just my shirt," I said, and allowed her to slip the soft heather T-shirt over my head. My breasts, free from their confine, swelled to greet her. Gently, at first, and then roughly, I rubbed my breasts against hers. Our nipples bumped and slid against each other. Deep inside, desire grew. As my chest collided with hers, the urgency inside me escalated. Higher and higher it bubbled up inside me. My clit grew hard. I could feel an answering urgency in Lilia.

She pushed my skirt up and brushed the inside of my thigh. I continued to straddle her, but now I moved back and forth against her feeling the material of my skirt rub against the solid bud of my clitoris. It pulsed and grew firmer.

Reluctantly, I made myself slow down. Again, I used the rose to arouse her. With it, I outlined her nipples and the gentle curve of her breasts. I found the hollow of her navel. I slid down her body to rest between her legs, and my rose followed. Winding a path across her stomach and down the length of her right leg, the rose continued its wanton caress. Finally, I spread her legs apart and revealed her wet and waiting pussy. Her vulva reminded me of my rose. Its delicate whorls were exquisitely formed like a breathtakingly beautiful flower—a rose. The soft brown of bush contained a single ripe bud, dark and dusky pink. A perfect bloom.

Gently, I flicked the rose against her clit. She groaned and moved against it. Her vagina opened in the warmth of her desire.

She squirmed when I circled her clit with the rose. Carefully, I pulled back its hood and assaulted it with the flower. Her pussy grew wet. Hot slick with fluid, she opened to the flower—to Pamela.

Pamela plunged into the depths of Lilia. Loving her, taking her, fucking her, Pamela made Lilia burst forth in ecstatic cries that prompted me to taste the sweet coming of their coupling. As Pamela continued to ravish Lilia, I began to lick Lilia. My tongue found every whorl, every hiding place. I licked the inside of her thighs. My tongue played havoc with the fleshy folds of her labia. She arched against us. I sucked her clit into my mouth matching my rhythm with Pamela's.

A stinging burst of pain brought delicious tears to my eyes. A thorn pierced my index finger. I brought the finger to my lips, tasting my blood, tasting the rose. The surprise of pain in the midst of such intense pleasure caused my pussy to begin to swell with the anticipation of release. First, however, I had a task to complete. No, a favor to bestow.

Lilia moved harder and harder against Pamela's thrusts. The resilience of the rose amazed me. I watched as Pamela went in and out of Lilia's pussy. It made me so incredibly hot.

"Watch," I whispered to Lilia.

She leaned up and saw Pamela coming out from between the tight lips of her pussy. Her eyes grew brighter. The lips of her vagina closed tight around Pamela, and she came. Over and over the waves of her climax washed over the petals of the flower, and then she was spent.

I could feel my own desire growing. Lilia rolled over to face me. She kissed me, and then she started to giggle.

"What?" I asked.

"Mmm. You taste like roses and pussy," she said. She licked her lips and smiled. "That's a delectable combination."

She pushed her fingers under the edge of my skirt. I started to take it off, but she stopped me.

"I want to put my hand under it," she said. "I want to feel the depths of you like you explore the depths of a rose."

As she kissed me again, she moved her hand up my thigh. Tantalizing me with her touch. Causing me to grow wetter with each stroke on my legs. Finally, she reached into me. Her finger-tips found my center, drenched in the dew of my desire. She played back and forth.

"Please," I begged. "Please, take me. Please, fuck me."

She began to move her fingers in and out of me. Faster and faster they flew. She pushed me back against the cushions. She shoved my legs up close to me revealing my naked pussy beneath my skirt.

She continued to push her fingers inside of me, deeper and harder they went. I could feel the warmth of the sun against my breasts. Her body moved against mine. Her nipples rubbed mine as her hand went back and forth inside me. As my vagina opened, I felt her move her hand into a fist.

"Wait!" I cried. I had never been fisted. But she stilled my protests. She moved the rose, Pamela, against my lips, and I was quiet. I could smell the heady combination of Pamela and Lilia. It caused me to open up even more. Lilia took advantage of my response, and moved her fist inside me. Never had I felt such an intense connection. Never had I felt so vulnerable, and at the same time powerfully desirable.

I felt everything within me give way to passion. I felt every-thing within me—bloom.

The Color of Her Touch

Rane Ketcher

Riding down the country road, Lisa is enjoying the beautiful autumn scenes from her motorcycle. Suddenly, she hears a loud clanking noise and immediately pulls off to the side of the road. She shuts the bike off, prodding the kickstand down with the toe of her boot. Kneeling down by the side of the bike, she realizes that the problem is the linkage. In one place it is snapped clean in half. She swears under her breath since she's in the middle of nowhere and about 250 miles away from home. With no cell phone, she prays someone will come along shortly. Just as she reaches into one of her saddlebags for a bottle of water, she hears the crunch of gravel and sees a car pulling up close to her.

Sylvia sits in her car for a moment, thinking that this is crazy; she never pulls over for anyone, and one can't trust a stranger. But she also knows that this road is not well traveled, and steps out of the car. Lisa stands up, takes off her helmet, and a tangled mass of black curls cascades down past her shoulders as Sylvia approaches her. Sylvia is momentarily stunned, thinking that this woman is beautiful.

"Hi there. Can I be of help?" Sylvia asks timidly.

"No, part's broken. The bike won't run without it."

"Well, I live nearby. I wouldn't mind giving you a lift. You can use the phone to call the town garage." Sylvia thinks to herself that she's crazy. She doesn't talk to strangers, much less give them a ride and let them into her home! Shaking her head, she waits for Lisa to respond.

"Gosh, I would really appreciate that. Thanks." Lisa pulls out a tote bag from one of the saddlebags and loads it up with clothes, her day planner, a small box, some toiletries, and then checks inside her jacket making sure her wallet is in the inside pocket, along with the bike keys. Satisfied, she walks over to Sylvia's car and lets herself in. "This really means a lot to me, um—"

"Sylvia. My name's Sylvia." She offers her hand and Lisa takes it, saying, "My name's Lisa." Sylvia mentions that she is on her way to her weekend home, so it's lucky that she happened to be coming at the right time. She was actually running a little late; she's a college professor and ran into overtime working with some students at the school gallery. Lisa nods, impressed. She glances over and thinks that Sylvia is really sophisticated, smart, and seems a little aloof the more she talks.

"Well, I'm pretty far away from home. I was on my way to a relative's house to deliver a couple of things. I think I only had another two hours to go. Figures." Lisa chuckles and Sylvia smiles. After a few minutes of driving, Sylvia turns the car onto a side road surrounded by trees, and drives up to a little clearing in the middle of the forest. She parks in front of a cottage seemingly made entirely of glass and stone. It is quaint and charming. Sylvia, smiling serenely, grabs two bags of groceries and gets out of the car. She leads Lisa into the house and shows her to a side table that has a phone book and a phone. Lisa is already on the phone while Sylvia goes into the kitchen and begins putting away some of the food.

"But you're there now, why can't I—? Oh. OK, well . . . all right. I'll be there Monday morning. Can you at least pick up the bike? I don't want it sitting by the side of the road all weekend. You can? Oh that would be great. I'll pay you for the towing when I see you Monday. OK. Yes, all right. Thank you." Lisa hangs up and looks around for Sylvia. Hearing noises coming from the kitchen, she finds her way and sees Sylvia shelving groceries.

"Sylvia, I appreciate the use of the phone. Unfortunately, the garage says they don't typically carry motorcycle parts and won't be able to get what I need until Monday. I was wondering if I could take up some more of your time and get a ride into town? I can stay at a motel for the weekend." Lisa asks this shyly, feeling guilty for asking this generous woman to do more for her, a complete stranger.

"Oh yes, not a problem. But would you like to stay and join

me for dinner? I've already started it. I think I would enjoy your company. I'll take you out afterwards."

"Really? That is so nice of you. I would love to, but only if you let me help." Sylvia laughs and they fix up an elaborate salad with grilled chicken on top. Then they set to work on making a home-made dressing. They begin eating, talking over red wine. They easily start a conversation about the house, the studio, what Sylvia teaches specifically, her artwork, and beautiful statues seen around the house. Then they talk about Lisa, how she manages a music shop, and teaches music lessons for virtually every modern musical instrument. They talk about where Lisa was going, and about what Sylvia was planning to paint this weekend.

Lisa asks where the bathroom is and while in there, Sylvia clears off the table, bringing everything into the kitchen. When Lisa comes back, Sylvia tells her the time. "Oh my," Lisa responds, with a surprised look on her face. Then concern furrows her brow. "I would hate to have you drive me into town so late. I could call a cab." Sylvia blurts out a loud laugh, covers her mouth at first, and then says that one doesn't get taxi service around here.

"No. The only taxi service around here is the generosity of some distant neighbors who happen upon the road you were on and are willing to pick up a hitchhiker. Listen, I have a nice guest room. It's hardly ever used, but you are welcome to stay tonight. I can take you into town in the morning. How about that?" Sylvia is amazed at herself that she'd let a stranger into her private sanctuary, much less have dinner with one and allow her to spend the night. *But there's something about Lisa,* she thinks, and then trails off.

Once shown the guest room, Lisa leaves her tote bag in there and comes back out into the living room where Sylvia is sitting on the sofa, drinking wine, feet up on the coffee table. For a second, Lisa hangs back and looks at Sylvia from behind. *So elegant, so classically beautiful,* Lisa thinks. Then she joins Sylvia on the sofa, where they ease into conversation once again, and talk until the wee hours of the morning.

Finally, they laugh, realizing how very tired they are. Sylvia gives Lisa a complete tour of the house, then bids Lisa good night and goes to take a shower in the master bathroom. She reaches into the open shower and turns on the water. Slipping out of her clothes, she steps in, and cool water sprays her back. She tilts her head back and allows the water to run through her hair. Sylvia turns around, adjusting the faucet to make the water a little warmer, then places her hands on the wall, above the faucets, her palms pressed flat against the wall. Only then does she allow herself to think of Lisa, her gorgeous hair and eyes, her fun personality, her beautiful lips, her body. Tilting her head back, she closes her eyes and concentrates on the water flowing from her chin, down her long, beautiful neck, slightly pooling where her collarbones stretch to meet. Shocking herself, she imagines Lisa's tongue being the water running down her neck.

Lisa, meanwhile, walks to Sylvia's bedroom in search of a towel, and knocks. Hearing nothing, she walks toward the bathroom. The door is open a crack and she peeks in, seeing Sylvia in the shower. She stands there quietly and watches as the water runs over Sylvia's body, unaware that Sylvia is fantasizing about her.

Feeling the water slipping between her breasts and teasing her nipples, Sylvia continues to imagine Lisa's mouth tracing the very course the water is taking. Her nipples hardening, thinking of Lisa's mouth on them, nibbling gently, Sylvia turns the faucet so the water is hot. She focuses on the water reaching the patch of hair between her legs and then, as she parts her legs slightly, she feels hot water dip into her already moist sexual folds. Oh how she wants Lisa's mouth cupping her, Lisa's tongue bringing her to orgasm.

Lisa goes back to her room before the water is shut off, for fear of Sylvia catching her. She lies in bed, thinking for a while. Sylvia is so sophisticated, but charming and, well, stunningly beautiful. Normally she wouldn't like someone like that, but all of a sudden, a very clear thought comes to mind: *I want this woman!* She closes her eyes and replays Sylvia's shower scene in her mind, and begins touching herself, needing that release, while imagining showering with Sylvia. *God she's beautiful!* Lisa thinks as she suppresses moans . . .

Lisa wakes up to the smell of coffee. She tumbles out of bed, and puts her hair up in a loose bun. She goes to the kitchen. Sylvia looks up and says cheerfully, "How about some breakfast before I take you into town?"

"You're so wonderful and I could easily feel spoiled. You'll make me not want to go into town!"

Before biting her tongue, Sylvia is already saying, "Then don't. It'll be fun. What do you say?"

"How generous you are. But yes, it indeed would be fun!" Lisa smiles warmly, surprised at this amazing woman.

So they talk over breakfast when Lisa startles Sylvia by asking about her personal life, the only subject not yet covered by either woman. Sylvia stammers but chooses her words carefully. "I haven't been with anyone for almost fifteen years, if you can believe that. I've been engrossed in my teaching, and helping with the campus gallery, and being out here painting." Lisa's eyes widen, mouth slightly agape. *Fifteen years?* she thinks to herself. "And what about you?" Sylvia asks.

Lisa looks down and then says, "It's been about six years since I've been in a serious relationship."

An awkward silence ensues and then Sylvia asks Lisa if she wants to go into town just to shop or look around. Lisa answers, "But you're here. Don't you need to paint?"

Sylvia responds, "Well, it's not like I have deadlines." They laugh, glad the awkward moment dissipates.

"Well, um . . . I would rather not go into town today, if you don't mind. Your place is so wonderful and warm and, well, I'm tired from staying up all night." Lisa adds, "Though I wouldn't dream of regretting it." Sylvia laughs and replies that she doesn't either.

"Of course you can stay here." She puts her hand on Lisa's knee. Then, as if her hand is on fire, she yanks it back. Lisa isn't oblivious to this reaction and smiles gently.

"So what would you like to do?"

"Well, actually, I'd love to watch you paint."

"Ah, well, um . . . that's interesting," Sylvia stammers. "I've never had anyone watch me. But I enjoy your company, so I'll certainly try."

"Great!" Lisa grins. They go into a glass-enclosed studio where everything is already set up. Lisa sits behind Sylvia as Sylvia puts on a smock. She flicks on her CD player, Rachmaninoff emanating into the room, lifts a brush, and puts it to canvas, painting a background wash in shades of white.

Overwhelmed by Sylvia's elegant looks, the music, the beauty of the woods outside, and the brush strokes, Lisa raises herself slowly out of her seat and walks to Sylvia. Before Sylvia can react, Lisa pulls Sylvia's hair off the back of her neck and kisses her, behind her ear, softly. Sylvia gasps and swiftly turns around, her eyes wide, seemingly with fear. Lisa jumps back at the stare and stammers, muttering apologies.

"I—I—don't be sorry." Sylvia stops, suddenly not knowing what to say, still holding the paintbrush. Lisa reaches up and touches her hair. The bun unravels and her hair once again flows down her back. She looks at Sylvia with beautiful blue eyes, now wet with brimming tears. Sylvia drops her brush onto the drop cloth and rushes to Lisa. Putting her hands on either side of Lisa's face, she bends and kisses Lisa's mouth. Lisa's arms wrap around Sylvia and she kisses back. They stand there kissing for long minutes, every kiss growing deeper, so much pent-up loneliness and sedate sexuality giving way to explosive passion and hunger for touch. Their hands explore and caress curves. Never taking her mouth away from Sylvia's, Lisa lets go long enough to shrug off her oversized shirt, leaving her tank top on. Sylvia feels light-headed and Lisa gasps for breath, not wanting to stop kissing.

They make their way over to the window seat and sit down, facing each other, not able to stop touching, caressing, hugging each other tightly, kissing with searching tongues, tasting each other. Sylvia takes off her smock. Underneath is a simple V-neck shirt, the beginning swell of her breasts and cleavage showing through the V-neck. Lisa feels a series of tingles in her stomach and her groin, and she touches the swell. Then she bends down and runs her tongue up Sylvia's cleavage. Sylvia tilts her head back, a single gasp escaping her lips. She closes her eyes and tears roll out of the corners. Lisa looks up and sees the tears. A concerned look on Lisa's face, Sylvia opens her eyes and murmurs that she is just overwhelmed with long-suppressed desires, she can't contain it. It's almost too powerful. This last part she doesn't say aloud.

An idea comes to Lisa. She gets up, picks up the dropped brush, and hands it to Sylvia.

"What?" Sylvia asks, confused.

"You have many deep emotions, feelings, and desires built up inside you. Like music, I'm betting this is the right time to express them through art."

"I don't think I could, not now."

"Worth a try, don't you think?"

They get up, and Sylvia places the brush back on the cart, temporarily. Standing face to face, their eyes locked, Lisa begins undressing Sylvia, pulling her shirt over her head, then unbuttoning her slacks, the pants slipping to the floor around Sylvia's feet. Lisa takes her eyes away from Sylvia's gaze and takes in the gorgeous sight that is Sylvia's body. She unclasps Sylvia's bra and pulls down her panties. Lisa stands back up and feels lightheaded herself with so much hunger for Sylvia. Sylvia's eyes are closed. Self-conscious of her body, she starts trembling slightly, her arms folded over her breasts. Lisa quickly pulls off her tank top and jeans, unhooks her bra, and kicks off her panties. Then, tenderly, she unfolds Sylvia's arms and turns her to face the easel, encouraging her to start painting. Still trembling, Sylvia takes the brush, dips it into some purple paint, and starts painting the edges of the canvas.

Lisa stands behind her and presses her body against Sylvia, her breasts against Sylvia's back, her face against her neck, kissing her shoulders, her arms reaching around her and her hands caressing Sylvia's breasts. "Paint whatever you're feeling," she whispers to her. Painting the edges of the canvas in purple, the purple being a warm color, representing Sylvia's tingling feelings, slowly opening up, her body relaxing, muscles loosening from self-conscious tightness. As Lisa continues caressing Sylvia's breasts, squeezing to show want, the purple becomes deeper, spreading to the corners while Lisa strokes Sylvia's nipples, gently squeezing them, one by one. She puts one arm around Sylvia, holding her up, as Sylvia's knees start to buckle.

As Lisa starts stroking Sylvia's stomach, going lower and

lower, Sylvia dips the brush into crimson and starts bringing the deep purples into a rich red as she slowly paints toward the center of the canvas, her breathing quickening. Sylvia feels fluid movements coursing through her entire body. She's even conscious of the pulsing feeling in her lips from kissing. Lisa reaches the area between Sylvia's legs and Sylvia's knees suddenly give way. Lisa tightens her grip. Kissing down Sylvia's neck, her other hand slips between her sexual lips and gently runs a finger from the clit down to a very warm and wet opening. Sylvia closes her eyes, feeling Lisa's breasts pressed hard against her back and the wonderful and exciting feeling between her legs.

Lisa whispers to please keep painting. Almost faint, Sylvia, feeling like molten lava is flowing through her, chooses a fiery red-orange and outlines the inner edges of the rich reds. Then, suddenly, Lisa's fingers are dipping inside and sinking into an incredible wetness; she brings one of her fingers up to Sylvia's clit. Sylvia grabs onto one side of the easel to brace herself while Lisa's arm stays tight around her. Lisa's lips are pressed against her neck, her tongue searching, tasting her skin, her finger circling Sylvia's clit, first slowly, then building up speed. Sylvia feels throbbing rocking her groin and, just as she splashes a bright white in the center of the canvas, she explodes, orgasmic, screaming.

After a few minutes trying to catch her breath, already sunk to the floor, lying on Lisa in a tight hug, tears flowing, Sylvia glances at the painting. It has chosen its name: "The Color of Her Touch."

Big Rigs Truck Stop

Rakelle Valencia

The rig was a fairly new Freightliner. I'd say it was made within the last few years because of the swooping lines, opposed to the blockier look. It was also bright purple, not a color splashed on eighteen-wheeler cabs five or ten years ago. The beast pulled up a few spots over to my right and slowly let the air brakes leak off; politely, I should say. The driver had probably noticed the horses inside my stock trailer and hadn't wanted to spook them.

My horses wouldn't have even batted an eyelash with a full set of air brakes releasing all at once. They were veterans of the road, with only one two-year-old colt mixed amongst them. I had been sitting on the flatbed of my mid-sized commercial hauler drinking a coffee while allowing my animals some rest, food, and water. Now I stared at the tinted windows of that purple cab and nodded my gratitude, figuring the driver could see me even though I could not see them.

She opened the door. Yes, *she* opened the door, fiddled with a bag and perhaps a wallet before clambering down from the heights.

"Thanks," I said, and raised my Styrofoam cup in salute to her. "You didn't need to."

"Ya'll never know," she replied in a distinctly backwoods, southern drawl. "Where ya headed?"

"Down the road a piece. Next rodeo." I really didn't think she wanted my exact itinerary and flight plan.

"Down the road a piece? Funny, me too. Does this piece have a name?"

"Maryland," I replied.

She flicked her dimpled chin in the direction of the truck stop station and asked, "This stop have a shower?"

"Yup. Lock's broke. So you have to jimmy the handle with a pocket knife or a nail file or something to hold it, then throw your bag against the door just in case. It's pretty safe if someone knows it's occupied. And there's no timer, just a flat fee." I swirled my coffee around inside its container as she stared at me. "You take the bad with the good," I said, breaking her stare.

"You showered already, I'm guessing." She leaned against the side of my flatbed, propping her bag there, and looked up at me once again, smiling. But I didn't think it was the smile of pure innocence. More like, it was a mischievous grin.

"Not this time. I know about the lock problem because I've been here before. Big Rigs is a chain. They're all about the same." And I knew what she was up to. It was what many truckers got up to before catching some shut-eye per regulations. Long-haul truckers have to log so much down time, but it doesn't necessarily mean they're sleeping the entire mandatory rest period.

Most rigs these days, costing as much or more than a house mortgage, have the full amenities inside: TV, microwave, small toilet, queen-sized bed, computer hook-ups with Internet access, and refrigerator; the whole works. Well, except for that shower, which she was headed to get.

"You wouldn't mind helping a girl who's all alone fend off those men that are bound to be eating slop in the diner?"

I took a serious look at her this time. I looked her up and down with an eye akin to a hungry wolf. She was heavy boned but not heavy. Her V-neck T-shirt was advertising Harley Davidsons and the top of her cleavage. She was well endowed, but still young enough to have some firmness, not hang in doughy globs.

Tipping my straw Stetson and placing my coffee on one of the trunks littering the flatbed, I said, "Always willing to help out a lady."

"Good. Then ya'll won't mind scrubbing my back." She winked. "Unless of course yer not wantin' to get wet."

I didn't know what she had immediately surmised of a tall, skinny drink like me but I wasn't stopping to ask. In a way, my sitting on that flatbed alone, sipping a hot coffee, was some sort of sign of availability—or desperateness. But I hadn't felt desperate. And this time, I truly hadn't meant to set up any signals.

With a shrug, I jumped down to land loudly on the tarmac with my booted feet. "Right this way ma'am."

"I'll pay and get the key," she said. "Be right out."

So, she knew all about this Big Rigs too. Which didn't matter much because the lock still wasn't going to work right, and I still wasn't opposed to getting wet.

I met her at the shower room door. Shoving it open, she sauntered past me with her bag in tow. The space was well lit and clean. Not like some of those greasy-spoon stops that have been around since trucking was invented. This one had a private toilet stall as well as a urinal on the wall, and a sink. Behind door number two, so to say, was a spacious shower that looked like it had been built for more than one, until the real reason—truckers— came to mind. Then it made sense. Most of them seem to be mighty big, beefy boys. But not all.

I jammed my penknife in the lock so it would hold, to leave the two of us uninterrupted. As I turned around, she was right there. She lowered her bag to the floor while keeping eye contact. "Ya'll did say to put my bag against the door."

I attempted to gulp saliva down a suddenly dry throat. She was a bit faster at the game than most. Hell, I hadn't even gotten her name, and didn't think formal introductions were on the agenda. The woman stepped up on her tippy-toes and kissed me gently, her breasts teasing against my own small, pert pair.

Before I could grab hold of anything fleshy, she spun around and whipped off her T-shirt, looking back over her shoulder suggestively down to her bra closure.

That I could do. I do so like to help. Cut loose, the two ends flew like a slingshot. I almost impulsively went to grab them at the front of her, momentarily thinking that those loose ends flying might hurt like getting snapped with a rubber band. I should have held onto the ends to let them slide oh, so carefully free, but man, I lack the couth or proper etiquette that I should have acquired as a birthright in being a girl.

With her back still to me, she dropped the satin underwire bra onto her discarded T-shirt, stepped out of her flip-flops onto her shirt while undoing her jeans, and bent over to pull them off, leaving a thong to peek out of her ass crack at me. Flip-flops back on, she went into the shower stall to start the water and adjust the temperature. "Mmm . . . it's gonna be hot," she said as steam rose above the dividing door.

She had me bewildered enough that I still hadn't even moved from my position guarding the door. Her thong sailed over the top of the shower divider to land at my feet. I picked it up, still warm, resisting the urge to sniff it, and placed it upon her pile of clothes.

As I stood up, she came through the shower stall door all soaking wet and waltzed over to me, once again standing shockingly close. On tiptoes, she whispered in my ear, "Let's get you out of those wet clothes." Then she dribbled a sodden finger down the front of my work shirt.

A trail of wetness ran the length of my pearly snaps. She stepped a foot back, took hold on either side of those snaps, and ripped them open, exposing only a serious, somewhat white, short-sleeved Hanes T-shirt.

"Now this just won't do." The woman grabbed at the worn collar and shredded the undershirt from my torso. "Mmm, better." She thrust her hot tongue out to sting each nipple. "I'll be waiting in the shower. I think you said you'd scrub my back."

Which I hadn't; she had. Regardless, I wrestled with the trophy buckle on my belt and ripped down the gritty zipper of my Wranglers while hopping first on one foot then the other to shuck my boots, jeans, boxer briefs, and Stetson.

My bare feet slapped across the ceramic-tiled floor where her flip-flops had left a watery path. As my hand hit the door and pushed it open, I had barely a glimpse of the water sluicing down her spine into the crack of her ass before she turned her head.

"Ya'll mind grabbing the soap out of my bag on your way in, sugar? Just help yourself to anything else ya'll think you might need in here."

I trucked back to the outer door, rummaged through the bag at my feet, and laughed as I pulled out a soap-on-a-rope she had kept in a Ziplock bag. The rest of the contents offered a promise of some pretty interesting sex play but I didn't have much time before I needed to check the horses again. I grabbed a sparkling pink waterproof vibrator and, with the soap swinging along beside me, pushed the door open.

She was facing me this time. Her head was tilted back, eyes closed, as she rinsed shampoo out of her shoulder-length, wavy brunette hair. I stepped in, placing the vibrator on the shelf behind her, and leaned to close my teeth on her exposed neck, grabbing just at the joint of her shoulder. She tensed. Her back arched at the pressure. I wrapped my rangy arm behind her and started soaping her back with long strokes of the bar, caressing and slicking from shoulders to the crease of ass and thighs, and into the cracks between. I released my teeth and turned to kiss her, running my tongue over her lips and into her mouth.

She parried, sucking and nipping my lower lip. I let the weight of the soap slip the rope through my thin fingers until it hit the end. My calloused hand eased down her curvaceous body, feeling the swing of the soap through the hemp in my fingers. I teased the rope between her butt cheeks in time with our probing mouths, swinging that soap just hard enough that it nudged her clit at the top of each arc.

Her hips started to gyrate with the rhythm of the soap. And just that little movement of hers sent my juices flowing out my twat. Undulating hips were always a wanton turn on for me.

Taking the sleeping vibe from the shower shelf, I gave the cap on that waterproof vibrator a quick twist with my thumb and brought it in direct contact with her pussy. The vibe did the work better than the soap and rope had. She started moaning into my mouth. I pushed her up against the tiled wall and hooked the soap on the shower handle. Then I started teasing that tight puckered asshole with my finger while I slid the vibe along her pussy. I felt her hand grab the vibrator from me and shove it home. So I reciprocated with my finger in her ass.

"Oh yeah, sugar, fill me up. Fuck me good."

I pumped her ass, throwing my body against hers to keep her from sliding, because my own fingers were reaching for my clit and a promised quick climax. She fucked her twat with the vibe. The turn on was more than I would be able to bear for long. Her other hand roamed over my back, fingertips digging into the rangy muscles below my shoulder, pulling me hard against her as she suddenly squelched, bit onto her bottom lip, then squirt in a tremendous eruption. Her ass chute spasmed to clench my finger in a velvety vice. With that, I orgasmed tense and fast, while stifling a yell.

I found the flesh of her neck again and bit, releasing my voice in a muffled scream until my body became less rigid. She bucked and continued to spasm in her own ecstasy.

Sweat beaded on her upper lip, as I'm sure it had on my forehead with the steam rising from the wasted stream of hot water. I ducked into the water, plucking the soap from the shower handle, and resumed sudsing, the both of us this time, while slowly working my finger from the clenching ring of her ass.

We cleaned up without a word between us. She mostly leaned against the tile and let me do the ministrations. When I stepped out after a peck to her lips, she said that there was an extra towel in her bag. Helpful.

I dried off, dressed, plucked my knife from the broken lock, and headed back to the horses, nonchalantly keeping a guarded eye on that shower door. I owed her that much.

Walking the right-side running board of my aluminum Featherlite stock trailer, I peered in at the horses, which were contentedly eating. When I got to the side door, I first noticed the lady trucker walking safely back across the tarmac, fluffing wet hair, then I unlocked the trailer, went in, and removed empty water buckets, cleaning hay from the others. Locking the trailer once again, I picked up those discarded buckets, climbed onto my flatbed, and stowed them in one of the trunks.

"Hey cowboi," I heard her call. "Are ya'll in a hurry?"

My coffee was still waiting for me. I spun, sat, and sipped while looking at that trucker over the Styrofoam cup. "No hurry," I replied.

"Why don't ya'll come on over." She had said it as if we were neighbors in suburbia who would sit down together over lunch or pastries. But what the heck, I was game.

Once again I hopped from my flatbed, this time to climb the heights of her rig, so to say. The interior was posh. I was guessing this was the only home she had. Much better set up than mine, if the road was a lifestyle. I felt a pang of jealousy. My own life entailed traveling from my ranch to give clinics at hosting farms and ranches that would put me up in bunkhouses or hotels, then on to rodeos where my horses and I lived a bit rough on the grounds until we left for a hotel to rinse off and get a quiet rest before moving on in much the same cycle. Truck stops just became a go-between and at times a longer lay-up. The horses were always well set. They rode loose in their own mobile home, which I kept as fresh, clean, and comfortable as possible.

In fact, there'd been times I had visited upon them, when having to sleep in some shabby truck stop that had no amenities. I found I preferred a bed of fresh hay under my sleeping bag even with the inquiring nuzzles and snorkels of fuzzy muzzles.

"Take off your hat and boots and stay a while," she said with a wink. "In fact, take it all off." She slammed the door and hit the electric locks. "Back there." She pointed. And I wouldn't have known the truck-driving aspect of the rig had existed once I entered the sleeper cab, though the room was smaller than that of one in a house.

She once again ripped at my pearly snaps when she joined me on her bed. Flesh, this time. Just flesh, as my shredded T-shirt had been lost to the garbage can in the shower room. She shoved me flat upon her bed with a palm to my chest, proceeding to attack my nipples with an inexplicable hunger as she yanked and tugged at my belt and jeans.

I lifted my hips to help slide unwanted Wranglers down my thighs, while my own hands roamed those recently familiar curves now disguised in clean jeans and tank top. Her damp hair trailed after her tongue as she worked away from my nipples and down the line to my navel. I buried my hands in the soft tresses at the nape of her neck. My eyes clamped shut with pleasure.

Her tongue pierced the tiny puckered umbilical pool in my skin and worked its way in and out with small circles, causing echoing repercussions eight inches lower. My body started to work on autopilot. Hips thrust and I pushed my flat belly to her face. Her head rode me smoothly. Her palms ran along my rib cage.

I was on the verge of flipping her over and returning the favor when one of her hands slid to caress the elastic waist of my tight boxer briefs, breaking my train of thought. A soft finger roamed along the line between cloth and flesh. Her touch, slow and light, raised goose bumps over my body. She started to trace that finger down the front seams, finding the pocket of those boy-briefs, and insinuated her digit inside to tease the top of my pussy lips. I felt the tip lightly caressing my dry clit shaft in time with her tonguing. Then it slipped down to draw some wetness from my hole.

"Sugar," she drawled, pulling her tongue from its work, "don't you move; I've got a little something in the side drawer I want to share with you."

She didn't have to tell me twice. Her talented finger kept me captive as she pulled her head back. My hands, tangled in those brunette waves too deeply to release, went with her involuntarily, making my body slam onto her finger. I bucked reflexively.

"Now, now, give a girl a second before you go popping off." She pulled her finger away. I heard a drawer open, some quick rummaging, and it snapped shut.

I groaned as she removed her hand completely from my tight, wet briefs. She laughed and disentangled my hands from her hair with a shake of her head.

The front of my briefs was stretched from my waist as I felt the unmistakable coolness of a condom-coated, silicone dildo shaft slide along my slit. The tip of its head bumped my clit. It was smooth; no ridges, and from the way I felt her hand angle and tug at my briefs, it was sharply curved.

She pushed it into me. The dong slid easily, the head hit me just above my G spot, and settled to poke upward toward the ceiling. I could feel a long, thick base that filled in between my lips and a nub that bumped my clit. If I moved ever so slightly, I would come. But that wasn't what she wanted, so I gritted my teeth and held off as best I could. She was working the pocket of my briefs again, and I opened my eyes enough to see a second prong of a double-ended dildo protruding from my boy boxer briefs.

"Well, cowboi. Let's rodeo. I sure hope you can last more than eight seconds, darlin'. 'Cause I'm gonna ride you until you're broke."

With that she sat back and started to unbutton her jeans. I noticed there was no belt to impede her progress. There were no panties to get in the way either. Her next move was so quick and fluid that I wasn't finished admiring it before I felt the heat of her pussy against the wet cloth surrounding the now buried dick.

When she hit bottom, the prong in me shifted and bumped my clit shaft and G spot at once and had me to bucking. "Yee haw, sugar. Let's ride!"

Her palms hit my shoulders and pinned me down as both she and my hips rose and fell in a hard, fast rhythm. I looked to see the white cloth go opaque as her pussy juice soaked it through. I felt her come pooling around the dildo base and running in little rivulets along the creases to mix with my own and coat my rear pucker. She threw herself back, sitting up where I could pluck and caress her nipples, watching the dick slip in and out as she bounced, humping and pumping. She leaned a bit farther and her hand slipped behind, yanked open the leg of my briefs, and insinuated a finger into the ring of my ass sphincter.

That was all it took to throw me over the edge. I couldn't hold off any further. I bucked like a pro-rodeo bronc, hammering her and me at the same time with that double-pronged silicone dildo. I yelled as I came hard, and yelled again as I felt her squirt warm wetness over my pelvis and groan her release atop me.

I rolled her to the side and humped her a few more times before pulling out, letting the dripping dick slap against her thigh.

She flopped over to lie against the backside of the cab, exhausted and readily falling asleep, but more importantly, leaving me an escape route. I peeled off my sodden shorts and left them, plucked the condom-covered end of the dick from my twat and jerked up my jeans, replacing my shirt and rescuing my abandoned boots and hat on the way out. I'm not one for long cuddles and even longer good-byes.

It was dark when I stepped precariously from the cab. Another truck had pulled in between our two rigs making me walk to the front of hers. It was light enough to admire details on the outside of her cab that I had missed on the way in. One such detail stopped me cold.

I turned around and headed for the Big Rigs store, yanking boots on and tucking my shirt in then buckling my heavy leather belt along the way. I found what I wanted pegged to the wall display, slapped down a few dollars, and borrowed some scissors to cut into that vinyl truck sticker sheet. I bought white; for the good guys.

When I returned, there was no sound emanating from the big purple rig. I walked to the nose, just ahead of her left front tire, and pasted my addition to her artwork of a torso, like those seen on restroom signs, with a lot of hash marks and slashes in groups of fives following the little half-person. I smiled as I leaned back and cocked my head to check my own work. The little torso was now wearing a white cowboi hat.

Noisemakers

Rachel Kramer Bussel

New York City apartments are notoriously small, with neighbors piled up next to neighbors, and thin walls and roommates making it difficult to properly fool around without fear of being over-heard. Luckily, for a little while, at least, I was able to turn what could've been a disastrous situation into one that allowed for maximum sexual entertainment. My roommate decided that his heavy metal band should use our apartment to practice; our two-bedroom railroad apartment, of which my room sat at the far end, while they'd be in the living room. I either had to leave while they played, or stay in my room and endure the ear-splitting and wall-rattling noise that simply could not be ignored.

I have never found it easy to turn down a friend in need, so I agreed that they could practice there, and found that I got used to the deafening noise level, for the most part. And then I met Maya through a friend of a friend. She was perky and adorable, with dimpled cheeks I just wanted to pinch, simple brown curls, and wire-rimmed glasses. She favored jeans and had a curvy body, like mine, that fit into them well. She was dating someone else, but it was an open relationship, so she had room to play. We geeked out together playing video games and flirting subtly, until finally she put the moves on me, wrapping her arms around me while I rocked my body to and fro indulging in an intense game of Ms. Pacman.

Then I found myself with a dilemma. We were near my apart-ment, and I of course wanted to take her home so we could see our flirtation through to its logical, and totally hot, conclusion, but I didn't want my roommate overhearing us, and I know I'm plenty loud when I get excited. Even though there can be a turn-on to deliberately trying to be quiet, unless I'm gagged, I can't

25

guarantee it, and something told me Maya would be a screamer, too. I turned her around so her back was up against the Ms. Pac-man machine, and pressed my body against hers, making sure she felt my knee between her legs. She smiled at me, that cute yet potentially evil grin, the one that said she wanted me to worship her and punish her at the very same time.

I leaned forward and whispered in her ear. "I want to take you home with me . . . but my roommates might overhear us."

"So?" she asked, grinning impishly and making a play for my ass. I was wearing a short schoolgirl skirt to her jeans and little white blouse, and it had ridden up in the back, conveniently allowing her hands to land directly on my cheeks.

"Well, it's not like they don't know I'm queer, I just try not to be too noisy when they're there. But . . . if you slept over, and were quiet, then in the morning we can be as loud as we want to be because they have band practice. I bet your hot body could distract me from what they call music."

She pulled me close for a kiss, letting her fingers slip beneath the elastic of my panties. I groaned against her mouth, and we made out like that until someone demanded to let Ms. Pacman rule over her rightful domain. "Rachel, I don't care if we have to be quiet tonight. You're not getting rid of me that easily." Maya traced my lips with her finger, then moved to sit on my lap. The pressure of her ass on me, her weight sinking me into the chair, made me long for her to be naked on top of me.

"Let's get out of here," I said, impressing her by managing to stand up with her in my arms and do a fireman's carry out the door, where I tilted her upright and deposited her on the ground. I only lived three blocks away, but three blocks takes a long time when you stop every few strides to make out intensely.

Finally, we got there, and managed to tiptoe past my room-mate's sleeping form before heading into my room and shutting the door. We giggled, then I stopped and just watched her laugh-ing. Those dimples were making me hot, and I wanted to see how she'd sound when she wasn't laughing, but moaning in pleasure.

"Take off your clothes," I ordered in a whisper. All of a sudden I knew I wanted her to perform for me, wanted to tell her what to do and have her obey. Maya looked at me skeptically for a second, as if I was playing some kind of practical joke on her. I reached for a ruler that I saw poking out from the corner of my desk and rapped it against my palm. "I'm waiting . . . ," I said, adding as much impatience to my voice as I could. The truth was, I kind of liked watching her decide, watching her figure things out, waiting for her to realize she wanted to obey me just as much as I wanted to order her around. She started unbuttoning the tiny pearls keeping her little white blouse together, and I was tempted to reach and rip them off.

I kept watching as the swell of her breasts was revealed, making my heart pound a little faster. Pretty soon she was totally naked. "Pinch your nipples," I whispered. Somehow, the constraint of us having to be quiet made the whole thing seem kinkier. Maya followed my instructions while I struggled not to get naked yet myself. Soon she was lost in her own body, pinching her nipples harder than I'd even planned to. I watched the pink nubs flatten between her fingers, her mouth opening, a tiny droplet of saliva forming at the corner of her lips. "That's enough," I said, rapping the ruler once again. She looked up at me, startled, then gave me a kittenish smile.

"Please?" she asked softly, then let her hand drop to between her legs. I moved forward and tapped her fingers with the ruler.

"No, Maya. You can't touch yourself, and I'm not going to either, even though I bet you're dripping wet right now. We're both going to wait until tomorrow. And you know what's going to happen then?"

My words had made me unbearably horny, and I hoped they'd had the same effect on her. Judging from the rapturous way she was watching me, I figured they had.

"What?" she asked, moving closer and closer until her nipples were pressing against me.

"I'm going to make you shriek. And scream. And come as loudly as you can, all to the soundtrack of heavy metal music. No one's going to know how hard I spank you or how much I twist your nipples." She gasped, her face going bright red, letting me know she was more than up for being spanked.

"Now get into bed," I said gently, as if to a child, pointing toward the far side. Maya clearly wasn't really that thrilled about stopping so soon, but I really didn't care. As turned on as I was, I knew she'd be worth waiting for, and having the power to make a hot girl like her obey me, trust me, do my bidding, was enough to content me for the moment.

I turned out the light and slipped off my clothes, then reached for any old T-shirt and boxers. I normally sleep in the nude, but in keeping with our kinky role-playing, I wanted to be clothed while she was nude, plus I figured that would help me resist temptation as well.

I slept fitfully, dreaming about doing all sorts of nasty things to and with Maya, and finally when I let myself open my eyes to the first streams of sunlight, I realized I was so horny I was frantic. I'd never done that before; taken a girl home and *not* fucked her. Wasn't that the point? But maybe I'd been missing out, because my pussy was throbbing, aching with wet and want, and I hoped Maya felt the same.

I traced her lips lightly with my finger until she finally opened my mouth and sucked lightly on the tip. I nudged closer, almost letting myself indulge in her beautiful body, but instead I pulled my finger away finally and whispered in her ear. "Let's have lunch in bed later, and breakfast now, at the diner." Then I kissed her ear, her neck, and rested my head against the comfort of her breasts for as long as I could without sucking on them. My hope was that by the time we returned, band practice would be in full swing.

I managed to coax Maya to the diner with the promise, or threat, that if she didn't go with me, I might choose to spend the day doing laundry and otherwise tidying up, sending her on her way. Why she believed me, I don't know, but over eggs and home fries, we got to know each other a little better. I mostly listened as she told me all about her family, who were far from New York in a small Washington town, though they spoke often. She had a kitten but wanted to get a bulldog. She was a librarian but had always wanted to be a writer. And yes, I know, these were all things I should've gleaned last night, but I was too entranced by her to properly get to know her.

The more we talked, the cuter I found her, which was a good sign; I like it when there's more to my lovers than just physical attraction, as powerful as that can be. I beckoned her to come sit next to me when we were done eating, and we squeezed into the booth together, our excitement palpable. She held my hand beneath the table and I gripped hers tightly. When she leaned her head on my shoulder, I thought I could get used to that. I still wanted to dominate her, but I also wanted to cuddle with her afterward.

We finally paid the bill and returned to the apartment. We were greeted by several male grunts from my roommate's band members. I tugged Maya by the hand into the apartment and away from their noise. They could be as loud as they wanted to be, because we were about to as well. I couldn't wait any longer, and grabbed her roughly, snaking my fingers through her hair. Her loud moan of pleasure made my nipples hard. "I've been wanting to spank you all morning," I said, getting straight to the point. We were both wearing jeans this time, and I ran my hand along the warm, damp seam of hers, pressing the fabric up against her pussy. "You'd like that, wouldn't you, Maya?" She agreed, then sealed the deal by spontaneously leaning down and kissing the tops of my bare feet.

I pulled her across my lap, her jeans off, panties pulled down to expose her ass. "You're going to count for me, and you only get ten, so I'm gonna make them good and hard. And feel free to scream as loud as you want." A shiver raced through me as I realized that I wanted to hear Maya scream, wanted to be the source of her pleasure and pain all tied up in one. I brought my hand booming down on her right cheek and she let out a wail. It wasn't fake or forced, but it was loud, and normally would've brought the neighbors knocking on our door, but I knew with the other kind of wailing in the nearby room, one I could both hear and feel, we were fine. I smacked her other cheek, watching the color rise to her skin. I kept going, making the most of my ten whacks to dole out louder and louder blows. By the end, she was calling out, not for me to stop, but for me to go. I'd chosen ten so as not to tire her out, but leave her wanting more.

And boy, did she beg for more. "Please, that just wasn't enough. You are the perfect spanker," she said, trying to suck up to me. She shifted so she was sitting next to me, my hand in hers.

"You've had enough for today, Maya," I said, staring deep into her eyes as she looked up at me. Then I pushed her hands away and brought my hand to her pussy. She was wet as could be, and I plunged immediately inside while shifting down so I could suck on her clit. Now her cries were louder, seeming to possibly rival the heavy metal music blasting though the walls. I kept going until she was simply wrung dry, limp. She begged to taste me, and I straddled her face, teasing her with brushes of my cunt against her lips until I finally allowed her to fully taste me. Her powerful tongue was soon coaxing forth my climax.

We settled under the covers and tried to fall back asleep, to a lullaby of power rock and metal ballads. And somehow, with her tucked against me, both of us naked and sated, they were as beautiful as any lullaby.

Crimson

Diane Thibault

It was her crimson-red lipstick that made me do it.

I would ask her if I could carry her books for her. I felt like a teenager in heat but this was not high school. It was a semiotics conference of international caliber. Ms. Lewis had been my semiology professor in university ten years before, to the day.

I remembered her sarcastic smile, her pencil skirt, her leather briefcase, her rigorous standards.

Whenever she asked a question in class, I raised a trembling hand and waited anxiously for her validation. I was usually right. When I was not, I delighted in the way she corrected me, always fairly but firmly. More than a few times, I rushed to my dorm room after class to jerk off. More than a few times, I fantasized about Ms. Lewis punishing me sternly with her hand, then forcing herself on me.

I had met my youthful crush again, and I wanted her. This time, I was determined.

When she finished her presentation, she gathered her papers. Her eyes surveyed the conference room, hoping no one would come up to her and ask her an asinine question. Or worse yet, drool over her mastery of the subject with all the fake admiration of a novice who wants a recommendation for her thesis. Thankfully, the crowd dispersed without a word.

Her hair was tied up in a severe bun, but a strand fell over her face. She looked up one more time and saw me. Her eyes tried to locate my provenance, lost in the mist of her past. She shook her head and prepared to leave.

I gathered my courage and approached her.

"Yes?"

"Ms. Lewis. I used to be in your semiology class. At Smith's. In 1997."

She considered me for a moment. A flicker of recognition lit up her eyes. She locked up her briefcase. Her hand caressed the leather. Her brief smile disappeared.

"I'm sorry. I don't remember you. It was such a long time ago and so much has happened since then. I'm so sorry."

She picked up her briefcase. Her eyes fell on the pile of books she had brought along. The strand of hair caressed her forehead. She frowned. I ached.

"Ms. Lewis. Please let me help you carry your books. You were such a wonderful professor. It's the least I can do."

My legs could barely hold me up. Did she bite her lower lip or did I dream it? Everything was happening so fast.

"Oh. Thank you. That would be lovely. What's your name again?"

"Chris."

"Chris. Nice to meet you."

Instead of extending her hand, she placed it on my shoulder. The warmth of her touch traveled all the way down my body. I composed myself while I focused my attention on her impeccably cut suit. It was European and accentuated the shape of her breasts. Her skirt flattered her ass in a sophisticated yet provocative way. When she moved, the fabric rustled against her nylons. My hands tingled as lusty thoughts raced through my head.

"Shall we?" she said, in her husky voice.

"After you."

As I walked behind her, I remembered my eighteen-year-old self being enthralled by her crisp enunciation, her classic glasses, her piercing brown eyes, and her sharp assessment of my papers. I yearned for her approval and worked harder for her than for any other professor.

Her mid-height sensible shoes echoed in the halls as we crossed one pavilion, then another, of this august institution. There was a chill in the air. The beginning of autumn. Leaves strewn across the immaculate lawns. She remained silent. My arousal kept rising.

"So. Chris." I felt a little more possessed by her every time she uttered my name. "Were you a good student?"

She did not turn to face me. I picked up the pace to keep up with her.

"Yes. I think so. I think I recall getting an A in your class."

We arrived at the parking lot. She turned toward me. Her face was flushed.

"Would you mind carrying the books to my car?"

"Of course not."

She smiled. Sarcastically? I couldn't tell. I never could read her. Another wave of lust washed over me. I wasn't sure if I was sweating or shivering.

Her car was a late model Jaguar. Tenured academia had its rewards. She waved toward the trunk, opening it with a click of her remote. I carefully placed the tomes inside.

It was getting dark. She came up behind me. I waited, unable to move. I felt her breath on my neck. She put her hand on my shoulder. This time, with a steelier resolve, or so I imagined.

"So, Chris. It is Chris, isn't it?" she teased. "Let's go for a drink. It's been such a long day."

I acquiesced even before she mentioned the drink. I would go anywhere with her. She smiled at me. She untied her hair, a deep auburn cascading down her shoulders.

After starting the car, she turned on the radio to a preset jazz station. She drew a sharp intake of breath and glanced at me.

"So, what have you been doing with your life since graduation?"

I shifted in my seat. The leather creased and creaked. The car glided along the highway like a bullet.

"I got another degree. In translation studies. I've been working in the field for, oh, about five years now. I love it."

"Really?"

I had piqued her interest. Her voice was softer, more even, and deeper. I looked at her and smiled. She glanced back at me. A warm, generous look.

"That's wonderful. Professional fulfillment is so precious. And so rare these days."

Her authoritative tone rose up again. My cheeks flushed with pleasure.

She took an exit onto a small service road. The forest grew thicker around us. Blue-black shadows towering in the early dusk. I was confused.

"Oh," she frowned, "I think I need to pull over."

I glanced at the dashboard and saw nothing wrong. The tank was three-quarters full. No warning lights were lit up. She gave me a little smile and slowed down. She put her hand on my knee, rubbing it.

"Ms. Lewis . . ."

"Hang on. Let's stop here."

I saw a garage on my right. Its doors were unlocked. She pulled the car into it. The door closed behind us with a soft thud.

"Ms. Lewis . . ."

"Don't worry, Chris. There's something I just have to do," she said, with the emphasis on "have."

"Oh. Can I help? I'm pretty good with cars. I took a mechanics . . ."

She undid her seatbelt and shushed me with her fingers. Her deep eyes bore into me. Her face glowed in the faint dashboard lights. She looked as beautiful as I remembered her; perhaps even more.

"You want me, don't you?"

I melted. Her clipped enunciation. The sweetness of her breath. The tightening grip of her fist on my knee.

"Well . . . yes . . . but I didn't think you were . . ."

"Sweetie, I noticed you watching me all afternoon."

She wrapped her hand around the nape of my neck and kissed me. I kissed her back with abandon. My seat inclined to a horizontal position. She climbed on top of me and lifted her skirt. I struggled to catch my breath as my hips bucked against her.

"That's right. Touch me. Come on. I know you want it."

I was overwhelmed. This was the same stern professor who always seemed poised and icy cool. Now, she was coming on to me. I marveled at my luck.

Her long hair rippled over my nakedness as she tore open my shirt and yanked out my undershirt. I unbuttoned her blouse and grabbed her voluptuous breasts through her bra. Her nipples were erect. I sucked on them with greed. Her moans echoed through the plush interior like an incantation.

"You're so sexy," I said again and again, admiring her body, and her boldness.

Her cheeks were flushed. She smiled at me. She bent down to lick my nipples. She ran her hand down my body until she sampled the wetness she had stirred up. Soon, I felt her tongue lapping at me, driving me into one orgasm after another. She finished me off by fucking me hard with her expert hand. I came again, twice.

When I was spent, she climbed up to my face and ground her pussy against my mouth. I felt her hips buck, twice.

"Are you ready? Are you ready to swallow?"

"Yes!" I screamed.

She let go and came into my mouth. Her juices spread all the way down to my neck, my ears, my hair. Everywhere. When she was done with me, she handed me a few tissues to wipe myself dry. She held out her hand and helped me up.

We sat back in our respective seats. She leaned over and kissed me lightly. She started the car and we rolled out of the garage.

"So, Ms. Lewis, are we really going out for a drink?"

I felt cocky and smiled. She grinned back at me.

"Well, Chris. I'll let you go if you want. But I'd still like to have that drink with you. And some more of what we just had."

"Yes," I exclaimed, "oh yes."

When we arrived at the luxury hotel, a valet parked the car. I carried her books and her briefcase to her room.

She poured us a couple of whiskies and sat down on the couch. She motioned me over. I sat beside her, still full of unspent desire.

She toasted her glass against mine.

"I do remember you, Chris. I remember you very well. And I'm glad I can finally do something about it."

As I gasped in disbelief, she took possession of my mouth with her fiery kiss. She grabbed my hair and pulled it a little.

"Chris?"

"Mmmh?"

She whispered in my ear, her mouth delightfully close, but infuriatingly far from my mouth. "Do you remember when you used to give me the wrong answer in class?"

I felt myself go moist again. *Please,* I wanted to say. I swallowed hard.

"Yes."

"Do you remember how if felt when I corrected you?"

"Oh, Ms. Lewis . . ."

"Yes? Do you have something to say, Chris?"

An electrical current ran through my body. Her other hand grabbed my crotch. I gasped again.

"I wished . . . "

"What did you wish for, Chris?"

"I wished that you would punish me for saying the wrong thing. I wished you would take me and . . ."

"And what? What would I do with you?"

I looked at her, helpless. Her eyes were assessing me, wondering how far I wanted to go. I felt adrift and powerless, yielding.

"You would . . . you would call me over to your office."

"Then I would close the door and lock it." She tightened her grip even more.

"Yes, please," I gasped.

"Then I would bend you over. And I would spank you. Hard."

She smacked my ass. A bolt of pain shot through me. A tear fell down my face.

"Oh, please, yes, Ms. Lewis," I continued, "I'll try harder next time. I'll study harder."

"Harder, you say?"

With this, she smacked me again, then slid her hand down and up. Her fingers entered me. I nearly lost my balance. She held me tightly. She was stronger than she appeared.

"And then, what would I do?"

"Ms. Lewis, you would force yourself on me. Please, fuck me."

"What did you say?"

"Please, oh please, Ms. Lewis. I'll be good, I promise. I'll work harder."

"You better," she said, and proceeded to fuck me hard, drawing my juices out freely. My breath accelerated, and I heard her moan.

"Come on, Chris. Give it to me. Give it up."

The orgasm seared through my body like lightning. I heard myself beg and scream. Still, she kept fucking me. I hoped she would never stop. And she did not, for a long time.

When we woke up in the morning, she smiled at me. I pulled her to me. She put her head in my nook, inhaling my scent.

"So, Chris. I bet you have plenty to teach me as well."

"Well, Ms. Lewis, I think I might. I think I just might."

"I'm open, Chris. I'm fully open," she teased, kissing me deeply.

I smiled and climbed on top of her. Room service would have to wait.

Sexploration

Sapphyre Reign

Being in a long-distance relationship made the needs of immediate sexual gratification somewhat challenging. But I tried to keep a positive spin on things as I stepped out of the shower thinking about all the wild, intimate, and freaky things and positions I planned to incorporate with and to my lover the next time we were together. All these desires made me hornier than most evenings. Just remembering the last time we were together and the wonderful things she did to my body—that and knowing she was my little freak in training—made me quick to pick up the phone and give her a call. I hoped I wouldn't be disappointed by her not being there. The phone rang and I held my breath.

She picked up on the fourth ring. *Finally,* I thought as I made myself more comfortable on the corner of my bed. "Hey you."

"Hi."

I could already hear the giddiness in her high, at times enthusiastic, voice. It amazed me, still, how coquettish she could be after all this time. She'd explained on numerous occasions that having me in her life was like being on an indescribable high. Still, you'd think after months of being together she'd be used to the bursts of tingles my voice sent through her veins.

Nonetheless I was pleased by her delight. "How was your day?" I inquired to be polite. Knowing how her day was had not been in the top priority of things on my mind. I'd been eager to get right to the order of business as my skin air-dried; just the sound of her voice made the diamond between my legs sparkle. I shuddered as she spoke.

"Better now that I hear your voice," she sighed.

"Oh?"

"Yes," she breathed in that lustful yet girlish moan of hers. "You've been caressing me all day. How do you do that?"

I smiled. I knew she meant that my essence had been teasing her here, tickling her there, and increasing her angst of missing me. We'd been here before, many times as a matter of fact. Our kindred connection, albeit long distance much of the time, was so in tune that I shivered when she was cold. "I really don't know what you're talking about, sweetie. But if it makes your panties wet and your nipples hard and your mind wild with wanton thoughts of me . . . I'll take it."

"Yes," she gasped. "Yes, it does just that. All of the above and so much more."

"Do you miss me?"

"Desperately."

"Do you love me?"

"Yes!"

I could almost feel her feather-light breath against my skin, cloaking me with her lust as she inhaled my scent. "How do you know?" I asked, knowing she hated it when I asked blatant questions like this.

She released a moan of desperation. "I do because my heart aches in your absence; my body feels naked without the comfort of your arms wrapped about it. My ears are hungry for your whispers, my lips parched without your kisses, my clit"—she whispered like an embarrassed child—"throbs for your strokes."

The melodic moan that followed her statement said all I needed to know. "Really?" I asked cynically.

Ignoring my antics, she continued. "But the main reason I know I love you is because my world would cease to exist without you!" Her tone was very serious, her voice stern.

Damn it! She'd broken me down. Played the trump card. Turned my insides into melted butter. "You really know how to turn a lady on don't you?" I asked with a weary sigh of my own. She giggled with delight. I didn't know how much longer I could stand being so far away from each other. Instead of focusing on that, I let my mind turn back to the reason I'd called to begin with. "Tell me, sugar dip," my voice became a beacon of lust and need, "what are you wearing?"

"Well," she drew the word out. "I just walked in not too long ago so I'm fully dressed."

"Humph. What color are your panties and bra?" I asked, wanting something to treasure in my mind's eye and somewhat disappointed that she was fully clothed.

"I'm wearing the lavender and black lace ones you sent last week."

I could hear her moving in the background and imagined she was undressing, as I shuffled through the pics she'd sent and pulled the one of her sexy, bodacious physique wearing the lacy bra-and-thong set.

"Oooh, baby, strip down to your undies. Now!"

"OK, I'm trying." Her voice sounded strained yet eager to please me.

"Hurry!" I urged.

"Wait a minute," she drooled sexily into the phone, pronouncing each word in that high yet aroused voice she used when she was feeling frisky.

I was having trouble waiting. To occupy my mind I lay booty-butt naked in the center of the bed. My legs were spread wide, my pussy juices marinating as my sensual scent permeated the room. I ran my fingernails across the middle of my stomach, imagining her hands exploring me as I waited for my baby to get sexy for me.

Minutes later she cooed, "OK lover," her voice caressing my ears like a tongue. It was that voice that sent a flash of sizzling white-hot heat shooting from the nape of my neck straight to the tip of my clit. It was a sound like no other I'd ever heard from anyone before. The first time she released it I thought she was crying, but she immediately followed it by a shuddering moan that let me know that ache was coupled by a desperate need for pleasure. "I'm here for you!"

"Good. Finally. Now, where are you in the house?"

"I'm on the futon in the office."

"Mmm, that futon knows and has seen entirely too damn much. Next time I'm there we might have to burn it." She laughed at my teasing. Becoming more seductive, I asked, "Are you wet for me, baby?"

"Yes," she breathed lustfully.

"How wet?"

"Soaked."

"How do I know that?"

"You'll have to take my word for it. But trust me, baby, I'm drenched for you."

"Oh really? Where?"

"Down there, between my lips."

"Where down there between your lips?"

"Where my thighs meet and my clit sleeps."

"WHERE!" I demanded in a harsh whisper, wanting her to release the power to me. To say the word that would take our sex-ploration to the tenth power.

"In . . . my . . . *pussy,* " she whispered.

"Say it louder," I demanded softly.

"In my *pussy.* "

"In whose?" I questioned with feigned intimidation, but now it was my turn to be coquettish and demure. I wasn't sure if she knew exactly what hearing her say that word in her reserved, almost modest, timid voice did to me.

"In YOUR pussy, sweetness."

"In MY pussy?"

"Yes, yes in your pussy, lover. Claim your pussy, baby. Your wet, throbbing, aching *pussy.* I want only you to have it," she confessed.

Just hearing her say the word *pussy* sent me into a state of delirium—orgasmic bliss. It was something about the way she pronounced it, coupled with knowing that she'd been a devoted nun at one point in life, that immediately sent my mind and sex drive into euphoria. I'd always been a sucker for profanity and dirty epithets during lovemaking. Her high-pitched voice, throaty lust, and desperate desire made the word sound like a wayward sinner on her deathbed calling for god. I'd planned on grooming her in the art of filthy word play the next time we met in person. For now, I settled for the exotic way she pronounced *pussy.*

I cupped my breast and twisted my nipple between my fingers. I wanted her so badly I could seize right there on the spot. A soft mew escaped my lips. "Lay back. Spread your legs. Wider!

Now palm *my* pussy in your hand," I requested as I simultane-ously followed my orders. "Now take your other hand and pull your nipple until it is hard and taut."

She let that intoxicating moan ring out over and over like a cadence. She knew exactly what I enjoyed.

"Bring it to your lips and flick that rock-hard tip with your tongue the way I did the last time I was there." I heard her lips part and imaged how sweet her tongue flicking across her beau-tifully big breast looked. "Now tell me, tell mamma what she can do to please her queen, baby."

"P-l-e-a-s-e," she begged in a shuddering voice, then filled the airways with that painful cry when making love is on the verge of being the next best thing to breathing.

"Please what?" I teased in a seductive voice I knew made her pimples goose.

"Please, love, douse this fire between my tiny wings, embed-ded in your pussy, before I burn up into ashes." The words came out in raspy breaths.

"We simply can*not* have that, now can we?" I licked my lips, making that slurping sound that love juices make when the kitty is being serviced correctly, stirred to a slow heat like a simmering boil. I squirmed on the bed as heat coursed through my veins. "Slide your middle finger inside my sweet cunt, baby. Yes, just like that. Deeper, deeper still, now bring it out. Just a little bit. OK, take the nub and tease the tip of that sweet, succulent, cherry pop. Yes, huh unh . . . Just like that." Her breath caught as I took in air while brushing my own finger against the soaked diamond between my wings. "Good baby. You like it like that? Yeah, me too. Now slide in two . . . three fingers and thrust your hips forward. Mmmn, yes that's it . . . faster baby . . . harder my love. OK, OK, wait, slow it down just a little bit."

Her breathing quivered as I remembered how delicious her sweet, pretty pussy was the last time I was there lying next to her, caressing it, memorizing it for just such an occasion. That delight-ful sob came out in a lush, orchestrated melody.

Annoying her, I said calmly, "I think we should stop, maybe talk about the state of the world. Explore today's headlines, but we shouldn't continue on *this* course of action." My fingers were embedded deeply in my sex. I wasn't about to stop but I loved teasing her this way.

A soft wail like that of a pouting, sleepy child hit my ears. "Noooo, please do not stop, sweetness. I'll beg if you want but do not stop loving me."

"Umm, you sound so sweet to me, girl. Shyt!" Her groans hastened. "Damn, you're bossy but I got you. Are you listening?" She purred. "Dip, dip into those hot creamy juices, now bring that finger back to the tip and stroke that sensitive nub in small, minute, quick flicks." Her cries accelerated. "Open those legs, baby." It was her habit to close or tighten her legs as our loving increased. "That's it, that's my good girl. Rub it, sweetie, faster . . . faster . . . faster. I feel you coming, baby. I feel you wanting to come for mamma! Are you gonna come for me, huh?"

"Yes! Oh baby, baby, baby, take it, claim it, mark it all up with your love. Lick it! Like that . . . yes, yes!"

"Oooh, you like that don't cha? The way my tongue flicks across your hard pretty glistening pearl?"

Her shrieks became louder, those groans sounded more painfully pleasurable as each minute ticked by. I knew she was on the brink of orgasm, but I wasn't ready for her to climax yet so I taunted her more and more until she reached the edge of that raging peak.

"Fuck my face, baby, throw them hips, lift that ass. Plunge it into me. Fuck my face. Come on girl, give it to me. You must not want me to have it, is that all you got? Surely, you can do better than that. GIVE ME MY PUSSY!" I breathed, stroking my clit, lifting my hips, thrusting my body into my fingers. "It's mine, let me claim it!" All I heard was her panting and the sucking sounds coming from my own sexy cunt. Both drove me over the edge and I screamed in sync with her cries. The melody was so erotic, operatic, and climactic as we exploded together again and again!

I heard her groaning and breathing heavily through my own high, pitchy wails as I tried desperately to catch my breath. But her mewling assured me there was more work to be done. I placed my come-soaked fingers into my mouth and suckled loudly.

She asked, "Baby, are you . . . ?"

"Yes, my love. I'm sucking your syrup the way you like to do."

The sound of my sloppy suckling caused her to release a hum so lascivious, so harmonious and loud I was certain her next-door neighbors were wondering what a single, seemingly shy woman was doing right about that time. My *phst, slurp, phisht, slurp, ptsk* flowed through the phone lines as she let go of that last bit of animalistic fight and slumped back, spent, against the cushion of the futon.

I imagined her body shuddering as it had so many times before to the eccentricity of lovemaking we shared as long distance partners. I breathed in heavily, still trying to regain a normal breathing pattern.

I giggled and asked, "Whose is it?" in a soft, delighted whisper.

"Yours. And only yours," she replied hoarsely.

"Are you sure?"

"Yes, my love goddess. This pussy is forever and always branded, seared by the heat of your essence. Eternally!"

"Good. I guess that's the power of the P, huh? Meet me in my dreams and we'll sexplore other options, sweet queen."

"Yes, of course. I love you!"

"I love you more!"

Where the Women Are

KR Silkenvoice

When I tell men that I attended a women's college, they usually say, in a voice heavy with innuendo, "I've heard about what goes on at those girls' schools." But what they imagine is from their masculine perspectives and fantasies, and so it is lacking in depth and breadth, not to mention out of touch with reality.

They imagine lesbian sex going on between busty sorority girls with Brazilian waxes in every room of every dormitory. They imagine the occasional lucky man tied to some girl's bed with women lining up at the door for a chance at him. But the reality is much subtler and far more interesting. Most of the girls at women's colleges are incredibly intelligent, the cream of the crop intellectually. Most of them are studious and driven: they had to work hard for the grades and test scores to get there. Some of them are from privileged families, but more and more, the student body has become a cross section of cultures, races, and socioeconomic strata. And most of the girls there are hetero. I figure that a minimum of one in ten are lesbian, and of the remaining 90 percent, probably one in five is willing to experiment, like I was.

While I was curious, I didn't start experimenting until my junior year. Early on, I'd found a boyfriend with a fascinating mind, an amazing mouth, a thick cock, and a willingness to learn to use them to maximize my enjoyment of him, and his of me. But Drew went off to grad school three hours away, and we commenced a weekend-only physical relationship that was insufficient to my needs and his. We admitted this to each other and spoke of breaking up, but there was love there between us, and we did not want to end our relationship because of distance. Yet, both of us were highly sexed and neither of us appreciated the fact that when we got together all we did was fuck like rabbits.

Whenever we saw each other, the sexual tension was so intense that even when we tried to go out and do things as a couple like we used to before he moved away, we ended up having sex. Restaurants, concert halls, parks, stairwells, swimming pools, classrooms, libraries, stores—it didn't matter. Our eyes would meet, or our hands would touch, and that urge to copulate would surge irresistibly through us.

We spoke several times a week, and one day, after a couple of months of separation, Drew spoke longingly of his attraction to some of the women he saw almost daily. I told him he should ask them out. He said that it would not be fair. When I asked him why, he said because it would not be fair for him to have sex but not me. I remarked that it would not take me long to find another partner, and told him of the dates I'd turned down. I've never been a sexually jealous person and the thought of him with someone else did not bother me—my only concerns were that he practice safe sex if he did sleep with someone else, and that he tell me about it, preferably beforehand. But Drew was not like me in that, and the thought of me with another man drove him nuts. So we dropped the subject.

Soon afterward, a solution presented itself in the form of one of the women in my house. Pilar was openly bisexual and quite a hot little number. She'd been hitting on me for two years, and at the beginning of our junior year, she'd begun doing things like sitting on my lap and feeding me bits of food, and slipping her arms around my neck and nuzzling me so I could smell the scent of the woman she'd just been with on her face. We went out dancing with a group one night as a stress break from midterms and she seduced me. It was beautiful and exciting and exhausting. The following morning I called Drew to confess what I had done. I expected a jealous outburst, but what I got instead was a barrage of questions. He admitted that the thought of Pilar and me together was very arousing, and we had phone sex as I described what had occurred the night before:

I had left the lab at about 10 p.m. on Friday night, utterly exhausted. My partner and I had been running PCR and gel electrophoresis on DNA from *Brugia malayi* for a project involving the development of a biological assay for diagnosis of lymphatic filariasis. I'd missed the traditional Friday high tea and dinner as well, so I was intent on finding something to eat and getting a few hours of sleep before I got back to work, this time on a lit paper that was due Monday morning.

When I let myself into the house, there were a few men and a dozen women in the living room. One of them was Pilar. She was wearing a little black skirt and a black vest, both of which showed off her golden skin marvelously. At first glance it looked like she was wearing a silk-screened tank under her vest, but she wasn't. She and Serena had painted the skin of her torso, front and back. She removed the vest to show me their handiwork, and I was impressed, not only by the artistry, but by the bounce of her breasts. Such perky little breasts.

They cajoled me into going out with them. Pilar dragged me upstairs and shoved me into the shower, and while I was shower-ing, she picked out my clothes. I balked at wearing a summer-weight dress in late October, but she reminded me that we'd be dancing at the Black Pearl, and we would be working up a sweat. When I finished dressing and looked at myself in the mirror so I could fix my hair, I groaned. Pilar had chosen a push-up-push-out bra to wear with the dress and I was showing some serious cleav-age. Which meant that guys at the club were going to think I was available, when I wasn't. Pilar wouldn't hear of me changing, so I sighed, then pinned my hair up to keep it off my neck and out of my way on the dance floor. Forgoing stockings, I slipped into some flats, grabbed a wrap, and away we went.

The Pearl was packed. Locals and people from all five col-leges in the area were there because it was one of the few places that the under-twenty-one crowd could go with friends who were of legal drinking age. The Friday-night DJ always played good dance music and this night was no exception. The group of us pushed our way onto the dance floor upstairs and started shaking it. Pilar had an amazing little gymnast's body and she had some serious moves. I remembered seeing her dancing with Serena and Melody, watching her weave her body around them like a cat. I loved it when she grabbed Melody's mane of waist-length blonde hair and bent her backward, exposing her midriff. Pilar's golden hand played across Melody's belly as she pumped her body against the taller woman's back, hips rocking, breasts bouncing, lips trailing along the exposed throat. It was a very sexually charged moment, and I got hot just watching them. I think everyone did.

We danced for hours, letting off our midterm stress. Pilar paired off with me several times, and inevitably she ended up grinding herself against my thigh or slipping her own thigh between my legs, bumping against my pubis. She was making me crazy. I hadn't seen Drew for two weeks and I was so sexually frustrated I was ready to hump my bedpost even before I went out dancing. Every brush of her body against mine sent a zing of pleasure through me. Mmm, yes, all that bumping and grinding to the powerful bass grooves on the dance floor was making me wild.

At one point Pilar worked her way down my body and back up, her fingertips trailing along the backs of my thighs, sending shivers through me and making my nipples harden. Her eyes fixed on my breasts on the way up and she pressed her lips to my cleavage, her tongue snaking out to taste my skin. I gasped at the sensation. A moment later, her mouth was just inches from mine. Her hand slipped up the back of my neck and she pulled me toward her, kissing me full on. It was probably a brief kiss, but it seemed to last several minutes. When her mouth opened and her tongue sought mine, I met it. She slipped her arms around my neck and arched her body against me, purring, then broke away, putting distance between us, dark eyes dancing in a merry face.

We closed the place down, then stumbled up the hill to our houses. Some of the girls paired off with each other. One of the boys got lucky; the other one who had been with us headed home, alone. Serena and her boyfriend asked Pilar to join them for a three-way, but she declined. Instead, she linked her arm in mine and we kept walking. I didn't think anything of it at the time, after all, we lived in the same house. We walked the solo girl to her house and made sure she was safely inside before we turned back to our own, just a few blocks away.

Pilar unlocked the front door and held it open for me to precede her. I, in turn, pulled open the entry door. As she passed me, she let her fingers trail along my back and waist. Her touch sent an electric thrill through me, making me hyperaware of my skin and the moistness between my legs. Our eyes met and without a word, she took my hand and led me up the stairs, stopping on the third-floor landing. My room was on the fourth floor.

Pilar raised my hand and pressed her mouth to my wrist. Her nostrils flared and I could feel her breath on my skin. "I can smell you," she said.

I blushed deeply. I was breathing fast, and it wasn't from the walk up. I was damp, and it wasn't from sweating. Pilar had teased me all night and I was in such a state that I was quivering inside. But I had no idea what, if anything, I should do. I hadn't touched another girl since I was eleven or twelve years old.

She smiled at me and tugged on my hand. "Stay with me tonight?" she asked. Her voice was sultry, her normally slight British accent more pronounced. Her eyes were beautiful and lustrous, long lashed, and so dark they were almost black. Her eyes drew me and I fell into them, willingly.

"I might"—I said the first thing that came to mind—"if you kiss me."

Another smile, this one slow and meaningful. She ran her tongue across her lips as she stepped nearer. Her fingers followed the neckline of my dress upward, teasing my bare skin, making my nipples rise. She put both of her hands on my shoulders and stood up on tiptoe to kiss me. It was a soft kiss, just a brush of her lips, really. It was tantalizing, a vivid reminder of the kiss we had shared earlier on the dance floor, making me want more.

Again! a voice in my mind cried. As she pulled away, I ran my hands up her arms and cupped her head, tilting it back. I pressed my lips to hers, firmly. She opened her mouth to me, but I ignored the invitation, nibbling and sucking on her bottom lip instead.

She moaned and sighed, and breaking away, practically dragged me toward her room. Once inside, she began undressing me, her mouth kissing every bit of flesh that she exposed. When she freed my breasts from the bra she ran her hands along the undersides, cupping them. Her hands were so small and my breasts so large in comparison, but she somehow managed to trap my nipples between her thumb and forefinger while still cradling them. A little bit of pressure and she had me gasping, pleasure singing along my nerve endings. My skin pebbled under the sensory onslaught of her hands and her mouth. She pushed me backward onto her bed and stepped out of her skirt, and then she was on me.

We touched each other, fingers exploring. It was such a wonder to me, the way she felt under my fingertips, the way she moaned and gasped—no rough rumbling from her—no, she was a bundle of breathy cries just waiting to escape her throat. I have no idea when my nervousness left me, but it did, driven out by such powerful longing for this little spitfire from Belize. Her body pressing into mine was a mass of contrasting sensations and expectations. Her skin was cool in some places and very warm in others. It was silky soft and hairless, so different from Drew's. Her cheeks were smooth, instead of stubbly. She was rounded and soft instead of angled and hard.

She lay atop me, her groin pressing into mine, rocking against my clit, making me gasp and writhe. Her mouth explored my face, her tongue tracing the curve of my upper lip. She could not seem to keep her hands away from my breasts for long. She bounced them and kneaded them, pulled on the long nipples, sensitizing me to the point that every brush of her fingertips sent stars shooting behind my eyes. She shifted a bit, straddling my thigh, and her mouth on my throat was hot, so liquid hot, that I felt branded by it. Her teeth nipped at my skin, making me moan and shiver. My hands rose, fingers tangling in her hair, and that beautiful chin-length silken blackness felt soooo amazing to me, such a source of sensuous delight, that it brought tears to my eyes.

She was slow and tender and yet so hot and passionate. Her thigh pressed rhythmically on my mound as she rocked herself against me, her hips dancing as they had at the Pearl. I could feel the brush of her pussy against the top of my own thigh, a moist teasing tickle. I lifted my leg a little, pressing it up into her, and she moaned, her breath puffing against my skin. She dipped her tongue into the hollow at my throat, then slid farther down on my body, leaving a trail of kisses behind as she worked her way to my left breast. Her pussy skidded hard against my thigh in the same moment that her mouth enveloped my nipple. Both were hot and wet and slippery, and combined with the intense stimulation of my nipple, the duality of the sensations over-stimulated me. I was full-body blinded for a few seconds: seeing nothing, feeling nothing, utterly blue-screened. I think I even forgot to breathe.

I needed a change, a break from the intensity, so I moved out from under her, lying on my side. She joined me and we lay facing each other, her head pillowed on my arm. With my fingertips, I traced the outline of her body, the curve of shoulder and waist and hip. I found myself loving the golden tone of her skin, which seemed so rich a color when contrasted against my own pale flesh. I admired the paint upon her skin, letting my fingers trace the sinuous abstract designs that served to camouflage her nudity. Again, my hand swept down along her curves, and when I reached her hip, Pilar shivered and made a little sound in her throat. She took my hand and parted her thighs, pressing my fingers against her. It was very foreign and yet oddly familiar, the feel of her. I had this odd flash in my mind, the thought that if I had no feeling from the waist down, this is what it would feel like if I touched myself.

Pilar moved to lie on her back with one knee raised, and tangled the leg nearest me between my own. Again, her hand sought mine, and again she pressed my hand against her mound, this time curling my fingers into her, pressing them between her labia, whispering, "Please . . . Please touch me, Kay."

God! She was liquid in her core, so hot and slippery that I sucked my breath in between my teeth. I marveled at how wet she was, giddy with the knowledge that *this* was what my lovers felt when they touched me. Before I knew it, I had raised my fingers to my nose. I inhaled deeply of her scent. She smelled quite different from me, musky and fleshy to my ginger and floral. I slipped a finger into my mouth. Piquant. Tangy. Different from mine, but not really, just stronger. More intense. Oralgasmic.

"You taste incredible," I said breathlessly.

I pressed my fingers to her mouth, smearing her juices across her lips, wanting to share them with her. She moaned and took my fingers into her mouth, sucking on them. Amazing! I closed my eyes and enjoyed the sensation of her tongue, warm and slippery against my fingertips. Like her pussy was. I slowly pulled my fingers from her mouth and ran them down her body, giving each nipple a squeeze as I made my winding way back to that enticing, moist, hot spot at the juncture of her thighs.

I touched my mouth to hers as I dipped my fingers back between her labia. She moaned and lifted her hips, pressing them upward, against my hand. Her mouth opened under mine, her tongue seeking urgently, penetrating me, searching for my tongue. I let it glide against hers, teasing her in the same way my fingers were teasing her, dancing around the opening to her vagina, tapping there, occasionally pressing just the tips of my fingers along the inner lining.

Her body was in constant motion next to mine, twitching and rocking. She whimpered and moaned into my mouth, turning up the sexual charge, making me ache inside. *So this is what it is like for my lovers when they pleasure me,* I thought, reveling in her abandonment.

I sent my thumb searching for her clit, and found it with some difficulty, even though I knew exactly where to go. *Such a little thing,* I thought to myself, thinking of my own clit. *Big anatomical difference there.*

Any other thoughts I might have had fled my mind as Pilar jolted and cried out when my thumb grazed her clit. She took my head in both her hands and kissed me hard, sucking my tongue into her mouth. I tapped her clit a few times with my thumb and then slid my first two fingers deep inside her. Her body went rigid and she broke the kiss, throwing her head back over my arm.

"Yes! God yes! Like that . . . Just . . . like . . . that!"

I pumped my fingers in and out of her, giving an extra little bouncing push when I could go no further. She was unbelievably hot and wet inside. Feeling the incredible liquid warmth of her vagina, I understood why men seemed so single-mindedly intent on getting inside women. If it felt this good with my fingers, I could only imagine how intense it would be with a cock. I felt a new appreciation for Drew's self-control and promised myself I would not get angry at him the next time he came too soon. Hell, I was ready to come just from the feel of my fingers inside her.

I leaned my head forward and took Pilar's bottom lip into my mouth, sucking on it. I pressed my thumb more firmly onto her clit and rubbed it in a circular motion, jamming my fingers as deeply as I could into her. I hooked my fingers in under her pubic bone, there, on that small rough spot on the top of her vagina, and rocked her whole body with the motion of my arm.

Pilar dragged in a deep breath and held it, her body arching as she came, her vaginal muscles clamping down on my fingers, fluttering wildly. Her legs kicked out and she let out her breath in short, sharp little gasps.

"Oh god . . . Fuck . . . Oh! Oh! Ah!"

A final forceful jolt of her hips against my hand and then she collapsed against the mattress, her chest heaving. I slowly slipped my fingers out of her and rested my hand on her belly. She tore her hair away from her sweaty face and looked up at me.

"I thought you'd never been with a woman before," she gasped.

I looked into her eyes, and a dark memory surfaced, only to be banished immediately.

"Not like this," I said honestly. "Not at all like this."

The Altar of New Orleans

Raven Black

(1989)

It all began on one beautiful autumn night on the outskirts of New Orleans. I was waiting on the concrete steps of the neighborhood library for Julia, my girlfriend, to pick me up for a night on the town. The sun had just begun to go down, and as I smoked a cigarette I watched the sky turn from blue to violet behind the oak trees. The air was unusually chilly that afternoon and I shivered as the darkness closed in on me.

As I sat on the steps, I thought about my relationship with Julia. What was I, a nineteen-year-old girl, doing with a thirty-seven-year-old woman? I turned the thought around in my head a few more times as I put out one cigarette and out of habit lit another. There was no definite answer. For every bad reason there were half a dozen good ones. In the short time that I had known Julia, she had always managed to keep the relationship rich and alive. There was never a dull moment with her around. I guess that was one thing that attracted me to her, aside from the fact that she was intelligent, domineering, and drop-dead gorgeous. It was our two-month anniversary this night and I knew that it was going to be a special one. Julia had informed me earlier that she had a surprise and not to expect to go home that night. I was all for it.

Not having much of an idea of what she had in mind, I wore my best clothes and tried to look a bit refined, expecting some fine dining to be part of the plans. I felt a bit odd in a dress but I knew that she'd be delighted to see me in one. I was always a bit of a tomboy but Julia brought out a side of me that I had rarely explored in my youth. Goose bumps began to invade my flesh and I pulled my skirt over my knees. I put my cigarette out and felt a grin spread upon my face as I saw a pair of headlights making their way down the winding road. I hadn't seen my love in over a week.

As the car got closer, I could see that it was indeed Julia's red convertible.

When Julia got out of the car she looked exquisite. She was wearing a sheer purple shirt with a skimpy black dress beneath it that clung to her curvaceous bosom and hips. Transparent black stockings and dark leather heels graced her legs and feet. Her red hair was pinned up in an attractive heap atop her head. I could hardly keep my eyes from her body or my hands from beneath her shirt. I wanted her at that moment, my body yearned for her the entire time that we were apart, but I contained myself. I didn't want to spoil the plans she had for this afternoon.

"Hello," she said with the cunning of a serpent dancing behind her emerald-green eyes.

I returned her greeting and reached out to kiss her but she wouldn't allow me that tiny bit of satisfaction. She just waved her finger and gave me a look as if I were being a bad little girl.

Before I could carry the conversation any further, Julia asked me to turn my back to her and close my eyes. And as I did, I felt a silken shroud cover my eyes. My body trembled with excitement as she tied the blindfold around my head. This was going to be a good night indeed.

She took my hand in her own and slowly guided me down the rest of the steps and into her car.

"Where are we going?" I said with a smile spreading further across my face, knowing damn well that she wasn't going to give me a straight answer. I always liked to toy with her that way. And she loved to play along.

"I'm going to take my baby for a walk," she nearly purred and then giggled sadistically.

I could hear Julia putting the keys in the ignition and starting the engine, and music playing on the radio. I tried to talk but she asked me not to.

She said, "The experience will be better if you don't say a word. Relax and enjoy it, let your other senses heighten, my love." I did just as she asked.

I heard a mechanical buzzing noise above me and soon figured out that it was the convertible top being raised. As the car took off, a sudden rush of fall air kissed my face. I could smell the water nearby, hear the ships signaling their existence and the chirping of the crickets. I was aware of my body slightly shifting side to side as we rounded the curves of the winding river road that ran beside the levee.

The sound of rushing traffic became clear as we entered the highway. Julia sang along with the song on the radio. Her voice was calm and confident. A strand of her hair whipped across my face, stinging my left cheek. The feeling excited me. I could picture her hair flowing in the cool wind; her wavy red locks caressed my imagination. I became wet thinking about her luscious lips, the way her pale flesh always looked in the moonlight. My eyes grew hungry for her. And I could smell her. The sweet smell of her perfume and her sex always stimulated me. The leather of the seat beneath me began to feel softer, almost one with my body. I found my hand wandering toward her thigh but only managed to fondle the gearshift in the process.

"Unh unh, you naughty little girl," she said as she slapped my hand away. Her nails scratched the surface of my flesh causing me to squirm in my seat. I let out a delicate sigh.

As the car continued on, I opened my eyes. My eyelashes fluttered against the silken shroud, comfortably tickling my eyelids. I began to see lights through the blindfold. I could make out the colors of the traffic lights and the white blurs of the passing streetlamps as the city grew near.

The car stopped again, and Julia took my hand once more and guided me from the car. I nearly tripped on what must have been a curb. She steadied me and we began to walk.

I could hear her heels on the sidewalk, cars driving slowly by, the sound of people talking, and the occasional clanging of a spoon upon a porcelain coffee cup or table. Smells of fresh coffee, alcohol, and magnolia filled my senses, delighting me. I had a good idea where we were—one of my favorite spots in the French Quarter near an outdoor coffeehouse. The combination of those scents was unmistakable to me.

The area had been like a second home at the time.

Excitement began to build within me once again as she tightened her grip. I thought of the total control she had over me and felt my nipples hardening beneath my thin knit dress.

I sensed a hundred eyes upon me, the warmth of bodies behind me as we stopped and waited to cross the busy street. The voices began to fade once more and all I could hear again was the rhythmic clicking of her heels on the pavement. The sound began to echo and I could feel the ground beneath my feet becoming uneven. It seemed as if we were walking on cobblestones. I could smell day-old garbage mingling with alcohol. We stopped walking.

"Do you know where we are sweetheart?" She paused, but not long enough for me to answer. "Do you remember where we first kissed?" she continued.

Julia began to gently push me backward and then I felt a brick wall behind me. I knew where we were. She had me pinned up against a wall in an alleyway, Pirate's Alley.

Before I could think another thought, her lips touched mine, kissing me once, her tongue teasing the hungry opening. I tried to stick my tongue in her mouth, but she backed away, smeared something all over my wet lips, and pushed it inside my mouth with one of her fingers. I found my hands pushing her skirt up around her thighs and grabbing at her buttocks as she kissed me again. My heartbeat picked up at the moment I realized what she had put into my mouth. It was cocaine. We had shared it a few times before, but never like this.

I wanted to take off the blindfold but she would not allow it. She pushed my hands above my head with her own and held them to the wall, pushing the bitter substance farther into my mouth with her tongue. She positioned herself up against my leg. I could feel the heat from between her legs moving upon my bare thigh. She planted many delicate kisses on my neck and then asked in a seductive voice, "Do you want me?"

She already knew the answer but I replied anyway as she continued to straddle my leg. "Y-y-yes Julia," I managed to mutter.

"Well, that's just too bad." She took me by the arm and led me away like an angry parent would an unruly child. She always had that sadistic streak in her. It only excited me more because I knew then that the surprise was going to be much greater than this.

We walked for what seemed like ten minutes or so and then I heard the jangling of keys and the sound of a door opening. We walked a few dozen steps and she sat me down in a chair and made me promise not to remove the blindfold. She said that it would spoil the whole surprise if I did.

I waited for what seemed a half an hour and had a hard time keeping still. I could feel blood coursing through my veins and rushing through my head. Breathing felt easier. It seemed like I was on top of the world, invincible.

Julia returned, led me down the hallway and into another room. The rich smell of incense hung heavy in the air.

"Are you ready?"

"Yes." My heart continued to flutter comfortably.

I felt her fingers brush the back of my neck as she undid the blindfold. Her hands were cold and slightly trembling.

As the shroud left my eyes I saw a platform before me, aglow with candles. And as my eyes adjusted to the light, I began to notice the many objects that covered the dark surface: crosses, both upright and inverted, skeletal remains, dolls, phallic symbols, statuettes, and many other items that I couldn't quite make out in the dark.

I looked back at Julia in amazement. "Surprise," she said with a thick grin.

At that point, I noticed that she had changed out of her clothes and into a sheer black robe. Her nipples began to peek through the thin material as she started to unbutton my dress. She kissed me softly.

"You know, I always wanted to make love to a woman on an altar," she whispered into my ear as she pulled down the top of my dress. I felt my nipples harden as they brushed against her gown.

My hands began to roam her body as I looked into her eyes. I was naked within a few moments.

I felt like her puppet; I would do anything she wanted me to. Anything.

Julia made it so that my back was to her and I was facing the altar as she kissed my neck and caressed my breasts.

"I have another surprise for you my dear."

I remained silent. I couldn't imagine what else she could have come up with.

"Don't you want to know who helped me with all of this?"

"Mmmm." My body was ready to explode with anticipation. She had teased me enough. I wanted her to make love to me right then. I didn't care about anything else. She mumbled something more and I couldn't quite make out what she said. Before I knew it another woman was standing next to me; it was her best friend, Victoria.

I was consumed. I didn't know what to do or say so I just stood still and stared at Victoria, waiting for someone to make the next move.

Victoria had the same sheer, black robe on except that it was open, exposing a rosary that hung around her neck, the cross falling between her ample breasts. Her nipples were full and dark, unlike Julia's. I could not believe what was happening and said nothing as Victoria put her hands on me. Julia was still behind me, holding me still so her friend could examine me.

After a few moments, they led me onto a large clearing upon the altar.

"Kneel down," Victoria said in a very soft voice.

I knelt down, facing Julia. I spotted many opened bottles of red wine, pictures of deities, and a figure of a wax hand with its fingers alight gracing the altar. Victoria stood behind Julia and gently pulled down her robe as Julia ran her fingers through my dark hair. "Let us pray," Victoria whispered.

She began chanting something foreign to me and pulled out an ornate knife. She positioned Julia's head to one side with one hand and cut Julia beneath her right breast using the other. Julia was ecstatic, writhing beneath the steel of the blade.

I was caught off guard by Victoria's dominance over Julia as I watched the blood well up and then cascade down her full body. Her life fluid looked black against her pale skin.

Victoria continued to chant as I began to take Julia's blood into my mouth, licking it off her belly and then tracing a pathway to her cunt with my tongue. The salty, metallic taste made me salivate, craving more. It was as if an invisible hand was guiding me, pushing me on. I wanted to make another incision in her flesh but I didn't dare.

Julia let out a soft, steady moan and I felt her legs go weak as she climaxed.

I gazed up and Victoria was no longer behind Julia. She was in the corner, praying with the rosary beads wrapped around her hands. Julia pushed my head back between her legs.

Shortly after that I felt Victoria's hands upon me, positioning me on my hands and knees. Julia sat on the altar in front of me as her friend knelt behind me. I began to lick my lover's wound and went down on her once again. Victoria performed cunnilingus on me as I serviced my lover. So much energy was passing between us. It felt as if the three of us had formed a circuit.

I gasped as I felt something penetrate my vagina. I looked up and then behind me. Julia was watching Victoria work a phallus from the altar in and out of my willing hole. And when I faced forward, Julia took a double-headed dildo from beside her and slid one end into her vagina and made me put the other end in my mouth. Julia put her hand on the back of my head so she could fuck my mouth.

As I worked it back and forth between my lips and into my throat, Victoria began to tongue my asshole.

I squirmed as I felt my virgin hole open up. I felt something rounded and slick penetrate it. I looked back toward her. She was sticking the bottom of a penis-like crucifix slowly in and out of my anus. The sensation of the phallus and the crucifix together felt extraordinary. I didn't want it to stop. I screamed out in pleasure and climaxed again as I felt the idol's feet and knees enter me.

Many minutes of pleasuring each other went on. I became lost in the warmth of the two bodies. It felt as if we had melted into one being.

Julia pushed me off, removed the dildo from her snatch, and walked away. Victoria took the two objects from my anus and cunt. I turned over onto my back and found Victoria licking the phallus. This got me extremely hot. I kept staring at her and she climbed on top of me, hungrily kissing me and fingering my insides. I returned the gestures.

Suddenly, I felt a lukewarm liquid being poured onto me. Julia was standing above us, pouring an entire bottle of red wine over both of us. I opened my mouth and allowed some in.

I began to lick the sangria off Victoria's flesh as Julia watched. I felt something come over me. I turned Victoria over and straddled her. I stuck two of my fingers inside her and began to take control of her body, to make her squirm and moan beneath me. I wanted to make her scream in ecstasy and I did. After she climaxed I started to eat her out. She smelled sweet, of decomposing flowers.

Julia was behind me again, lapping at my hungry cunt.

"Mmmmm, you're mine, bitch!" Julia said forcefully as she entered me with the head of her strap-on. She put her hands on my hips and pushed the entire length of the shaft inside me. She began to shove it in and out slowly and then faster until I threw my head back in ecstasy. I could tell that she was really getting off by fucking me in this position. The motion of her hips was smooth and rhythmic. She continued fucking me until Victoria and I climaxed again. Between the three of us, we sounded like a bunch of felines in heat.

When it was all over, I noticed that the candles were nearly to their end and most of the smoke from the incense had left the room. My head and body were drunk with delight.

Afterward, we all took a shower and got dressed. The three of us went out for a very late dinner, coffee, and dessert as if nothing out of the ordinary had happened. Just three lovers out on the town, enjoying one another's company.

The night seemed so surreal to me. My head finally felt as if it were swimming back into reality as the sun began to rise. We were at a twenty-four-hour coffeehouse, spoons clanking against coffee cups once more. Last night's drunks were being woken and pushed out by the demand of the nine-to-fivers wishing to start their day without blemish to their sight.

There was a lull in the rigmarole.

Julia turned to Victoria and me, sported a sly smile, and said, "Wanna do it again?"

And so it was.

Sometimes I feel guilty for what happened. But, to this day, I cannot pass an altar without getting excited. I would do it all over again if given the chance. In some strange way, my body felt cleansed in a city that is supposed to be known for sin. I will never forget that blessed night on what I consider the altar of New Orleans.

The Visit

Lora McCall

Many times I imagined myself unbuttoning Anne's soft silk blouse, pulling it off her shoulders, reaching behind her back, and unhooking her bra. Even in my fantasies, my breath caught as I imagined how her breasts looked when freed from their restraints. Then, bending over, and with one hand caressing one of her breasts, I would slowly circle the other breast with my tongue—narrowing the circles until I found her nipple and covering it with my mouth. Slowly, I would kiss my way over to the other breast before moving up Anne's neck and ending my fantasy with caressing kisses on her eyelids, her cheeks, her lips, before a final, passionate, full-mouth kiss.

It didn't seem possible I was now spending a week alone with Anne—no husband, no other friends.

The third afternoon of my stay at Anne's beach house, she suggested we walk to a nearby restaurant for dinner. I had forgotten my hair dryer so Anne said I could borrow the one she had with her. I showered, dressed, and waited for Anne to finish drying her hair. Within minutes the whirring stopped so I tapped on her bedroom door and asked, "May I use your hair dryer?"

The door opened and Anne stood there in white cotton pants, one hand on the doorknob, the other holding the hair dryer, bare footed and bare breasted. The breasts I had been fantasizing about for years were now in front of me: firm, rounded, as darkly tanned as the rest of Anne's body. Even her nipples were tanned.

Speechless, I could not stop myself from staring at her breasts. Anne casually held out the hair dryer. "Here it is."

Stepping forward, and without thinking, I took the dryer and then kissed Anne on the lips. Stunned, I turned to make my retreat but Anne's hand on my arm stopped me. I thought I heard her say, "Lynne, don't go," but I couldn't be sure since my head was now buried in the curve of her neck.

I had been sexually attracted to my colleague and friend for several years, but never acted on my feelings. Anne, happily married, knew I was a lesbian but was unaware of my feelings for her. I did not want any friction between us at work so I told no one of my attraction, not Anne, and not my lesbian friends.

With the clean scent of Anne's hair blending with the sweet fragrance of her body, I quickly overcame my years of restraint, and returned the hug.

Oh my god, I thought to myself, *I'm holding Anne Durrant.*

Instinct took over and I started to softly kiss Anne's neck. Dropping the hair dryer, I put one arm around her shoulder, while my other hand lightly caressed her breasts. I heard Anne catch her breath, but felt no resistance to my touch.

Somehow we managed the few steps to her bed. Gently, I pushed her backward while still gliding my hand from one breast to the other, caressing each while I continued to lightly kiss her neck, cheeks, and eyes. My lips brushed across Anne's lips, before my tongue moved searchingly inside her mouth. I found her tongue waiting and the passion of the moment was exhilarating.

Anne's aroused response emboldened me, and I got lost in kissing her. How long I kissed her, I don't know. Without letting go of her, I drew my head away and started to slowly trace my tongue over her jawline, licking her ear, her neck, and moving down her throat. I could feel her irregular breathing and I thought I heard a low moan come from deep inside her throat.

Cupping her breast in my hand, I pushed it upward so my tongue could easily trace wide circles around her nipple. With each completed circle, I narrowed the circumference until my tongue flicked her nipple a few times before taking it into my mouth.

I could feel a quiver go through Anne's body and I thought, *I'm living my fantasy!*

The sexual tension was exquisite.

I felt overwhelmed by the beauty of her full, rounded breasts. I started to pull down her slacks when her hand stopped me. "Don't you think you should take off your clothes, too?"

LORA McCALL

It was a fair question. "You're right, but I am more focused on you than me."

"Then," Anne offered, "why don't I help you?"

I remembered my own small breasts, not nearly as sensual as Anne's, *but too late to do anything about that,* I thought, as my clothes landed in a pile on the floor next to hers.

Anne lay crossways on the bed, with her head on the pillow. I stood above her for a moment reveling in her nude body. Then I crawled next to her, put one leg between her thighs, and slowly lowered myself on her. Being several inches shorter than her, my toes pressed against the tops of her toes, my head fit nicely into the curve of her neck, my breasts pressed against her breasts, and I moved my thigh against her clitoris. I use my body to cover Anne's body with a gentle, undulating massage.

"It's been years since I have been with anyone," I whispered in her ear. "I hope I remember what to do."

Laughing, Anne whispered back, "Isn't it like riding a bicycle; once you learn how, you never forget."

So true.

Until totally exhausted several hours later, I luxuriated in touching, kissing, caressing Anne. My tongue followed the path my fingers took, gently kissing her lips, sliding across her breasts, brushing her nipples, traversing her stomach, teasingly going into her belly button, stroking the gentle curves of her hips, and then tantalizing myself with feather-light strokes on her inner thighs.

I could sense the tension growing in Anne's body, her back arched and relaxed, then arched again. Her breathing became staccato, and her head turned from side to side.

"How did you do that?" she asked. I sensed it was a statement of wonderment more than curiosity, so I didn't stop to answer her.

My hand pushed Anne's thighs farther apart, and my fingers quickly found her erect clitoris. I stroked her wetness before gently separating the warm folds of her swollen vulva so my tongue could easily find its target. By now I was as sexually aroused as Anne. With my mouth engulfing her clit, my fingers glided downward, finding her vagina and exploring the area before I entered her. Within seconds a flood of wetness covered both of us. Anne's hips rose and fell as her body went into the rhythmic throes of an orgasm.

Finally, her body went limp, and her hand motioned me to come to her.

"Hold me," she said. "I need to feel you next to me."

I entwined my arms and legs around her and held her until I heard her whisper, "I can't believe it. I have never climaxed so quickly. What did you do?"

"I wish I could tell you, but all I know is that it felt like the most natural thing in the world for me to make love to you."

Anne shook her head slowly but said nothing.

We rested, and then I made love to her again before she insisted it was her turn to touch me. I was the beneficiary of her sensual exploration of a woman's body. A bit tentative at first, touching me as I had touched her, Anne soon followed her own intuition.

Fatigue finally took over and we both fell asleep.

In the early morning light I felt movement. I was alert enough to see Anne pulling on her running clothes.

"Are you really going running?" I mumbled.

She leaned over, gave my head a gentle tussle, and said, "See you later, Lynne."

When I awoke several hours later, the condo was quiet. Throwing on my T-shirt and shorts, I looked over the balcony but could not see Anne on the beach or the lawn below us.

Umm. How strange, I thought. *Maybe she's sitting in the coffee shop across the street.* I knew she liked to read a newspaper while she had her coffee, but it didn't take long to discover she wasn't there.

Returning to the condo, I decided to wait another thirty minutes then I would have to take action. First, call the hospital to ask if a woman fitting Anne's description had been admitted. If no, then call the police and report a missing person. I started to look up the necessary phone numbers as the front door opened and Anne entered.

"Where have you been?" I asked, relieved to see her safe. "I have been so worried."

"I told you I was going on a run," she said coolly.

Her aloof response set the tone for the remainder of the day. Any effort to talk about our night together was met with obvious disinterest and a change of topic. It was a long day so after dinner, I went to my bedroom. Tired, frustrated, and angry, I just wanted to be by myself. Chastising myself for not keeping my emotions in check and my hands to myself, I realized this visit had turned into a disaster. Nothing left to do but catch an early flight home and deal with the consequences later. I turned off my light and thankfully fell asleep.

The sound of music awoke me a few hours later. It was after midnight but the lights from the parking lot illuminated my room so I could see Anne standing in the doorway. Slowly pulling down her white strapless shift, I could hear the song "Music of the Night" coming from the living room stereo. In a soft, husky voice, Anne asked, "It's the music of the night, Lynne—come to bed with me?"

"Dammit Anne, what are you doing? You disappear this morning, and won't talk to me this afternoon. Now you want me to have sex with you? I need to understand what is happening here."

"Please . . . I promise we'll talk in the morning."

Seeing her standing naked in front of me was too alluring. I got out of bed, pulled off my T-shirt, and followed Anne into her bedroom.

"No running tomorrow morning," I said in a firm voice, "we are going to talk."

A bottle of wine and two wine glasses were on Anne's nightstand. As she poured the wine, I said, "If I knew this day was going to end like this, I could have enjoyed it a heck of a lot more."

"Shhh, we will talk about it in the morning, but not now, OK?"

For the next few hours, we made love as though the previous day had never happened. It was as sexually exciting to make love to Anne the second time as it had been the first. We both admitted to being sore, but not *that* sore. Anne was more demanding than the night before, which made it even more pleasurable for me, but I, too, was determined to cover her body with kisses, spending time caressing her breasts, finding her nipples with my tongue. At times she guided my fingers over her body, or asked me to be lighter or more forceful with my touch.

Oral sex had never been my favorite thing, but I loved moving my mouth and tongue over Anne's clitoris and feeling it harden. It was sexually exciting for my fingers to explore her vagina, and finally put my mouth on her clitoris as my fingers entered her. The strong gyrations of her hips forced me to take my mouth away from her clit and lie next to her as she climaxed. I kept my fingers inside her vagina, moving with the motions of her hips, until she could no longer endure it, then she pulled my hand out so she could calm herself.

As we reclined against the pillows and drank wine, I gently traced my fingernails around her breasts and down her stomach, until I reached her clitoris. Anne's hand reached for me, but I said, "Let's try something a bit different." I cupped my hand over her hand, with my fingers on top of her fingers, so we were both stroking her clitoris.

I guided our fingers downward, playfully touching the tip of her vagina and then withdrawing. "Shall we both go in you?" I whispered in her ear.

"Yes, oh yes, let's do it."

Anne's reaction to our touching her was electrifying. Her body started convulsing after a few thrusts, the wetness squirted out of her vagina, and her moans turned into a low shriek as she climaxed, throwing her body into the bed, grasping a pillow to muffle her increasingly loud screams.

After several minutes of calming down, Anne took my head in her hands, and leaning close to me said, "I have never had an orgasm come so quickly—what did you do?"

Laughing, I said, "We'll talk about it in the morning."

We continued to make love to each other several times throughout the night, and whenever I pulled away to look at Anne, her head would shake in disbelief. Finally, fatigue took over. We straightened the bed as best we could without getting out of it and spoon-held each other until we fell asleep.

When we awoke many hours later, we both felt fuzzy from lack of sleep, too much wine, and too much sex. Gingerly we walked across the street, bought our coffee, and returned to the lanai before Anne started talking.

"After years of great sex with a man I love, I'm experiencing something entirely different with you. The sensations started the moment you put your arms around me, and then you were kissing me and touching my breasts and my mind was going wild. I couldn't stop you and I didn't want to stop you. I am usually slow to get wet—in fact, my husband uses gel to ease my soreness—but I'm wet within seconds after you touch me. And, I have never experienced orgasms as quickly, as often, or so totally consuming as I did with you—and it happened again last night." She paused. "Lynne, I am trying to understand what is happening to me, but I just don't get it. Why do I respond so easily to you?"

"Anne, you are the first married woman I have made love to, so I don't know what to tell you. Maybe the newness of it all enhances the sensations. After all, being touched by a woman is different than being touched by a man."

She shook her head in disbelief. "I just don't understand it."

"There's something I don't understand," I said. "If you felt so conflicted with our first night of sex, why did you come into my bedroom last night?"

"I tried not to, Lynne. I went to bed, couldn't sleep, tried to read, couldn't do that either. Then I asked myself 'what's happening here?' That's when I realized I liked sex with you. I approached your bedroom several times before I got the idea of the music. I was already drinking wine so I just added another glass and decided to go for broke."

I forgot about taking an earlier plane as I leaned over, kissed Anne, and said, "Thank you for a gutsy move. It was another wonderful night, and I loved it, but I have to admit to being totally exhausted."

"Me, too," said Anne.

"I suggest we skip the beach today. Let's find some shady lounges on the grass and read and sleep."

Later in the afternoon we wandered into the condo to get a cool drink. Anne looked sexy in her bikini, but even sexier without it. She was standing in the small kitchen holding two beers when I entered. I placed the beers on the countertop behind her, pressed her against the refrigerator door, and kissed my way up her neck to her lips while my hand pulled down her bikini bra to stroke her breasts.

Then I slid my fingers down her belly, nuzzling her belly button before slipping inside her swimsuit. I felt her wetness quickly flood her clitoris and vagina. My fingers gently separated the folds of her vulva, flicking her clit before sliding lower to enter her. I could hear Anne's soft moans getting a bit louder, and at the same time, we could hear people talking outside of our opaque kitchen window that was slightly ajar.

Anne started to draw back, but I whispered in her ear, "They can't see us but they can hear us." By now I knew how to touch Anne's body to bring her quickly—or slowly—to climax. I covered her breasts with kisses and took delight in cupping my fingers around her fingers so we could both enter her together. She struggled to remain standing while she climaxed, but finally collapsed to the floor. After a few seconds I stopped hugging her, reached for our beers as she again shook her head in wonderment.

I had no answers.

Our remaining days were spent on the beach, and our nights—and some afternoons—were filled with exciting sex. Then, it was time to leave. Anne's husband was arriving the next day so she drove me to the airport and gave me a final hug.

Settled in my window seat, my pillow tucked behind my head, my eyes closed, I shook my head in amazement as the big plane rumbled down the runway.

Did this really happen, I wondered, as images of my lovemaking with Anne filled my mind, *or was this one of my fantasies?*

Sea Life

Shannon McDonnell

The one o'clock penguin feeding show started typically enough. Alex stood before the exhibit window and posed simple questions to the crowd. Kids sat on the floor, endlessly fidgeting, while their parents hovered beside them, looking mildly interested or bored. A group of teenagers slouched at the back, captivated by the rockhopper penguins but trying not to show it.

Alex adjusted the microphone at her mouth and glanced behind her. Two of the animal husbandry staff had entered the enclosure, holding buckets of small fish. "Does anyone know what penguins eat?" Alex asked, turning back to the onlookers. As an aquarium tour guide, she had posed these questions hundreds of times before. The kids' answers were seldom amusing anymore.

"Pizza!" someone shouted. The crowd tittered.

Alex sighed, then remembered to look patient and friendly. It was an effort today. The whole tour guide thing was getting old. She needed a vacation, or better yet, a girlfriend. It had been six months since she and Abbie had broken up, six long months devoid of companionship. Devoid even of sex. Sex with Abbie had been mind-blowing while it lasted. Alex needed that again.

"No, not pizza," she told the crowd. "They eat fish, and crustaceans called krill." Inside the habitat, one of the workers was handing out fish to the penguins, which crowded around and snapped up the little silver treats in their beaks. The second staffer made notes on a clipboard.

A chubby boy raised his hand. "Why does that penguin look so terrible?" he whined, pointing.

Before Alex could answer, the kid's dad said, "Bad hair day!" Wiseass, playing for a laugh. Alex waited for the crowd to quiet down, then explained that Fezziwig, the penguin in question, was molting.

Then she heard: "How do penguins mate?"

The crowd fell silent, except for the giggles of a few children. The adults looked amused or embarrassed. The teenagers were hanging on Alex's answer.

The speaker, Alex saw, was a young woman, early twenties at most. She wore a sweatshirt and jeans, and a backpack over one shoulder. Probably a university student, Alex guessed. The nearby campus had a major marine biology program.

"How do penguins—mate?" Alex repeated. "You mean, physically?" The girl nodded, and a mischievous little smile tugged at her lips. Alex couldn't look away. The questioner was strikingly good-looking: shortish but fit, with full lips, a smattering of freckles across her pale cheeks, strawberry-blonde hair pulled back in a ponytail. And in her eyes, there was something for Alex only. Alex felt a stirring in her stomach and a liquefying jolt between her thighs.

No clever quip came to her. "They, uh, mate in pretty much the same way all birds do. The female lays on her belly; the male mounts her from behind—"

"Come on, Billy," a mother hissed. She shot Alex a baleful glance and stormed off, pulling the disappointed boy beside her.

Alex laughed and felt better. The workers had disappeared from the penguin enclosure, and the rockhoppers were waddling off, their stomachs full. When Alex turned back to the audience, the stranger was gone. In fact, the crowd was breaking up. "Well, that's our penguin feeding program for today," she said. "Be sure to check out the other exhibits."

As the visitors dispersed, Alex moved among them, searching. The girl had vanished like a ghost. Alex gave up and headed for her scheduled talk at the otter exhibit, feeling depressed again.

She was getting a cup of coffee at the aquarium's cafe the following afternoon—another raw, blustery day that promised rain—when her glance turned to the glass wall and the sea beyond. Yesterday's visitor was lounging against the railing of the observation deck, her face turned up to contemplate the heavy sky. Her figure was ripe with youthful ebullience: sweater stretching snugly over smallish, perky breasts; cargo pants hugging her cute ass; ponytail tossing in the wind. The bench where the girl had been sitting was strewn with textbooks. A mountain bike leaned against the bench.

Alex paid for her coffee and hurried outside. Despite the chilly weather, her palms were sweaty and her face felt hot. Moving up softly behind the object of her attention, she said, "'How do penguins mate?' That's a good one."

The younger woman turned, and Alex nearly fell into her eyes—slate gray like the ocean behind her, and just as deep. Recognition dawned immediately. *Had she been thinking of me already?* Alex wondered.

The girl smiled. "So? It's a legitimate question."

"Yeah, but in that setting, kind of provocative, don't you think?"

"That was the point. You looked like you needed someone to shake things up."

"I did?"

The girl laughed. "I'm Olivia. You want to sit down?"

"I'm due for a presentation at the shark exhibit," Alex said.

"Please, just for a minute."

Squeezing onto the bench beside Olivia's stuff, Alex introduced herself. "But you know my name already," she said, fingering her name badge. "So . . . you're a student?"

"Yeah, I'm a senior at the university. Final exams coming up." She sat down close to Alex. Very close.

Alex swallowed nervously. "What's your major?"

"Comparative psychology."

"Hmm. The minds and behavior of animals, right?"

"You must have studied something similar, to work here."

Alex shook her head. "Hardly. I was an English major. Just sort of fell into this." Her glance fell on Olivia's hand, barely an inch from hers. It was decorated with freckles. "So you dropped that penguin question on me just to get a reaction?"

"Yeah, partly. All those kids gaping and their parents looking mortified." Olivia rolled her eyes. "Come on, you loved it."

Alex had to laugh.

"Besides, I really wanted to know." Olivia brushed a stray lock of hair off her forehead. "That was nothing compared to what I *might* have asked."

"Oh? Such as?"

Olivia said, "Well, are there gay penguins?"

Alex had been about to take a sip of coffee, but that stopped her. "I don't know. Same-sex preference does crop up in other animals, and some fish." Eyeing her companion over the rim of her cup, Alex saw that Olivia's expression had turned cagey. Did she know Alex was gay? She had always thought she was hard to read that way.

Olivia nodded toward the ocean, which was rough with whitecaps. "Some of the female seagulls on the Santa Barbara Islands practice lesbian mating." Her eyes slid back to meet Alex's. "They go through all the motions, even laying sterile eggs."

"Really?" All Alex wanted just then was to lay with Olivia, the Olivia underneath the backpack and sweatshirt and jeans. She imagined them both nude, hands caressing, exploring curves and secret recesses . . .

Olivia was watching her closely, and just for an instant, Alex saw the want in Olivia's eyes, the desire simmering just beneath the surface. Alex felt a tremor of excitement.

But she was late. "I have to go," she said, rising from the bench. "You'd better get inside, too. It's going to pour." She hesitated, unable or unwilling to walk away. "See you around?"

"Yep. I ride my bike over here a lot," Olivia said. "This is my favorite place to cram."

Cram. Alex imagined other places where they could cram together, body to body, her own dark bush tangling with the other's reddish mound. Alex wanted to slide her tongue into Olivia's sex, taste her, satisfy the craving. She sighed. And then she had an idea.

"We're opening a new exhibit next week. If you can be here Friday, a few minutes after we close, I'll give you a sneak preview. Interested?"

Olivia's face lit up. "Love to."

Alex wrote her cell phone number on the back of a business card. "The security guys lock up promptly. Just call me when you get here so I can let you in."

"OK. Thanks."

Alex hurried back inside the aquarium to talk about sharks, feeling a bit like a shark herself.

Friday was the one evening that Alex could be sure the other employees and volunteers would leave more or less on time. There would still be a small night shift, since some exhibits needed attention after dark, but those were in a completely different wing. She and Olivia would have privacy.

Alex didn't see Olivia before then, not even once. By the time the aquarium cleared out on Friday afternoon, everyone wielding umbrellas against the rainy twilight, she had convinced herself that Olivia wouldn't show. She was sitting in the employee break room at ten after six when her phone rang. She flipped it open with trembling fingers.

"Hi, Alex? It's Olivia. I'm at the main entrance."

"Great! Be right there."

Feeling a surge of nervous energy, Alex bolted from her chair. Out among the galleries, all was quiet except for her echoing footsteps. The building seemed larger now, cavernous. The overhead lamps cast soft pools of light on the slate floor, giving the place a romantic quality. The effect was enhanced by the glow of fluorescent blue fish tanks in the walls.

Olivia was standing with her bike under the overhang. She had ridden through a downpour; water dripped from her nose and chin, and her hair hung in drenched strands around her face. Hastily, Alex unlocked the glass door and swung it open.

"No car," Olivia said, in response to Alex's unasked question. Her breath condensed in the chilled evening air.

"Come in," Alex said. "Yeah, the bike, too."

Olivia stepped past Alex, who caught a whiff of floral-scented shampoo. "It's a short ride," Olivia added, propping her bike against the wall. "Besides, I like the rain."

Alex closed and relocked the door. "Let me find you something to dry off—"

"That's OK." Olivia shrugged out of her jacket and hung it on her bike's handlebar. Then she pulled her sweatshirt over her head and used it to dry her hair. A close-fitting black T-shirt hugged her slender midriff and her jutting breasts. Watching her,

Alex felt a flutter in her stomach and a corresponding twinge in her groin. Olivia caught her staring and smiled. Alex felt her face flush.

"So, where are we going?" Olivia asked, laying her sweatshirt on top of her jacket.

"I'll show you." Without thinking, Alex took Olivia's hand; the gesture was accepted without a word. Feeling more excited and tense by the second, Alex led Olivia through the empty main hall, then into the aquarium's catacombs. Finally they arrived at a makeshift door that the construction crew had erected to hide the new exhibit until its grand opening. Inside, all the work was done. Alex held the door open for Olivia and followed her in.

The younger woman gasped. Alex knew the feeling; she had experienced it herself the first time she saw it.

They stood in a circular chamber under a vast glass dome. On the other side of the glass, thousands of shimmering silver anchovies glided round and round the room, all swimming in the same direction, their shiny bodies sparkling in the indigo water. The room itself was bathed in dim yellow light. Alex turned away from Olivia for a moment and regarded the curving glass, briefly lost in wonder.

"It feels like we're underwater," she heard Olivia say. "Like we're in the ocean. It's beautiful."

There was a long silence, during which the sexual tension Alex was feeling seemed to expand and fill the room. After what seemed like an eternity she forced herself to turn around.

Olivia, she saw, was watching her, not the fish. Olivia took a step toward her, and Alex saw the desire in her eyes again, the same desire she had glimpsed in Olivia's face a few days ago—only this time it was bold, raw. Olivia wanted her to see. To know.

"Can we stay here awhile?" Olivia asked, so close now that their lips were almost touching. Alex felt her cunt respond with a gush of wetness, and her breath caught in her throat. Olivia's hand was on her arm; she leaned forward and Alex kissed her, long and deep. Finally they broke apart, panting.

"I knew you felt it, too," Olivia murmured. "I've watched you, wanted you—"

The rest of her sentence was lost as she crushed her lips

against Alex's again. Their hands met, clasped, then separated to roam over each other's body. Olivia reached under Alex's shirt and unhooked her bra. Alex searched for Olivia's and found nothing; she wasn't wearing one. Alex grabbed Olivia's shirt and lifted it over her head. Olivia raised her arms to help, freeing her buoyant breasts to Alex's eyes, her hands, her mouth. Olivia's head tipped back and she sighed, pressing her breasts into Alex's hands. Her sighs became moans as Alex rolled the stiff nipples between her fingers. Alex bent and took them between her lips, one after the other. Olivia arched her back, feeding her flesh to Alex. *Her breasts are like candy apples,* Alex thought as she suckled. *Candy apples with cherries on top.*

Coming up for air at last, Alex said, "Get out of these wet jeans." Olivia was already working at the buttons. She tugged the soaked denim down, and Alex reached for her panties, which were soaked, too—but more from desire than from the rain. For a moment, Alex rubbed Olivia through the wet fabric, making the desperate girl quiver with frustration. Slipping her hand inside her lover's undies, Alex discovered that Olivia's labia were perfectly smooth, hairless. Just above, she felt a strip of trimmed pubic hair.

"Oh God," Olivia breathed, pushing against Alex's fingers. "I need to feel you. All of you." Kneeling, she pulled Alex down beside her, and they practically tore the rest of their clothing off. Alex's breasts were large and soft compared to Olivia's. She leaned into Olivia for a kiss; Olivia shuddered as their nipples rubbed together.

Olivia lay back on the floor, looking flushed with need. She reached for Alex, but Alex wanted a moment to admire Olivia's beauty, from the tidy curves of her hips and breasts to the neatly groomed patch of honey-blonde hair between her legs. At last, Alex eased into Olivia's embrace. As they slid against each other, the anchovies continued their endless rotation around and above them, gliding along obliviously. Or were they watching? *And,* thought Alex, *were any of* them *gay?*

Olivia's skin was smooth and warm. She wrapped her arms around Alex, and as their breasts crushed together, Alex felt Olivia's heart beating in her chest. Alex used her knee to push

Olivia's thighs open, then pressed her own thigh to the slick spot between Olivia's legs. Olivia pushed back, grinding. Alex's cunt throbbed wetly against Olivia's hip. Soon they were both trembling, and the room filled with the heady scent of sex.

Alex was desperate to taste Olivia. She turned around and cleaved her body to her lover's once more, this time with her thighs on either side of Olivia's head and her belly atop Olivia's breasts. Olivia's lovely vulva was right below Alex's face, the lips thickened and glistening. Alex filled her nostrils with Olivia's aroma and then dove in with all the pent-up excitement she'd been holding inside. Her tongue slid up, down, inside Olivia's fleshy softness. Her taste was redolent of salty brine, like the sea. Heaven.

Then Alex had to stop and refocus, for Olivia was nosing into her own cunt, her breath falling in warm, rapid little puffs between Alex's folds. Olivia's mouth felt like a nibbling fish as she sought Alex's nerve center. They both knew she'd found it when Alex jerked and rose halfway into a sitting position over Olivia's face. Sparks of exquisite sensation radiated from the point of contact out to every nerve in Alex's body. "Harder," she urged, grinding down onto Olivia's mouth. The flutters of Olivia's tongue against her clit became thrashings that threatened to dissolve her. Olivia moaned, responding to Alex's pleasure, and pushed her face deeper into Alex's sex. Olivia's hands curved around Alex's buttocks and spread them open. A moment later Olivia's tongue slipped, eel-like, into her ass, even as Olivia pumped two fingers in and out of Alex's cunt.

"Jesus. You're . . . driving me . . . insane . . . " Alex's words sounded strangled, but Olivia understood. Her fingers and tongue worked Alex's two holes with a practiced touch. She pressed her thumb to Alex's clit, pulsing it back and forth, and Alex knew no more for the next few moments. The room faded, her body quaked, and her mind retreated into primal bliss.

When Alex came out of it, Olivia's slit still filled her vision, waiting for her to return the favor. Alex spread the lips with her fingertips and raked her tongue through Olivia's pink cleft, making Olivia's whole body undulate. Faster and faster Alex licked, giving special attention to the little peanut emerging from its hood. Taking a cue from Olivia, Alex pushed her thumb into her ass. That sent Olivia sky high. She thrashed and squirmed below Alex, and her throaty cries reverberated through the domed chamber. Alex couldn't help worrying that the sounds of Olivia's climax might bring the night crew to investigate. But the danger passed. Olivia laid her cheek against Alex's inner thigh, still breathing hard.

Alex rolled onto her back and they lay together on the sweat-dampened floor. Staring up at the dome of silver fish, Alex thought about all the people who would walk through this space soon, marveling at the spectacle surrounding them but never suspecting what she and Olivia had done in there. Round and round the anchovies swam, perhaps hoping for an encore performance. Or, if they were magnanimous creatures, maybe they hoped the two women would take their show to the rays, or the sea horses, or the octopuses.

Alex had no doubt that she and Olivia would accommodate them.

Never Taste the Fruit

Morgan Aine

"If you don't want to crave the flavor . . ." she said coyly as her eyes burned holes through me, "never taste the fruit." Her long blonde hair cascaded down around her shoulders. It caught the light and reflected rays around her face. In her presence, I was blind to the others around us. The library was full of people. She caught my gaze and I stared at her ruby lips.

My voice caught in my throat. I had come here to do research for a paper, not to be seduced. She had asked to share my table and now she was pressing for more.

She grinned at my obvious discomfort. My panties dampened as her meaning soaked in. I could feel the energy radiating off her. Little beads of perspiration covered my palms.

"Don't tempt me to taste you. I will. You'll be mine, once my tongue enters you." She paused before adding, "And never taste my fruit. You'll crave it the rest of your life."

I couldn't figure out how we arrived here. My simple question regarding books on computers opened the door for introductions. Abby, Vale, Vale, Abby-type of thing.

How did a simple conversation take such a sharp turn?

She took my innocent question of "Do you have a boyfriend?" into an open response of "Hardly," and led to me to this.

I laughed faintly before responding.

"You act as though it's manna from heaven. Surely, you're not that vain."

I tried to joke off her statement but she continued to elaborate.

"It is manna, in a manner of speaking. A golden syrup that will flow into your mouth, down your throat, and throughout your veins. You can fight against the addiction, but it'll be useless. You'll give into it again and again."

Images of her mouth against my clit invaded my thoughts. Was she serious? I tried to imagine lapping her cunt. Could something so simple capture me so completely? I imagined kissing her.

I had always considered myself heterosexual, open minded, perhaps, but very attracted to the opposite sex. Never once had I considered being with a woman.

So, her advances were foreign to me; her frank statements rare to my ears.

Suddenly, I stood up. My throat closed and my tongue became too large for my mouth. I wet my lips seductively, instinct making me flirt even with the danger signs flashing. I reached down, placed my palm on top of her fingers, and gave a little squeeze before releasing them. The heat radiating off her flesh burned my hand. I felt a longing gnaw at my belly.

"Think what you like." I grinned more confidently than I felt. "I'm sure I can handle you."

"If you're sure it won't ruin you, take me home."

"Don't be frightened, little girl."

Her grin rose from her soul; a devilish glint filled her eyes. She blazed wickedly and stood up as well.

My heart pounded, a bass drum inside my chest, issuing warnings of her intent. Her heavy breast brushed against my arm as she reached behind me and wrapped her arm around my waist.

Silently, she led me from the table to a hidden alcove behind a large flowering gardenia. The sickening sweet scent surrounded us. It filled my nostrils making me almost gag.

Her palms pressed into my lower back, drawing me to her, breast to breast. My nipples tingled and strained against the tight fabric that stretched across them.

I half parted my lips before her mouth crushed mine, her tongue darting hard as she sucked the air from my lungs. My tongue fought back, pushing through her teeth.

A sharp pain registered as her teeth gnashed down around it, eliciting a moan. This excited her more. She bit harder, holding me by the tip of my tongue.

I rose up on my toes as she held me there. The nerves in my

body flashed points of light in my eyes; my mind whirled at her dominance over me. Quickly, she released me, her lips brushing my tongue's tip before it recoiled to the safety of my mouth.

Her smile spoke volumes. I stood panting, knees trembling as the sweet nectar of her filled my mouth and dripped down my chin. My eyes widened as her tongue jutted out again; one single lick under my lip gathered her wetness back to her own mouth.

I stepped away, moving back as if she'd burned me.

The fragrance of the flowers was bitter on my lips.

She collected herself, repositioning her shirt collar.

Her fingertip stroked my cheek.

"Next time you get close, I shall bite your neck and take you as my own," she warned.

I shuddered and turned, scurrying back to my chair a frightened mouse, knowing, without the bite, she already had me.

I trembled and kept my eyes down as she gathered her things, turned heel, and walked out the door.

I hurried from the library promptly at 9 o'clock.

The library staff was ready to leave, clicking off the lights as I exited. I had delayed as long as I could.

The librarian locked the huge wooden doors on my coattails. The sidewalk was empty. Not a soul was around, only the wind and the trees for company.

The earlier encounter with Vale was fresh on my mind.

I recalled the events. Her mouth bruising mine, her teeth against my tongue, all worked to keep my pussy throbbing. Who was she anyway? For all she knew, I had tasted a woman before. Arrogant bitch. She had me shaken.

I turned the corner onto Elm Avenue. A dog, face pressed to the glass, watched me walk past. As I neared the window, I noticed his gaze fell short of me. He wasn't watching my path at all but rather several steps behind me. I sneaked a glance over my shoulder. There was no one there.

Shivering more from fear than from the frigid wind, I pressed on. The leaves clattered together creating a buzzing chatter that highlighted my solitude. I hurried faster; the wind slapped my skirt against my ankles. Angrily, I steeled myself against letting my imagination get the better of me.

Whipping wildly, a piece of paper slammed against my cheek. Startled, I screamed, then laughed. This was out of hand.

Rounding the next left, I headed up the short flight of steps to my apartment foyer. I almost fell over her. Vale sat huddled, midstep. She hopped up immediately, her hand extended to me. In her palm, she gripped one of my research books.

"You forgot this, Abby."

I stared at her in disbelief.

"You left before me, Vale."

"Oh, yeah. Well, I picked it up by accident."

"I didn't see you pick it up."

My voice sounded accusatory; hers remained steady.

"Well, I must have. It was in my book bag."

She motioned to the ground. A small, black leather bag lay crumpled there, at her feet.

"How did you know where I live?"

"Your library card was inside, marking your place in the book. When I noticed the time, I knew I would miss you. The library closed at nine."

I felt lightheaded. Wavering slightly, I grabbed the handrail. She reached out, steadying me by placing her fingers along my forearm.

A calmness covered me. Suddenly everything seemed right.

"I'm sorry."

The words were flat.

"You made me a bit jumpy at the library. I'm tired, I guess."

I headed past her up the steps, reaching for my book as I walked.

"Thanks." I tossed the word over my shoulder. She didn't speak. I half turned and spoke again.

"Do you want to come in and warm up? I can offer wine to shake off the chill." My heart took off, racing. I couldn't believe I had asked her inside. Half of me hoped she would say no; the other half begged her to say yes.

Her smile went straight to her eyes, and the green darkened. She nodded and followed me down the hall to my door.

My hand shook as I slid the key into the hole, turning until the bolt fell. I pushed the door open; she was inside on my heels.

I continued through the small room to the kitchen, dropping my bag to the floor and my coat on the chair.

"Red or white?" I half yelled from the kitchen. "It's cheap. Don't expect a lot."

"Red," she answered, sounding far away.

I sneaked a glance around the corner and saw her studying the paper strewn across my desk. Her eyes moved up as she examined a few photos pinned to the board on the wall above my monitor.

I reached for a couple of glasses and hurried to her.

Her perusal of my personal effects unnerved me. She turned smiling as I reached her side. Sweeping her hand up, she motioned to a particular photograph. A picture of me, just the breasts exposed, creeping over the top of my bustier.

"You?"

"Yes," I admitted. My cheeks reddened as a grin tugged the corners of her lips upward.

"Do you often pose like that," she questioned harder, "or like this?"

Again, her fingers swept along a photograph. This next one was a full-body picture, my fingers buried inside my wet cunt.

"I do some modeling for extra money," I explained.

I placed the glasses on the edge of the desk, pouring each full before re-corking the bottle and setting it aside.

"I'd like to get you in that position myself."

Her voice was barely audible. I wasn't sure if I had imagined the comment.

It was as if she put the words directly into my head.

She picked up the wineglass by the stem, sipping as she walked to the couch. Dropping down, she made herself comfortable, tucking her legs underneath her.

I moved to the stereo, flicking the switch and hitting the play button before following her to the couch. A saxophone whined out a few notes. I sat on the opposite end of the couch, nervous. In her presence, I was totally spellbound.

"So, what's the big research project? Are you writing a book or what?"

Her voice sounded like that of an old friend. I smiled as her entire stance changed. She was a chameleon, changing in the blink of an eye. I watched her face as it altered. She appeared soft pink, for an instant.

"Yes, a book. I'm working on a book."

"Anything I would read?"

"Probably not. It's a study of the Internet, the communities on the Net."

"Perhaps you should write something darker."

I laughed. It erupted from deep inside me.

"This is mostly light reading. More like a study."

"I prefer dark."

Her red lips pouted. I wanted to kiss her.

The small talk was innocent. I dropped my guard, relaxing onto the couch as she sipped her wine, stem held elegantly between two fingers. She peered at me over the rim of the glass, green eyes flecked with the gold powder of conquest.

Moving feline-like in slow motion, she lowered the wine glass to the coffee table.

She leaned to me and brushed her lips against mine. I whimpered as the ache deepened.

She sucked softly and bit my lower lip. Nipping harder, I felt her tooth pierce my flesh. The salty mix of blood and saliva filled my mouth. She sighed as I gave in.

Working herself up onto her knees, she crawled the short distance between us and ended up on top of me.

We became a mesh of tangled arms and legs in an instant. Her scorching mouth blazed a trail along my flesh.

Tugging and working, she slid my dress up, my arms pinned above me, the material twisted. Her mouth and tongue explored my breasts. She circled my nipples delicately before raging down onto them. Her fingernails scraped the top layer of my flesh as she pushed her hands up under my hips.

As she devoured me, I worked the dress off my wrists.

Her fingers slid along the crack of my ass cheeks; she was already knowledgeable of my wants and needs.

Inching her tongue along my folds, I inhaled sharply as she drank me in. I tried to arch my hips up to her but her nails dug into me, holding me in place.

With piercing stabs, I felt the tip of her tongue enter me. Moaning and thrashing, I fought for air.

Her attack was relentless. Her mouth pressed tightly to my folds. She used her teeth to nibble my clit. She pressed the barest tip of her finger inside my anus, rimming it lightly before sliding it farther in.

My breath came in short gasps now. I couldn't find air. She dove between my thighs again, her fingers and mouth combined.

The orgasm started as a shiver and grew stronger. The throb pulsed through me as I hovered on the brink of climax. A finger pushed against my inner spot. I was trembling and begging as she pushed me over the edge.

I raised up off the couch, back arched to meet her mouth, a wildcat for the feeding.

Panting harder, eyes closed, I let her carry me there, again and again. I road the waves of her mouth as she pulled each pulse from me. Finally, her hands lowered my ass to the couch again. Covering my naked body with hers, she waited as I regained my senses.

Without speaking, she stood, pulling me behind her toward my bedroom door. I was caught in her spell.

There was no way to refuse her. Her mouth still dripped evidence of her feasting. I padded behind her, mouth aching to taste her fruit.

She led me to my bed as if she owned the place, pulling back the covers and settling me underneath before moving around, lighting the scented candles that spotted the bedside table and the dresser. The aroma of blueberry and melon mixed, creating a delightfully seductive odor that permeated my senses.

She slipped out of her clothes quickly. I lay there, marveling at her features. Her heavy breasts belittled mine. I stared mesmerized at the darkened areolas. Long blonde hair cascaded over her shoulders. Her eyes were forest green, almost black.

They remained unreadable.

She crawled onto the bed, queen of her kingdom.

Laying her head to the pillow, she pulled me on top of her. Her body was alien to me. I was used to a man's hard body; her softness enveloped me. I sank into the cushions of her breasts, my back arched atop this foreign soil.

Planting kisses along her neck and collarbone, I worked my way down her body. Her fingernails drew slashes along my shoulders as she pressed me downward.

A soft mound of hair covered her sex, trimmed close to the skin. My fingertips rubbed her folds until she parted her legs farther, giving me entrance to her ripened need.

The tip of my tongue danced in circles around her clit. I felt her shiver as I shoved it deep inside.

She tasted of sweet cider, a musky aged blend. Her gasping moans told me my ministrations were worthy.

Gaining confidence, I tenderly fed my fingers inside her with my tongue on her clit. Inching them, in and out, I closed my eyes. I played her sex. Her panting joined in. Together we coupled our sex.

Her body trembled as she moved closer to orgasm. I knew the movements well, so often had I mimicked these motions myself. She rocked her hips forward, grinding against my lips and chin.

The sudden throbbing of her clit gave way. Her climax sucked my tongue deeper as I strained my lips to her pussy. My tongue stopped moving; I focused on her inner spot, feeling her strain harder against me.

My face wet with her come, I rested my cheek against her thigh. She tangled her fingers in my hair. My skin along my shoulder blades burned; my flesh buried under her nails.

As we relaxed, she tugged on my hair, pulling me up to her. I rested my cheek to her chest.

"That wasn't so scary, was it?"

I mumbled softly, "Umm . . ."

A laugh dripped from her mouth. I felt a chill work its way down my spine. Catching my chin in her fingers, she turned my face to hers.

"Now that I've had you, you're mine."

Her confidence was unnerving. I didn't respond but rather lowered my face back down, drifting between conscious thought and sleepiness. She was right.

After tasting her fruit, I would crave it forever.

Finally, sleep won. My body grew slack in her embrace.

Knowing Marie

Charlotte Dare

I'd wasted the entire Saturday fuming in my cramped third-floor apartment, repeatedly replaying our conversation in the hope of uncovering some clue I might've missed.

"I can't wait to get my hands on you," she'd purred through the phone the week before, and her low, throaty voice got me moist.

"When do you get back from that seminar?" I asked, tantalized by visions of the reunion.

"Late Friday, but I'm all yours Saturday night."

Even Nancy Drew couldn't detect anything awry in that.

The laptop keyboard bore the brunt of my intense frustration as I struggled to compose the last poem needed to complete my creative writing thesis due that Monday. After years as an English major and Starbucks barista, I stood on the cusp of a college teaching career that might actually pay the bills. A hearty dose of writer's block was just what I needed. Thanks, Marie.

Between each fit of hammering the delete key, I had grabbed my cell phone and engaged in the ultimate woman versus self conflict not to hit Send. I wanted to forget Marie, erase her, to obliterate every trace of her cascading raven hair, tight blue jeans, and minty-fresh breath. I then went as far as enlisting Mrs. Farinelli, simmering a vat of marinara in her apartment two floors below, to hold my phone so I could focus on something, anything other than Marie. I didn't stop thinking about her, but at least I couldn't call her.

After polishing off the meatball sandwich Mrs. F. delivered earlier, I revived myself with a splash of cold tap water and called it a night with nothing to show for the day except a Word file scattered with mixed metaphors beneath the title, "I Hate Her," and a meatball splat on my favorite Calvin Klein V-neck.

I retrieved my cell phone from Mrs. F. and stepped out into the misty night air. There were three missed calls from Marie sent earlier in the evening. Now I was ready to press Send.

"Why didn't you tell me you were doing a guy," I seethed, marching down Chapel Street in the dark.

"What are you talking about?" Marie countered, mounting a futile defense.

"I saw you last night leaving the Marina Pub, walking arm in arm with some dude, and don't tell me you were just having dinner with a friend because I know what I saw. You went home with him and fucked him. This I know because I called your house until about three this morning."

She was so quiet I thought I might've dropped the call.

"What's the matter, cock got your tongue?"

"Look, I'm sorry you found out that way," she came clean with an irritating calm. "But what difference does it make if I screw around with a guy once in a while? I am bisexual."

"You're bisexual?" I'd hoped it was the wrong number. "Why the hell didn't you bother to tell me that before any one of the numerous sexual encounters we've had in the last three months?"

"You never asked."

"Fuck you, Marie," I spat and flipped my phone shut. I wasn't sure what pissed me off more, the idea of her fucking a man or that she never told me she was bisexual. The whole thing sucked eggs.

As I trudged down the sidewalk along Wooster Square, my phone sang with "You Sexy Thing," the signature ring Marie had downloaded onto my phone. How true it was at the time, but now the tune ground my nerves to a pulp. I contemplated not answering it, a small victory in this power struggle I was clearly losing, but I couldn't *not* answer it. We weren't done with this, no matter how queasy it made me picturing her with some beefy guy with a Harley tee stretched across his broad chest.

"What," I shouted.

"Come over," she insisted.

"Come over? Look, Marie, it was fun while it lasted, but I think I'll pass on the psychosexual drama. We're done."

"Just like that? Charlotte, I don't get you. We met in a bar and fucked each other's brains out that same night. Our relationship has been nothing but booty calls and random hookups, and now you're acting all freaked out because you've discovered I'm not exclusive. We never said we would be."

"I know," I bellowed, ripping mad because she was right.

"Do you want to be more? Is that what this is about?"

"I don't know, Marie. I just know I can't crawl into your steamy bed sheets knowing I may be second in line."

"Are you on your way over?" she asked, not getting me at all.

"No," I insisted. "I told you it's over."

"Then I'm coming over there. We need to talk about this in person."

"I said no. It's late, I'm tired, and I don't want to deal with this crap." I flipped the phone shut with authority and stuffed it into the side pocket of my cargo pants. That time I sounded like I meant business, but knowing Marie, she was only letting me think I was the one calling the shots.

After circling my block a few times, I returned to the solitude of my apartment and continued to wade through the deluge in my head. What was I doing? I should've known from the start all that hot, meaningless sex was going to come at a price.

Home for about thirty minutes, I was convinced Marie had decided to wash her dirty hands of the situation, and then came the rapping on the door. Power play number two: don't answer it.

"Open the fucking door!" she demanded through intermittent pounding.

"My neighbors are gonna call the cops."

"Fuck them!" she wailed and then simmered down to a dull growl. "Would you just open the door?"

I complied with her demand, and she stormed in with this inflated sense of indignation, as if I'd perpetrated some heinous betrayal against her. What a piece of work.

"Charlotte, don't end this over Rad. He doesn't mean anything to me."

"Rad? That guy's name is Rad?" I mocked.

"It's Henry Radcliffe. He's a biker. I don't give a shit why he calls himself Rad," she spat, getting flustered. "That's not why I'm here."

"Why are you here, Marie?" I challenged, popping open a can of diet Sprite like I was James Bond swirling a martini.

"I don't want you to end what we've got going. It's too good," she whispered, attempting to sway me with her wicked sensuality.

"Yeah, so good you were getting it from someone else last night."

She looked pissed. I'd actually rocked the Ice Queen's pedestal. What a feat.

"Can we not do that sarcasm shit, please," she barked, jolting me out of my moment of private revelry. "I'd like to have a serious conversation."

She then slowly inched me back against the counter, a shrewd maneuver to knock me off my guard, and it was working.

"Would you mind having a seat over there then?" As I gently pushed her away, I noticed she was visibly chilled by the night air blowing in over the sink. "If you get any closer to me, your nipples will be poking against *my* shirt."

"Fine," she huffed and plopped down on a barstool at my breakfast counter. "Why did you rip me a new one over this, Char? Is there something you haven't told me? Are there feelings involved here that I'm not aware of?"

She was so smug and so sexy I couldn't stand her. "You're awfully presumptuous this evening, Marie. I don't have to feel anything for you to be mad about what I've discovered and the way I discovered it. Maybe I just don't like being played. Maybe I'd like to avoid the human papillomavirus, thank you very much."

"I'm always safe, and besides, it's not like I'm out fucking anything that moves."

"It's not?"

She didn't fire off an acerbic reply like I'd expected. A simple, vanquished lowering of her eyelids was enough to make me feel sufficiently like shit.

"Sorry. We said no sarcasm," I offered, but I wasn't sorry at all.

Marie got up and sauntered toward me again.

"Where are you going?" I asked, alarmed those piercing eyes were going to bewitch me right off my preeminent position by the refrigerator.

"I'm coming over to say I'm sorry. I am, you know," she drawled.

"I can hear you from there." My hands started to tremble. I extended my arms to keep her at bay, but she forced her shoulders against my palms.

"How long do you think you can stand like that before your arms get tired?" she challenged.

"I'm prepared to stay the course."

She broke into a smile. "You gotta stop leaving CNN on for background noise when you write."

"I know."

"This is stupid, Charlotte. What are we doing? You know you don't want to end this anymore than I do."

"I think I need a definition of what *this* is," I countered.

"Let me think about it for a minute," she replied and began gently kissing my neck. She then started squeezing my triceps and rubbing my shoulders, and I could feel the rush surge through my whole body.

"You're wasting your time," I protested weakly. "I'm not in the mood."

"I bet if I shoved my hand in your pants I'd prove what a damn liar you are," she whispered in my ear.

"It's not your hand I want you to shove in," I breathed and lunged for her mouth, jamming my tongue in as far as it would go. She whimpered with pleasure and draped her arms around my upper back, pressing me against the counter.

"Marie, why are you doing this to me?" I asked, knowing it was too late to stop what she'd started.

"Because you want me as much as I want you," she replied, opening my pants. She dragged them down below my knees and, with my assistance, lifted me up onto the counter.

As she kissed my stomach, I gripped the edge and flung my head back into the cabinets. She spread my thighs apart and dove in, licking me all over, teasing me with soft strokes over my labia until her tongue, a warm wet tidal wave, at last rolled up and down my aching clit. I clutched her mane of hair and pushed her head closer, feeling her tongue slip inside me. She thrust it in and out and then back over my clit as my legs started shaking.

"Marie, you're driving me insane," I complained, panting in ecstasy.

"Patience, honey. It's gonna be well worth the wait," she echoed from below and then plunged her tongue back inside.

My wild groans signaled her to stay where she was, and soon the intensity of a swelling climax gained momentum from vigorous thrusts of her stiff tongue.

"Oh, Marie, this is so fucking good!" I cried. The rush swept slowly up my legs, and I finally came like the crash of a violent wave in a hurricane. "Damn!" I exclaimed when I caught my breath, my pussy still pulsating in ecstasy.

"I told you so," she teased. She brushed the back of her hand across her lips. "Are you about ready to reconsider?"

I slid off the counter and quickly zipped up. "Reconsider what?" I asked with a defiant glare. "Sharing you sexually with someone else? Well I can't. I can't know that what just happened here also happens with somebody else. I don't want you doing that with anyone else."

I stormed out of the kitchen to the refuge of the sofa's plush arm, sure of even less than when Marie barged in and seduced me. I couldn't let her see the emotion she stirred in me, not until I understood it myself.

She strategically placed herself on the coffee table across from me so I'd have to face her. "If you're asking me to choose between the two of you, I will. I'll choose you."

"I wouldn't ask you to choose."

"Why not?"

"Because it has to be yours, and if it's me, it has to be because you want me and because I'm enough."

"Charlotte, I'm doing the best I can here," she said. Agitation overtook her voice as she sprang from the coffee table and paced the area rug. "My thirty-one years haven't exactly been a smooth ride. A failed marriage to a man, a failed relationship with a woman . . . I seem to have the best luck keeping it uncomplicated, like we are."

"We're not uncomplicated anymore."

"I see that."

"What is it that you want, Marie? Forgive my ignorance, but I don't get the whole bisexual thing. I mean if you like men and women, how can you be satisfied with just one?"

"I don't think orientation has anything to do with it. You like who you like. I was married to a man for four years and unhappy for most of them. Then I met Sharon and things were great for a while until they just seemed to implode. Maybe it's just me. Maybe I can't commit."

"You're not making a very persuasive case for yourself here," I drawled, but Marie's eyes were dim, floating in lakes of self-doubt.

She took a deep breath and sat back down on the coffee table, placing her hand on my knee. "If you're asking for a guarantee that we'll live happily ever after, I can't give you that, as much as I'd like to believe it myself . . ."

I never imagined she could possibly have a vulnerable side. Yet there she was, sitting across from me, gazing back with those fiery, plaintive eyes, her soul laid bare, and she never looked sexier.

I reached for her, grabbing her satiny white shirt and pulling her on top of me. Kissing her pouting lips with reckless fervor, I pleaded, "Just be with me and nobody else, for however long it lasts."

She reached across the couch and snagged her purse while still kissing me, and then proceeded to take out a colossal strap-on dildo complete with rubbery appendage for its captain.

"Will you put it on?" she politely requested, and stripped her jeans off before I could utter my reply.

"Well if this is what's gonna keep you off Rad," I teased.

"Shut up," she demanded. She had my pants in a ball on the floor in a microsecond.

I wriggled into the curious contraption, placing the tickler right where it belonged, fascinated by the new experience.

Marie straddled me and eased herself down, riding it in a

slow, sensual rhythm as she closed her eyes and savored the exquisite feel. She shook free her midnight tangle of hair and leaned back, balancing herself with her hands on my thighs. She began panting louder as she pumped up and down with unrestrained vitality.

"Can you feel it, baby?" she asked. Her thrusts got wilder, and her hard nipples pressed against the thin material of her blouse.

"Yeah," I whispered as the rubber tickler sent flickers of pleasure through me with each of Marie's thrusts.

"Oh, yeah baby," she groaned as she pounded my lap so hard I thought she was going to break my sofa.

I studied her face as she lost herself in climax. Her eyes squinted tightly shut as she gasped for breath and luxuriated in raw physical pleasure. I never took my eyes off Marie, watching every undulation of her body until it convulsed in orgasm.

After a moment, she collapsed beside me on the couch.

"That was so hot," she said, exhaling deeply.

We sat beside each other for a long, quiet moment, our arms lazily entwined.

"Oh, I wish I could spend the night with you," she then announced, "but I can't."

"Why not?" Already I was rankled with suspicion.

"I have to be at the Farmington Marriot for an early brunch with my aunt."

The old "I have an early brunch with my aunt" escape hatch. How perfectly unoriginal. That's the female version of the guy's "I have an early meeting." Did she think because I don't sleep with men I wouldn't recognize it?

"Do you want to get some dinner this week?" I asked, baiting the trap.

"Sure, how about Saturday?"

"Why not sooner?" I tried to be subtle, but the words were spilling out of their own volition.

"Starting Monday, I'm taking Steve, the new guy, out on the road for the week. My schedule's very hectic, but I'll save the weekend for you." She winked and sashayed to the door, entirely unmoved by my angst, and I wasn't sure if I should be relieved or furious.

After watching her taillights disappear down Chapel Street, I hauled out my laptop and clicked away at the keys until the amber sun rose over the cherry blossom trees. I titled the poem "Orgasm," and explored the metaphor of a bomb exploding, decimating multistory brick façades and those of once self-assured women who used to know how to resist a woman like Marie.

Remembering When

Jules Torti

The fantasy that is you replays in my mind in fast-forward, but I always rewind if I'm not ready yet. The Virgo perfectionist in me needs to set the scene exactly; everything must be accounted for. I am the set dresser in this movie of you, and you love, are my star.

Your quick smile enters my thoughts and slides into that familiar expression I know like my own. That expression you have when you are on the teetering brink of letting go, slipping from a body in control to a vulnerable woman influenced by a relentless, exploring tongue.

There are inches of you that I savor like dreamy end-of-summer days, where all is buttery and the sheets on the clothesline are dense with fresh air. Other parts of you I turn rabid on, feeling compelled to squeeze and bite with hungry gnashes. In the dark cloak of night I sometimes want to sink my teeth so hard into your milky smooth skin that you yelp. I need to be reminded that you are real, that in the thick of stars and blackness, you exist beneath my fingertips. In the hours that we are apart, I think of strokes and licks that will make you shudder and arch your back in the flood of a sedating climax as I order color ink jet cartridges and memo pads for the office. Oh, and UHU sticks for Jackie in Admin.

It would be easy to do this forever. Love you. Our landscapes are each other and we are new blank canvasses, taut and full of possibility. The hands on the clock are ignored as the warm hands I place on your hips suspend minutes of our lives.

There is a restless throb that we both need to swallow back. Between our legs, in the wettest part, a recurring hum seems to overwhelm the clarity of anything. Distinct lines blur like vision after eyes rubbed hard with knuckles. Blurry, soft edges, like a charcoal sketch, humming parts and lines that never end. We are combustible anticipation, jittery, spinning faster than a carnival ride.

My eyes travel across your limbs, scanning for reference points, the crooks and dips and curves that I have memorized like my debit card PIN, VISA numbers, and mother's maiden name. I can spit these answers out fast, without any conscious thought. Just like I can close my eyes and trace your fine lines, even when you're not there.

Your eyes follow mine, and the weight of your vulnerability becomes palpable. Everything you do is gentle, unassuming, and patient. Your pupils constrict as you step closer to the bright candles, your eyes that are the color of Coca-Cola.

Most of the candles have burned low, the flames responding to the breeze sweeping through the open window. I watch you bring the glass of red wine to your pouty lips and brush your hair back behind your ear.

"It feels like fall," you whisper, and I can tell from your nipples that you feel the coolness of night fighting the day's heat inside the house. I imagine your nipples in my mouth, the pebbly plum texture, and the direct channel of arousal that swims from my lips to your pussy when I suck on them.

You lick your lips in that sultry cover-girl way, and set the glass carefully on the shelf as if it is a fragile egg. You place it between the purple starfish and the neat stack of old atlases from your aunt.

For the first time we hear the low thump of music. It's the band you love from the East Coast, Madviolet. Their vocals are syrupy and remind me of the night we had our First Real Date at Hugh's Room. I met you outside the bar; you had a bag of pomegranates and a bike seat in your hand. You bought the pomegranates for two bucks in Kensington and the guy tossed in a head of elephant garlic for free. We stained our fingers with the wet fruit, sucking the fleshy, crimson seeds, and drank gin until the whole world was smiling and pretty. And then we fucked like we might not see each other again on your new leather couch that was the color of dark chocolate. The Madviolet CD was on repeat, and we knew all the lyrics by morning when we hugged hot cups of coffee with creamy condensed milk and ate raisin biscuits, refusing to leave the sheets we were wrapped in.

I don't think I left after that night. Once a week we would visit my "old" apartment to water the drooping plants. We would pour out the sour milk and watch dumb cable that I continued to pay for even though I hadn't been home for weeks. We'd have long hot baths with frankincense oil and listen to the neighbor have screaming sex to Stevie Nicks. We fed each other take-out Thai, chopsticks full of noodles and prawns. Salty kisses peppered in between as we glowed with our unconquerable love for each other.

We always went back to your place, because of the stillness, because you had grass in your yard that we could walk barefoot in. We could lay topless in the backyard and drink pink lemonade full of pulp and tease each other with sticky ice cubes. We read old Nancy Drew books and Archie comics out loud to each other, and tried to outdo each other with stories of past sexual conquests, threesomes, and summer camp fumblings.

Tonight, there is change. I no longer have the apartment; this is my home. The purple starfish is mine, I have carried it with me since I found it on the Sunshine Coast when I was fifteen. Fifteen and fighting to not be gay and wanting to save the world and kiss my best friend Penny Sanders everywhere. The atlases are yours, but the yours and mines have become *ours*. This is *our* home with bowls of crisp, green apples on the table and jars of acorns and hazelnuts that we filled our pockets with on long fall walks. *Our* house with bars of anise-studded hand soaps made by that lady who sells clover honey and catnip at Riverdale Farm in the summer.

We have tins of loose jasmine tea and oily Oso Negro coffee beans that we grind on Sunday mornings to sip with the cornmeal blueberry muffins you bake. We have eucalyptus and camphor massage lotions for long foot rubs, three antique telescopes, all of Jamie Oliver's cookbooks (now pesto and tomato sauce splattered), passports stamped with fuzzy Brazil and Venezuela stamps, and six dildos that we keep in the top drawer with your boy-cut underwear and wool socks.

The dildos were housewarming gifts from our jaded single friends and sexless couples who live vicariously through our stories that we tell after too many tequila shots on a Friday night at Slacks.

Remember how we met? Remember when? That sex shop on Queen, red-faced with vibrators in our hands. I told you not to buy the warming-cherry-pie lube because it tasted like cough syrup, and it tended to get really warm with friction. Too warm, like jalapenos between your thighs. There was one other customer in the store, a woman with Colonel Sanders eyeglasses on her head, and another pair of cat-eye frames swinging around her neck. Her shirt said something about someone pissing in her cornflakes that morning. The store manager was in the back, checking out the centerfold in the latest copy of *On Our Backs*.

Minutes passed, and after we had exhausted everything we could say about the weather, you pointed out a dildo as big as your arm. You covered your mouth and communicated horror with wide eyes, imagining the penetration of it. I did too, and winced. We touched the new line of dildos with "fleshy realism" and agreed: they were fleshy, and real! Too real for something fake.

You tucked your vibrator behind your back, but I already recognized the packaging. It was the same ribbed, sparkly one that I had chosen. You picked purple; I went with the electric blue that matched my alarm clock. There was a picture of a woman with long red fingernails sucking her index finger like a popsicle, trying to be suggestive in a lacy set of bubblegum-pink bottoms. Ew, we decided.

Laughing, we were impressed that we had the same great taste in dildos. Then I thought out loud, or you did, that if we were a couple, we'd only need to buy one.

"Let's be a couple then."

So, we were. I allowed you to buy the purple one, and we tossed copies of *Curve* and *Girlfriends* on top of the heavy-duty, plastic-entombed dildo. The employee was all teeth and gums, her faux hawk falling limp with the heat of the day. "You two make a cute couple." There, it was settled.

Before "my place or yours," we stopped at Starbucks. Me: tall tea misto, nonfat, half shot sugar-free vanilla. You: same. Us: kind of falling in love.

I carried the bag with the vibrator; you were a little shy to tote around the bag with COME AS YOU ARE emblazoned on the side. I was twitchy with speculation of what would come next and naked thoughts of you banged around my head like bumper cars. People didn't meet like this. And they certainly didn't have anything meaningful after. The pattern was formula: two girls, a random meeting + undeniable attraction + great length since last sexual encounter = drunken, regretful night of unstoppable sex. The one-night stand was predictable. We would end up avoiding each other for years in cramped bars and dreading Pride day run-ins with new cheek-dimpled girls on our arms.

We bought mood rings for a dollar at the store on Church that smelled like curry, mothballs, and patchouli. The sun was hot and bright for the first week of September, and it seemed only right. We admired our newly ringed hands and interlocked fingers, sweaty and clammy, biting back the desire to just tear off each other's clothes in the alley and fuck against the dumpster and pigeons pecking at pizza crusts.

You drank your Starbucks like it was a glass of expensive South African wine. I downed mine like it was sunshine and shortbread, possibly giving me the superhuman power to swallow you whole, right off the street so you'd be mine, all mine.

The summer had been sexless for the both of us, save for a few kisses that I now sneered at with disappointment and disgust. You had fucked your ex in June after one boozy night at the Rivoli. Elvira Kurt was doing stand-up comedy and you said to her after the show that you'd "like to see her laying down instead of standing up." She said she was married and you were dropped like luggage in the trusted hands of an airport baggage handler. Your ex showed up moments later, bought you a Red Bull and double vodka, and she looked like an OK alternative for the night. Especially after the second Red Bull double. You had sloppy sex, fought like a rutting deer over who the Iron and the Ferron CDs belonged to, cried, and left her condo with a door slam. But forgot your wallet, and pride.

I went home with my ex's ex who just broke up with my

ex that night after their third attempt to be monogamous. We watched *The Breakfast Club* in beanbag chairs, fooled around on the Ikea lime-green shag carpet, but mutually decided the movie was more interesting. She faked an orgasm à la *When Harry Met Sally,* but I couldn't be bothered. She passed out, half on the beanbag, half on the shag, and I fantasized about you. I rubbed my clit hard and fast like I was in the path of a twister. Careful not to make a sound, careful not to squeak the beanbag pleather against the wall and wake her. You were good, even then when you were imaginary.

I had seen you seven times before we bought matching vibrators: twice on rollerblades, once with a golden retriever and girl with her hair in a tight ponytail, once talking to a cop on a motorcycle on Bloor, and three times in the window of Ginger, looking out blankly over a bowl of steaming broth. You said you'd never seen me before. Damn. But you couldn't wait to see me again. Good.

And here we are naked again. This is our home. This is our love life. Your eyes seem distant, darting, but I know you're preoccupied with work. Sex always makes us better though, "connected" you say.

You smell like melon soap, your skin pink from the hot shower. Your lips meet mine and our tongues slide together. We smile and feel the anxious heart pounding even though we're not that new anymore. I lick the tattoo on your upper arm, desperate to taste the black ink, the ink and blood that makes you, you. Turning away from me, you spread your arms across the window, splaying your fingers against the wood frame, your breath fogging the glass.

My hands slip over the fullness of your breasts and run along your rib cage to your tight ass. I push my pelvis into you, imagining that fantasy you told me of in halted whispers. You know the one, with the helicopter pilot in fatigues who takes you from behind. How she smelled like power and diesel, hands rough from outdoor work and grease. Her hips that pumped you hard, slamming into you like a cowboy on a wild horse across the open fields, pumping you until you felt weightless and dizzy in her strength.

I will be the helicopter pilot tonight, forearms rippled with broad tendons that flex and extend over your body. Your face squeaks against the glass as you turn your head, embracing the cool relief of the window.

Tonight we are in Alto Cuen, Costa Rica. The jungle is wet and dripping, fog hanging on the river like all of San Francisco. The jungle is a thousand shades of pulsating green, and the humidity is oppressive, clinging like Saran Wrap. The altitude makes your head spin, and the sounds of the jungle are throbbing and vibrating like amplified heartbeats. The pilot keeps her fatigues on and penetrates you like a sailor on shore leave. Desperate. Feverish. Hungry for wet flesh. Your ass, your legs, all of you opens up to accept me and the fantasy. You feel the hot metal of the Chinook on the burned-out helicopter pad and smirk to think that you're about to be penetrated by the pilot.

That wet sucking sound gets louder and faster. Like boots stuck in mud. Your moan is heavy with satisfaction and hearing it makes my body rage with an internal fire to be so far inside you. It is a wet fire; the slippery strands leave my body and cling to my legs as I push into you again and again. My breath fogs the window with yours.

I know you're thinking of her, I know. Not the helicopter pilot; that stupid theater director with the PhD who you think is so funny and so smart and so awesome for building her own log cabin on some stupid lake up north. Whatever.

Fine. I think of her too, and the helicopter pilot and Ivan E. Coyote reading her stories to me in the back of a rusted-out pick-up truck while we smoke unfiltered Camels. Yeah, that's right, I have fantasies of my own. I think of Sheryl Crow in scuffed cowboy boots and threadbare jeans, the sun on her face, and her teeth and glossy lips on mine. Oh, and I think of that girl from Laide who just came back from Afghanistan and has a scar on her hip from getting grazed with a bullet from an AK-47. We fucked in the washroom: did you know that?

The faces flash and fade, the bodies turn and toss and cloud in my memory. But yours is the body I love most, with the tiny knot of an umbilicus, sinewy arms, and strong, wide palms that massage me perfectly. You have just enough freckles and Coca-Cola eyes that tell stories to me even when you are sleeping.

"Harder."

Always harder. I push your ankles out farther and you bend at the waist. I fall to my knees to lick you. I love licking you from behind. Like coconut gelato in August. We're sweating and salty and I taste melons and that coconut gelato, and all of your dreams.

Maybe you're doing Carmen, oh curvy *L Word* Carmen with the flat stomach and come-hither lips and hips. Sometimes you're so involved with the rhythm of penetration I wonder if you remember that I'm behind you. Say my name. Pound the glass with your open hand and scream it so I can feel like I'm here and you are too. Your quads quiver and I feel the taut bands of muscle as you squat and take in my deep thrusts.

The music repeats, a candle spits and flickers out. I wonder if this is a sign, or just the breeze.

"Faster."

I go faster, gripping the hardwood under my bare feet. I am Carmen and the helicopter pilot with the forearms that distract your eyes. I'm Miss PhD with her stupid Harley all polished up and black as oil. I am your ex and your next and your first and all the tongues that have licked your expanse.

You come and fall backward into me. Sweat trickles down to your navel and you run your hands over your own breasts, not mine. You drink the rest of your wine and leave it in your mouth a moment before you swallow. You're going to tell me something, I can tell in your Coca-Cola eyes that are glossy and staring at our toes touching.

You pull the window down and lean back against it, sweeping your hair out of your eyes. The wetness between your legs is like silver in the candlelight. Your hand rubs across the fine trim of your French wax and you hold your palm there, as if to hold it all in. To hold the hum there.

"I'm hungry," you say, and we pop popcorn the old-fashioned way like we always do. You pour out an inch of oil and I drop in the kernels. This is our routine. I cut a generous wedge off the block of cold butter and let it fall into the hot pan. The butter thins into liquid and we drizzle and salt the hot popcorn in silence. We eat not so politely, in the matter that you can after six months of living together. Popcorn falls to the floor and skids across the tile. We'll get it tomorrow.

"I haven't forgotten about you," you whisper, but your eyes don't meet mine. Your cell phone rings in the other room and you ignore it. But you change. The distance between us is elastic and you are pulling, pulling. We will snap. Your Coca-Cola eyes say sorry, and your body tries but you're no longer fucking me. I don't know who it is, but it's no longer me.

I fall to sleep in the bed that is no longer ours. It's mine. You're sleeping with her and I am stuck with all the images of you. All the sex we've ever had passes back and forth in my mind like a tennis match that never ends.

You make me wetter than you should, because you are no longer mine.

Finding My Feet

Shanna Germain

They say that the thing you want is right in front of you, if only you know where to look. But there's the rub: how do you know where to look when you don't know what you want? Or worse, when you know what you want, but can't have it? Where do you look then?

I thought I couldn't have what I wanted, but what did I know—I was looking at the wrong thing. I was looking at my own face in the mirror, lining my blue eyes, putting on coral lipstick, brushing my light brown hair back off my face. I was looking at Sun's dark eyes beneath her darker brows and the way her teeth showed, small and white as Chiclets, when she smiled. I was looking at her curves beneath her wraparound skirt while she poured our chai. I was looking at the tapestries on Sun's walls, the fabrics she'd brought back from Singapore.

I moved around her dining room, touching a red-and-orange fabric, a green and gold. A blue one that matched my eyes. I dared to imagine her there in the bazaar, touching the blue and buying it, thinking of me.

"The place looks amazing, Sun," I said. "I can't believe you've only been back two weeks."

She pushed the air away from her face. "Oh, thanks," she said. "There's still a lot more to do."

Sun would tell you that she's goal-less, she would lament over her inability to find her type-A gene, but then she'd spend a year in Singapore doing relief work before coming home to repaint and redecorate her house. I could almost hate her for it if I wasn't convinced I was in love with her. Her year away hadn't changed that, despite my—hope was the wrong word—half-wish that it would.

I sat back down at the table across from Sun; put my hands on my warm mug. I had to keep my fingers moving—without something in their grasp, they threatened to get away from me, to reach across the table and wrap themselves in Sun's dark, straight hair, to close her dark eyes. Sun didn't know how I felt. We'd been friends since college, when we played together on a beach volleyball team. And we'd stayed friends through all of her boyfriends, through all of my boyfriends and girlfriends.

Most times, it was enough to know that I could be here, across the table from her, with my eyes on her face. Now that she was here, though, after so long away . . . I looked down and counted the dark specks of spices that floated in my chai.

From the ceramic bowl in the middle of the table, Sun picked up a piece of candied ginger. She dropped it into my chai.

"Sweet and spicy," she said. "That hasn't changed, has it?"

I swirled my mug, letting the ginger sink. Then I took a sip: sugar-sweet, with that lingering spice in the back of my throat.

"No," I said. "That hasn't changed."

"Good," she said. "Some days, I feel like I've been gone forever."

I kept my eyes on my chai, the way the spices met and swirled at the top.

"So, I have a surprise for you," Sun said. "I brought it back from Singapore."

Her at the bazaar, choosing something just for me. It was better than the blue tapestry. I pressed my palms tighter to the mug. *Stay still.*

"You didn't need to do that," I said.

Sun laughed, husky and rich.

"Maybe you don't want it then?"

But she didn't wait for me to answer, just stood and lifted something from a side table—a silver tray holding a squeeze bottle, some cotton balls, a clear glass bowl of liquid. Sun set the tray on the table between us.

I picked up the squeeze bottle. The dark liquid inside smelled like cloves and ginger.

"What is it?" I asked.

Sun's smile reminded me of Mona Lisa. Half smile, just her lips, sly.

"Henna," she said.

"Like body paint?"

"It's more like a stain. More permanent."

Sun flipped her hand over—on her palm, right in the center, a cluster of small flowers in reddish-brown. Tiny, intricate. I wanted to feel them. I squeezed the bottle so hard that a bit of henna came out the top. *Stay still.*

Sun leaned forward and put her fingers over my fingers around the bottle. "I want to henna you."

I was distracted by her warm fingers. Maybe I could feel her fingerprints pressing into the back of my hands. Maybe I could feel the henna design scratching lightly. I couldn't be sure.

"What? I mean, you do?"

Sun took the henna bottle from me. She turned the bottle over and over in her palm, watching it spin.

"Yes," she said, "but only if you don't mind. I saw this woman in Singapore, and she had her whole body done for a wedding. Hands, face . . . her feet."

I dipped one fingertip into the clear bowl on the tray. The liquid smelled like lemonade.

"Sugar lemon water," Sun said. "It helps the henna set."

I put the fingers wet against my chai mug, let the heat seep in. I didn't dare move—I didn't want to distract her from her story. It was selfish, but I wanted to hear her tell how she'd thought about me in Singapore.

Sun turned the bottle over, pressed in the sides and some henna came out of the metal tip onto a napkin. The henna was even darker against the white napkin—the color of clay mud.

I stayed quiet, waiting.

"Her feet . . ." Sun said. "They were so beautiful, and they . . . they made me think of you. When we used to play beach volleyball. Remember?"

Sun looked up then, her dark eyes on my face.

"I remember," I said.

SHANNA GERMAIN

"I always watched you when we played. Your feet," she said. "You had such beautiful feet."

Something started in my belly, worked its way into a giggle.

"My feet?"

Sun poked the metal tip of the bottle against the napkin. Made three small dots in a row.

"Don't laugh," she said.

I had to take her hand then, put my fingers over her fingers on the bottle. Hold her still.

"I'm not laughing," I said. "Well, OK maybe a little. But my feet, Sun? I've been . . ."

I stopped. How to tell her I'd been lusting after her for all these years—her eyes, those small hands, her laugh—when she'd been . . . she'd been watching my feet?

Sun pulled her hands out from under mine, leaving only cold air. She put the bottle back on the silver tray.

"You're right," she said as she lifted the tray from the table. "I'm sorry, that was stupid. Let's just have our chai. You can tell me about the teaching, how that's going."

"Sun, wait." I reached for her hand, for her arm, but only caught the corner of the tray. Liquid splashed onto the silver, sending up the sweet scent of lemon and sugar between us.

Keeping my hand on that tray, just on the corner, feeling the carved designs, feeling Sun pulling away from me, I thought it was the hardest thing. And then I realized that I had to say something. That was so much harder.

"Sun," I said. "Yes, I'd love to have you paint my feet."

"You'll be cold," Sun had said. She was right. Now, I was on her living room floor, leaning against the front of her couch, my jeans rolled up to the knees and a blanket wrapped around my shoulders. A thick towel was folded beneath my feet.

Sun was on the floor, cross-legged in front of me. She lifted my foot, held it with her palms under my heel. Her touch sent shivers up my leg.

"OK?" she asked.

I nodded, but didn't trust myself to speak. Her hands on my

109

feet, her eyes there too, I had never imagined. I'd always thought my feet were ugly—tiny and short, the way they curved out near my big toe. But Sun's hands told another story, her fingers around my toes, sliding up over the ball of my foot.

"You have to stop shivering so I can start," she said.

I tried. Held my teeth together tight but it just made the rest of my body shake harder.

Sun snuggled my foot against the inside of her thigh, right up against the thin fabric of her skirt, and held it until it didn't shake anymore. My foot was still, but the inside of my body was all shakes. Sun picked up her squeeze bottle, moved it in circles over the top of my foot without touching the tip to my skin.

"I'm just working out the design," she said. "Some people use books, but I liked the way the women did it, just stared at the skin until they found the pattern there."

I must have looked skeptical, because she said, "Close your eyes, relax. Have faith."

I did as she said. At least the close-my-eyes part. I wasn't sure the ability to relax was an option for me. But I willed myself to breathe slowly, in and out.

Soon, the cool point of the bottle touched the side of my foot, near the instep. The metal tip traced my skin in a pattern that I couldn't distinguish. After a few twists and turns of the tip, the still-warm henna pulsed into my skin. It was like a massage, but with lines of henna instead of fingers. Warm and tingling with spices, the henna patterns made my foot feel alive.

I realized I didn't pay attention to my feet, not ever. They got me from one place to another, they sometimes wore cute shoes. That was about it. But with Sun's attention—the way she tilted my foot to get better access or the way she pressed her thumb to my instep to hold me still—I wondered. What was it about feet that made her want to do this? Was it just a friendship thing? Or was it something more? I wanted to ask, but I was afraid. And so I just stayed still with my eyes closed and my feet in Sun's hands.

When she finished with the henna, Sun dipped cotton balls in the lemon sugar water and patted it all over my feet. The gentle way she applied the cool, sticky liquid made me feel once again like I was being pampered. When she stopped, the skin on my feet felt like it was hardening, like if I moved, it might crack and slough off like an old shell that I'd outgrown.

"All done," Sun said.

I opened my eyes. I'd been in that half-dozing state that comes with massages and day dreams. My feet were covered with intricate brownish patterns. Flowers and twirls and other things that I didn't have names for.

"They're beautiful," I said. I thought I meant her designs, but maybe I meant my feet too. The patterns and the sticky sheen of the lemon juice seemed to bring out the curves of my feet and toes. Seemed to make them sensual. Not mine, but someone else's.

"I told you," Sun said. Her throaty laugh. "So, you can't really move for a while. You want a book or something?"

She had her hand still on my leg, between my ankle and the bottom of my rolled jeans.

"We could just . . . talk," I said. It sounded like something out of a bad movie. I wanted to take the words back as soon as they were words. My face burned hot, even as my feet were freezing.

Sun didn't seem to notice. She scooted next to me on the couch, her shoulder pressed into mine. Her feet sneaked under the blanket that covered my legs. She leaned her head on my shoulder so that her long hair fell against my neck.

That's the thing they never tell you about being a girl who likes girls. You get to have another girl pressed up against you, have a friend who hugs you to her, or who dreams about painting your feet in a faraway market—and it might mean everything. Or it might mean nothing. Just friends.

"Sun," I said. My eyes focused on my new feet. Sometimes you changed one thing and the whole world looked different.

"Hmm?" she said.

"Have you ever, you know, liked a girl?" I wanted to stop talking as soon as I started, but—words; you can never take them back. Before, I'd had to force the words out, how I'd been OK with her painting my feet. Now, I couldn't shut up.

Sun was smarter than I was. I'd known that for a long time. She didn't say anything. She turned her head toward me until her breath was warm against my neck. Her lips pressed warm against my skin. First kiss. It wasn't even on the lips, just against the pulse that beat fast in my neck. Yet my skin tingled just like it had beneath the henna.

She shifted her weight until she faced me, and then brought one leg over mine to straddle me. Her skirt covered my legs and hers.

How often had I dreamed of this moment and not of this moment over the years? In my dreams, I was always the perfect lover, could tell by Sun's body how to touch her. But this wasn't a dream, this was Sun, rising above me. Real as day.

I didn't know what to do. My hands were so still at my sides that it was as if they were the thing painted, the part of me that should be immobile. Sun settled herself against me, her body warm where it met mine. She picked up my hands and put them beneath her skirt. With the flat of her palms, she pressed my hands to her thighs. Her skin was smooth and muscled. When she was convinced my hands would stay there, she let go of them and leaned over and kissed me. This time, on the lips. This time, pushing her tongue between my lips into the corners of my mouth.

My mouth filled with the tang and spice of her tongue. Ginger and cloves. Her fingers on the edges of my lips as she kissed me added the flavor of sweet lemon. Beneath it all, there was the taste of Sun. It was a flavor I'd smelled for years—alderwood soap and lilac lotion.

She pushed her thigh hard against my hand. I took it as the hint that it was, and let my fingers explore the skin there. I brought one hand into her V, expecting panties. Her lips, clean-shaven and silky, met my fingers.

We both moaned as I touched her there and ran my finger up the shallow groove between her lips. She was wet already and when I ran my finger up and down, she grew wetter still, covering the end of my finger.

As we kissed, Sun's fingers traveled down from my lips and across my shoulders to find their way to my nipples. She feathered them with her thumbs, touching me so lightly I thought I might be imagining the movement of her fingers. But my nipples knew better, hardening and pressing toward her soft touch.

I entered Sun with two fingers and she broke the kiss and sat up straight, sighing. I wanted to see her—all these years of dreaming of what she looked like, and I didn't know if I'd get another chance. I untied her skirt and pushed the fabric back until I could see her lower half. In her belly button, a small red stone. Her hips spread over my legs. The bare, shiny cleft of her pussy, the same dark brown as the rest of her.

I dipped two fingers inside her to watch them go in. Just the tips. With her hands on my shoulders, Sun lowered herself slowly over my fingers. I could feel her skin sliding over them, stretching around them. It seemed she was going to make it last forever, but then she was down on my hands, my fingers all the way inside her. She stayed that way for a second, then rose and lowered herself again.

"Don't move . . . your feet," she said, as though I was the one moving and not her. I wiggled my fingers inside her, just to show that I had the power to move something. I loved that the movement made it hard for her to get the rest of her words out. "You'll ruin . . . all . . . all my hard work."

"OK," I said. Which sounded stupid. I would have given her the moon if she'd asked. Not moving? That was a cinch.

She pressed her fingers to my lips, and I opened my mouth. My tongue on her fingers was lemon pucker and soft skin. Pulling her fingers from my mouth, Sun leaned back a little, opening her center to me. I could see her pussy lips and the hardening pink nub of her clit. She put her wet fingers there, back and forth. I worked my fingers harder inside her so she didn't have to move so much and she let herself go slack a little.

"Don't stop," she said. "Don't . . ."

Her eyes were closed and I watched her. Watched the way her thighs tightened as she rocked back and forth. The way she lowered herself over my fingers, sucking them inside her. The way her clit glistened and peeked beneath her fingers. And when she came, the way everything quivered and flowed, skin and arousal and breath.

After a few minutes, Sun rolled to the side of me. Her breath still moved in and out of her in fast little gulps. She pulled her wraparound skirt around her lower half like a blanket and rested her head on my belly. My T-shirt had ridden up, and her cheek on my belly was warm and damp, like she had a fever.

My insides felt all twisted up, trying to take everything in: my arousal, my disbelief that this had actually happened, my fear of the future. I didn't know what to do with my hands, still damp from Sun.

"Sun, why now, after all this time?"

She was quiet for so long that I wished I hadn't asked. Why couldn't I just shush and let things happen? What if this was a one-time thing? Now all I would remember about the ending of it was how I'd pushed.

Sun's head stirred on my belly, but she didn't look up.

"I just . . ." When she exhaled, her breath tickled my skin. "I thought about you a lot in Singapore and I realized I was just afraid. So I made up this plan: I'd offer to do your feet and if you laughed or freaked, then I'd be able to say it was just an idea. And we could just stay friends."

Another small silence. This time I was able to keep my mouth closed. I stayed still and waited while she kissed the skin above my belly button.

"But you didn't laugh. Well, OK you laughed a little, but you were willing. You didn't make me feel stupid."

She scooted up and put her head back on my shoulder. We both looked down at my feet, white beneath the hardening henna. They say that the thing you want is right in front of you, if only you know where to look. But sometimes it takes the thing you want to show you where to look, so that you're both looking at the same thing.

I wiggled my toes, careful not to crack the drying henna. "How long will they last?" I asked.

"Depends on how well you take care of them."

"And if I didn't? How soon would you have to do them again? Like, what if I took my jeans off right now, messed them all up?"

I couldn't see Sun's smile, but I could feel her cheek as it pushed out against my shoulder. She didn't answer my question. She just sat up and reached for the button of my jeans with both hands.

Mon Amie

Josephine Boxer

I quickly stopped to use the ladies' room in the arrivals terminal at McCarran International Airport in Las Vegas after a short, three-hour flight. I wanted to freshen up before meeting her for the first time.

I retrieved my luggage, went through customs and immigration without a hitch, and now began my search for her.

We had met online fifteen months earlier during a fanisode scriptwriting contest for *The L Word* television series. Ashley always gave my scene submissions high scores with positive comments. After the contest ended, I e-mailed a few of the contestants—all complete strangers—through the fanisode Web site to thank them for their support. Ashley replied with her private e-mail address, and we kept in touch as pen pals.

Little did we know then that these early interactions would later set the stage for a blossoming romance—but not one without its obstacles. Ashley was married with kids, living in California. I was single with no kids, living in Canada.

The long distance and complicated circumstances initially deterred me from any involvement with Ashley other than as friends.

Eventually, our e-mails turned into phone calls, photo exchanges, and cellular text messages. When another *L Word* scriptwriting contest was announced, we decided to collaborate on a scene, based on our online friendship and our "real life" connections to other women. We did extremely well in the contest, and soon thereafter expanded our mini-project into a two-hour feature film script.

During this time, it became apparent that our friendship and writing partnership were transforming into something more—but it was "something" neither of us ventured into discussing. We didn't want to jeopardize our relationship by doing anything foolish—crossing boundaries and having sex. But after months of debate and mutual resistance, we decided to meet in person.

I instantly spotted Ashley just inside the terminal's crowded exit. She was a delightful image of European descent, smaller in stature than I had envisioned, exuding warmth, confidence, and sensuality. She stood near the far wall in a cozy summer outfit, her dark, curly hair resting on her bare shoulders, holding her cell phone in one hand and sunglasses in the other. I wondered if she shared my slight nervousness.

Ashley scanned the crowd. Our eyes finally connected. Her radiant smile and the beautiful, warm, brown mirrors of her soul confirmed that we would share a magnificent vacation together in Las Vegas.

"Hi, Carly," she greeted me with open arms.

I set my luggage upright, kissed her cheek, hugged her, and said, "Hi, it's great to see you."

After climbing into her sexy, black Mercedes in the 128-degree summer heat, Ashley reached into the backseat cooler and offered me a bottle of cold water. She was incredibly thoughtful, sweet, and lovely. And she was mine for an entire week.

As Ashley drove through the parking lot, I caressed her hair and neck, eventually resting my hand on her thigh. She took my hand and played with my fingers.

We soon entered her spacious time-share, and the delicious aroma of homemade pasta sauce simmering on the stove permeated the air. She had arrived before me with groceries, wine, and candles, and had converted the condo into our very own romantic oasis. I was impressed, but also relieved by the comfort level between us.

Ashley prepared dinner while I unpacked. I wandered around in my Prodige boxers contemplating what to wear: shorts since it was scorching outside, or long pants since the indoor air conditioning was quite chilly.

"Are you sure you're a real Canadian?" she joked. "You're awfully wimpy about the cold temperature in here."

"I'm freezing my nuts off, and can't believe my California girl isn't cold."

But then again, she was slaving over a hot stove. And that's when I stole my first kiss.

Ashley looked so beautiful in the kitchen, tending to every detail with such care to ensure our first dinner together was perfect. I found it tremendously nurturing when a woman cooked for me, and I wanted to demonstrate my appreciation for all of her efforts.

She was stirring the pasta sauce. I had uncorked the wine and poured two glasses. I wrapped my arms around Ashley's waist, pulling her close as my lips reached for hers. She was briefly taken aback, but pressed her warm lips to mine. It was a delicious kiss—an exquisite icebreaker—and an exciting sign of what the night would hold. By then, our agreement to be there "as just friends" went up in smoke, and we knew that we'd make love that night.

After a leisurely, candlelit dinner, we took our wine and some romantic music into the bedroom. Ashley showered while I finished tidying up the kitchen and lighting more candles.

I crawled into bed after my shower and waited for her. I didn't know where she was. Finally, I heard her soft voice call out, "Carly, what are you doing?"

"Waiting for you, baby, in bed."

All the while, Ashley had been waiting on the living room sofa for me to seduce her. We laughed.

The first time we made love was sheer bliss. I knew she had limited experience with women, and I wanted our lovemaking to be magical. We kissed and caressed for a long time before clothes were slowly removed. I enticed her onto her stomach to sensuously massage her back and tickle her with my long hair. I love foreplay—the longer it lasts, the better—and Ashley had never enjoyed so much of it. Initially, she thought I was being nasty by torturing her with foreplay and making her wait to climax.

Ashley was dripping from her pleasure palace by the time my hand slid between her thighs. I climbed on top, tenderly kissing her from head to toe, exploring every inch of my exotic lover. My eyes and hands rested on her gorgeous, soft breasts each capped by a large, dark areola.

"Your breasts are beautiful, babe," I whispered. "They really turn me on."

"I'm glad you like them, baby," she sighed. "They certainly respond to your touch. I've thought about this moment more than you know."

My thumbs delicately brushed over her slightly protruding nipples, and circled her puckering areola. I wanted to savor the special moment of my initial time latching onto her nipples—and delayed doing so to build the momentum, and subsequent pleasure.

I cupped her breasts in both hands, caringly squeezing and massaging. Ashley moaned and arched her back, lifting her body and grinding her hips into mine. I softly and slowly kissed her breasts, then worked my way across her chest and up her neck to nibble on her ear. My hair swept over her body with my trail of kisses.

She eventually untangled my hair and pulled me into a deep, passionate kiss. Ashley had sumptuous, full lips that I could kiss all night. Our hungry tongues waltzed in each other's mouths, until we were breathless; we had to break away for air. I slid down her body, leaving alternating kisses and tongue strokes along the way.

I licked and kissed a circle around her right areola, teased the edges of her nipple with the tip of my tongue, and then took the entire nipple-areola complex into my mouth.

"Oh God, that goes straight to my clit," Ashley gasped.

I alternated breasts, admiring the ample size of her erect nipples. I sucked firmly, gently kissed, lightly bit, and feverishly licked her nipples and breasts. I could feel my own vulva drip with desire.

I covered her torso with butterfly kisses and fondling fingers, as she spread her legs, inviting me in.

I navigated her silky, swollen vulva with my lips, tongue, and fingers, teasing her opening and blowing on her clit, then kissing, licking, and sucking my way down her thigh and behind her knee.

I returned to her breasts, squeezing them together and taking both nipples into my mouth—flicking my tongue over them and sucking vigorously.

"Yeesss." Ashley's body twitched, desperately wanting to come. "I'm so ready for you. Now, baby."

I held her breasts, tweaking her nipples between my thumbs and index fingers. She parted her pussy with both hands, allowing my tongue to lap up her juices, leisurely jetting inside of her, tracing the edges of her labia, and sucking her vulva into my mouth. I progressively tickled her clit, feeling it engorge under my tongue.

She came in my mouth. And a second time on my hand—she had never before been fist-fucked. Her body was relaxed and aroused enough to ease my hand into her womanhood where time stood still and we became one.

Her fingers explored the river she had created between my legs as she entered me. I sucked on her nipples and rubbed my clit until my body convulsed in ecstasy. We collapsed side by side, and then she snuggled peacefully into the crook of my arm—her "spot"—where we fell asleep.

In the morning, we made love again.

Prancing around topless and wearing my Canadian-flag boxer shorts, I served my sweetheart coffee and cookies in bed. We talked, touched, and cuddled for hours—something we did for most of our Vegas vacation.

That week in Sin City was filled with romance, passion, adventure, and laughter. Ashley pressed her breasts against my arm and back as our bodies swayed to the music of Gwen Stefani at the MGM Grand. We tore through Caesars Palace like mad women to get to our Canada Day Céline Dion show—three songs late—as we had lost track of time during a romantic dinner in the Paris Hotel, complete with being serenaded by our talented singing waitress.

"I'm never late," Ashley mused, as we ran in the blistering heat to find the box office. "I only lose track of time when I'm with you."

Even though we missed the extravagant opening of my Canadian sister Céline's concert, I could do nothing but smile. I was happy. And I was falling in love.

There were so many highlights to our time together.

We flew in a helicopter over and into the Grand Canyon, followed by a boat ride along the Colorado River and lunch over-looking this World Wonder. We visited a *Titanic* exhibit on the Fourth of July followed by another romantic, serenading dinner date at Le Provençal, where the song "For Good" will now hold a special place in our hearts.

We spent hours cavorting in the pool—oblivious to onlook-ers—and plenty of time around the pool with piña coladas, vodka coolers, and beer. Unwittingly, I even added to the entertainment by toppling ass-over-tea kettle on my lounge chair, laughing hys-terically.

We got caught necking like teenagers in our condo elevator—twice! And giggled every time the automated elevator voice, which we named "Veronica," would announce "going down."

Our condo felt like home—our home—and we were clearly living in domestic bliss. We slid into our roles naturally, cooking, cleaning, barbecuing, and doing laundry together. We went gro-cery shopping like an old married couple. We fit together, per-fectly. And I knew it was right. She was right.

When we pulled into our parking spot at a sex-toy store, Ash-ley was self-conscious and giddy. She had never gone toy shop-ping, whereas I had an entire "tickle trunk" full of toys at home in Canada. I decided that with 9/11 security measures in full force, bringing a dildo across the border may cause an international relations nightmare—not to mention the embarrassment and risk of confiscation—so we thought it best to buy a new toy on our trip.

Back in our bedroom, after sharing a sensual, candlelit bub-ble bath and more wonderful foreplay, I fastened my harness with a modest-sized dildo.

"You look so sexy with your cock, babe."

I stroked my cock seductively while Ashley watched lascivi-ously.

I slowly mounted and deeply penetrated my woman, com-pelling a small orgasm.

We spooned and scissored. She rode my cock while I rocked her hips and enthusiastically watched her breasts bounce. She came hard on top of me, falling forward where her breasts land-ed in my face and I took her nipples between my lips.

We fell asleep briefly, and woke up wanting more. We sensuously washed each other in the shower before returning to our den of desire.

She straddled my face, holding her balance on the headboard. I wrapped my arms around her thighs, sliding my hands up to play with her breasts and nipples. I devoured her pussy as she gyrated above me. Her soft, slick vulva dancing over my cheeks and chin was pure paradise. I latched onto her clit and sucked until she exploded. Her body shook pleasurably for several moments as our bodies entwined and recovered.

Then, I eagerly parted Ashley's legs again.

"Will you open yourself for me, baby?" I asked, gazing intently into her loving eyes.

She moved her hands between her legs and spread her labia. I outlined her wet crevice with my finger, and then entered her. I added two more fingers and quickly penetrated my lover, enraptured by the sounds of her juice, the softness inside her walls, the tightness as she pulled my fingers deeper into her, and the thrill of stroking her G spot.

I removed my fingers, opened my own labia, and mounted her. We rubbed our drenched and throbbing cunts together.

"I don't wanna come yet, baby," I whispered. "I wanna watch you touch yourself."

We pulled apart to lay side by side on our backs in opposite directions. We slid our fingers into each other, and massaged our own clits while watching one another. We tried to come at the same time, but I trailed a few minutes behind as I observed every second of my lover masturbating to orgasm. I came intensely as Ashley's body still rippled with aftershocks.

We sighed and laughed.

"Now, honey, don't you fall asleep," Ashley ordered, as she molded her body into mine for snuggle time.

Within seconds, my lover was sound asleep in my arms. I held Ashley in that post-orgasm euphoric state until she awoke. The smile never left my face.

On our second to last day, we were quieter than usual, sensing the other's sadness at our pending departure. We spent a lot of time lovemaking and memorizing each other's body.

"Baby, I want you to wake up," a soft voice roused me on our last morning together.

"OK, baby," I replied, rolling over to meet my woman's lustful stare. "Good morning, sunshine."

Ashley climbed on top of me, already wet and ready for love. I sucked on her nipples and explored the level of arousal between her legs. She was saturated. I thrust four fingers into her and stroked her clit with my thumb. I lifted her hips and slid completely inside, closing my fingers into a fist.

"God, baby, that feels good. How many fingers do you have in me?"

"All of them," I whispered into her curls.

I fist-fucked my lover with one hand, and stroked my clit with the other. We came fast and feverishly.

We cuddled, and then Ashley disappeared into the living room. I could hear her rummaging around searching for something. She returned with a felt pen.

"Can I draw on you?" she asked.

I smiled and nodded my approval.

"OK, but don't look."

I laid flat on my back while my sexy woman in her black nightgown began carving into the skin near my right hipbone.

"Do you know what I'm drawing?"

"No, baby, not a clue."

I was thoroughly enjoying the sensation of Ashley leaving a mark on me, and watching the lovely smile on her face as her moist pussy gripped my thigh.

When finished, she revealed a perfect red Canadian maple leaf.

"I've been practicing drawing this. Does it look alright?"

"I love it, babe. It's perfect. Now, let me draw on you."

Ashley smiled and reclined on the bed. I slid the left strap over her shoulder, and began my body art on her upper breast near her heart.

Our bedroom was candlelit—since we hadn't opened our curtains to let the outer world into our romantic oasis—and therefore, Ashley couldn't see my "art."

Curious, she vanished into the bathroom to unveil my skin carving on her breast.

In mere moments, Ashley leapt back into bed, sprawling across my stomach. "I love you too, babe." We kissed and held each other in silence. No further words needed to be spoken. Everything we needed or wanted was in our arms.

As Ashley's plane took off into a clear blue sky, I felt an ache in my heart, my soul. I held back tears. And I stood in the terminal for twenty minutes watching planes land and take off.

When I boarded my plane, I reflected on our body art: her Canadian maple leaf on my hip; my words I LOVE YOU on her chest. I smiled at the romance of it all.

But then reality came crashing in. I knew that aboard her flight, Ashley would be returning her wedding band to its proper place, and I speculated on what she'd do about her body art. Would she leave it as a hidden remembrance of our special time together, or would she scrub my words of love from her breast before crawling into bed with her husband?

I sighed. But this was, after all, our mutually agreed arrangement. We could only be part-time lovers—for now, anyway. We had to take things one day at a time, one trip at a time.

I closed my eyes and fantasized about my special friend, my writing collaborator, my lover. I felt happy and completely satisfied with our love. And I started counting down the days until our next, already-planned romantic getaway.

Pool Girl

Sheri Livingston

"Oh, pool girl. I need more oil rubbed on me." Madison stretched against the lounge chair, pushing her barely covered breast toward the sun-lit sky.

Banana plants whipped in the warm afternoon breeze, their wide green leaves cascading shadows against the white-pebbled border surrounding her pool.

At the edge of the deep end stood Jodi, the pool girl. Madison was sure she was the sexiest woman she'd ever seen. Standing several feet away, she stole the breath right from Madison's lungs every time she pushed the skimmer pole across the bottom of the pool, flexing those toned arms.

Long, tanned legs ran from beneath a pair of brown Bermuda shorts. She had small breasts, held snug inside a lone white sports bra. Madison wanted to see them, to pluck at their hardened tips, gently suck them between her teeth. And from the discreet glances Jodi kept tossing her way, she was sure she could do just that.

But first, she had a game to play with that sexy piece of female flesh.

Jodi leaned the pole against the edge of the diving board and started walking toward Madison, her eyes hidden behind a pair of Oakley sunglasses. Submissive, just the way Madison wanted her. She loved being in charge. It gave her a rush beyond description, made her pussy weep with need.

"Faster!" Madison barked the order like a drill sergeant.

Jodi rushed her steps. A tentative smile stretched her thin lips.

Madison remembered just in time not to return that smile.

Instead, she reclined in her chair and angled her face toward the rays. After all, she was the mistress. Above all, she must remain stern and demanding, just like a true dominant.

Jodi stopped beside the chair and picked up the bottle. She poured suntan oil into her palm and slowly massaged the liquid into her mistress's legs, looking down submissively. Her hardened nipples pushed against the confines of her damp sports bra.

Madison smiled. *Oh yes. That's one hot and bothered pool girl kneeling at my side. Time to up the ante and watch her squirm.*

She leaned forward, untied the string at her back, dragged the loop over her head, and tossed the bikini top to the concrete.

Jodi's application slowed. She tilted her face toward Madison's chest.

"Did I give you permission to look at my tits, pool girl?"

A sexy flush darkened Jodi's cheeks. She dropped her gaze obediently. "No, ma'am."

"Call me 'my queen'." Madison enhanced her dominance, wanting to see how far Jodi could be strung along.

"No, my queen." Jodi kept her sights on Madison's long legs, her fingers working the oil into her flesh.

"That's better." Madison parted her legs and cupped her breasts. "Do you like looking at my tits, pool girl?"

"Yes, my queen."

"Would you like to touch them?" Madison pinched her nipples until they hardened into tight peaks.

"Yes, my queen."

"What would you do with them, pool girl?" She gently twirled the tips until a streak of fire rushed to her pussy.

Jodi looked up.

Madison scowled at her. "Are you disobeying me?"

Jodi quickly resumed her proper submissive position, eyes averted, and continued her circular motions against Madison's skin. "I would lick them until they hardened, slowly circle my tongue around them, and when your mouth parted on a strangled whimper, I'd guide them between my teeth and gently suck and nibble on them." Timidly, Jodi whispered her promises.

Madison quirked her brow. She reached down and dragged Jodi's sunglasses off her face, needing to see the obedience in those blue eyes. "Would you like to play a game, pool girl? For a chance to do those things to my tits?"

Jodi nodded, keeping her gaze trained on Madison's legs, already working those fingers past her knees.

"Strip!"

"Ma'am?"

"You heard me. Take off your fucking clothes."

Jodi took a step back, her expression clouded with confusion, though edged with lust.

Pool girl was enjoying the game. Madison could almost smell her arousal.

Jodi watched Madison through lowered lashes. Slowly, she unbuttoned her shorts and shucked out of them, standing before Madison in nothing more than a pair of women's briefs and sports bra.

Madison pointed. "All of it."

She held her breath while the band of Jodi's bra passed her small breasts. Dark areolas circled hardened nipples, begging Madison to suck and pinch at them.

Finally, Jodi slid her snug briefs down her legs, displaying a patch of black wiry hair.

Madison raked her gaze up and down Jodi's body, eating her alive with her eyes. "Nice. Verrry nice." She leaned up on her elbows.

Jodi brazenly stepped forward. "What would you like me to do, my queen?"

Madison grinned. "I'm feeling generous today. Why don't you humor me and tell me what game you'd like to play?"

Jodi's gaze disobediently dropped to Madison's breasts, before flashing back to her face. "I once made a woman come without touching her pussy."

Madison pursed her lips, different punishments rushing through her mind that she should bestow on the object of her infatuation . . . if her words hadn't made her pussy throb with need. "Hmm." Feigning boredom, she studied her red-polished nails for a second before turning back to Jodi. "I don't believe you."

Surety washed over Jodi's face. She resumed her abashed

expression, ducked her head, and lowered her voice to a properly humble murmur. "Then it's a challenge?"

"It'll take more than the sight of your tight body to make me drip."

Jodi stepped to the end of the lounge chair. "Will you remove the rest of your swimsuit, my queen? I promise not to touch." Her eyes roamed with wanton intent over Madison's body.

Madison swallowed, feeling her hold on the game loosening.

"Can I watch your pussy moisten, watch it tighten with need?" Jodi stood strong in front of her, no doubt anticipating her strings of restraint vanishing.

Madison's insides clenched just thinking about Jodi staring at her cunt, watching wetness seep to the edge. Taking a deep breath to steady her racing heart, she hooked her fingers into the hem and shoved her bottoms down her legs and off her feet, too trapped by the game not to play along.

Jodi knelt. A cute dimple formed at the corner of her mouth.

Madison resisted the urge to lean forward and touch the indention, to swipe her tongue across those inviting lips. She couldn't give into such temptations when the game was on, when time was ticking.

Jodi nipped Madison's big toe then, while those piercing eyes pegged Madison. Her half-smile vanished within the sharp intentness of her gaze. She sucked the flesh into her mouth.

Madison's insides burned and pulsed, though she kept an unaffected expression on her face. She couldn't let Jodi know how close she was to coming under her servant's attentions.

Jodi's tongue swirled around the tip of her toe, then she slowly loosed her suckle. "Please spread your legs, my queen."

When Madison didn't move, Jodi wrapped strong, lean hands around her ankles, slowly pushed her fingertips up her calves, past her knees. "I can't see your wet pussy unless you open for me."

Without will to stop them, Madison's lips parted while she spread her legs for Jodi's gaze. Her cunt clenched with need. Damn it! She was in over her head already. Perhaps it would be better to find a way to halt this game before she came out the loser.

Never one to accept defeat easily, she looked to the sky and sighed. "You're boring me, pool girl."

Quick as lightning, Jodi slid her upper body along the lounge chair, between her legs. Her hands pressed against Madison's inner thighs, spreading her wide. Her gaze speared Madison's pussy before her soft blue eyes rose. "Your dripping cunt says you're not quite so bored. Want me to taste you?"

Heat swirled in her gut. Madison tried to close her legs. Strong hands kept them pinned apart. "No. I want you to make me come, just like you boasted you could."

A grin dominated Jodi's face. "Patience, my queen." She ducked and blew hot breath against Madison's pussy.

Madison bucked her hips, reaching for satisfaction. She wanted to cram Jodi's face to her crotch, grind against her until an orgasm rocked her body.

No! If I do that, I lose.

She squirmed out of Jodi's firm grip and shoved out of the chair. "Pool girl, you're wasting my time." She walked toward the pool and dove in, praying the cool water would take away all evidence of her arousal.

When she emerged on the shallow end, a splash sounded behind her. She turned to find a naked body swimming beneath the water toward her.

Jodi stopped just shy of Madison's crotch and rose, her height taking her a good three inches above Madison. Water ran down her face and neck, droplets dripping from the tips of her nipples.

She leaned forward, her minty breath feathering across Madison's face. "Can I feel how wet your pussy is, my queen?"

Madison backed up a step. Maybe she underestimated the difficulty of harnessing her arousal.

"That's not part of the game. I won't allow you to touch my pussy." She grinned with false bravado. "You can't make me come without touching me, can you?"

"I never lie." She ducked and slurped at Madison's earlobe. "My fingers will never touch your pussy, but you're going to come, and come, and come."

Madison closed her eyes against the hot whispered promise.

Slowly, Jodi pushed Madison with the tips of her fingers until her back struck the edge of the pool. The force of a water jet rushed against her buttocks, making ripples swirl around their sealed bodies.

"Can I kiss you, my queen?"

"Yes . . . I mean, no, you cannot."

"But you want me to."

Lava-hot anticipation snaked through Madison like a fever taking over her body.

Blast her! Jodi was too good at the game, too sexy, too fucking hot.

Jodi lowered her mouth to Madison's. She licked her bottom lip, from corner to corner, then tenderly sucked it between her lips.

Madison opened her mouth in invitation, completely at Jodi's mercy now.

Jodi stared down over Madison with thick lust filling those beautiful eyes, then she sealed their mouths together.

Madison released a soft cry as Jodi's tongue slipped inside her mouth, her thrusts caressing, exploring, tasting.

When Jodi eased back, Madison was weak kneed, wild for the game to continue, yet needing it to come to an orgasmic halt. Her pussy clenched, a wire of heat traveling through her gut, spearing her core with a craving need.

Jodi spun her around, and eased Madison against her chest. "I think you've lost control, my queen." She lowered her voice into a husky whisper. "I promise not to take advantage of your weakness."

She leaned back until Madison floated just beneath the water, her head resting against Jodi's shoulder. The force of the jet shot against Madison's crotch, pulsing pleasure straight to her core.

"You have beautiful breasts, my queen. As soon as you come, I'm going to lick every drop of water from them. I'm going to suck your clit until you come again and, when you recover from those spasms, I'm going to finger-fuck you until you scream that you can't take anymore." She pressed her lips against Madison's cheek. "I may stop. I may not."

Gut-wrenching sparks erupted through Madison's cunt. Even with her body submerged in cool water, the arousal overpowered. She clenched her insides to sizzle the glorious pain, but that did little to extinguish the brutality of the inferno devouring her cunt.

Madison licked her lips, arching her hips toward the strength of the jets. "You're cheating. Why don't you just put me out of my misery now?"

Jodi chuckled. "Unlike you, Madison, my queen, I don't want the power. I just need you begging."

Madison knew she was only seconds away from doing just that, from whimpering like a newborn pup searching blindly for mama's tit, from pleading with Jodi to extinguish the heat wave raging at her pussy. As much as she needed an end, needed her insides to pulse with an orgasm, she couldn't bring herself to beg. She was determined to prevail.

"You'll be waiting a long time for me to beg you, pool girl." Madison reached behind her, slipped her fingers into short hair, and tugged her head around. She swiped her tongue across Jodi's lips, knowing full well she'd been conquered.

Jodi pulled out of her grasp. "You will beg me. You wouldn't want to go inside all by your lonesome and put out your own fire, would you?" She sucked Madison's earlobe between her teeth, and nipped. "Your vibrator can't make you scream nearly as loud as I can."

The water pulsed against Madison's pussy, pushing her arousal to the brink of pleasure. She bucked her hips against the penetrating waves.

"Your nipples are hard as rocks. I can't wait to chew on them."

Madison pumped her hips, riding the invisible pleasure. She tightened her hands into fists, desperate for the abyss.

Jodi pulled Madison away from the water's force.

Madison scoffed and tried to slither out of her grasp.

Jodi wrapped her arms around her chest, fingers on either side of her breasts, hovering, but not daring to touch. "Let me hear you plead, my queen."

"You're a fucking tease!"

"Quite the contrary. You're the only one keeping yourself from satisfaction." She smiled against Madison's cheek. "Beg me to let you come. You're so close, so near. I bet your pussy is slick as glass. Let me feel you, Madison."

Madison squeezed her eyes, beyond hopeful for relief, yet more determined not to give in.

"Beg me, Madison. Let me taste those nipples while you come, while I plunge my fingers between your sweet folds, then inside your tight ass."

Madison's insides tightened, pulsed, and before she knew it, her orgasm shattered. She screamed and thrashed in Jodi's grasp.

Jodi leaned over Madison's body and sucked an erect nipple between her teeth. One hand slid between Madison's legs. Before Madison could catch her breath, Jodi drove her fingers inside, renewing her wild, orgasmic pumps. Her other hand slid down Madison's back, between the cheeks of her ass, supporting her weight. She dipped a single finger into her pussy, reversed, then shoved the digit into Madison's ass.

Madison loosed another scream, arching back and forth, deepening the thrusts in her cunt, in her ass, fucking herself with Jodi's fingers.

She whimpered and quivered until the orgasm weakened, leaving her drained of energy, floating weightlessly in Jodi's arms.

The water softly sloshed against the edges while Madison regained normal breathing.

"You're such a lush." Jodi chuckled and hugged Madison to her body.

Madison pushed away from her and planted her feet flat on the bottom of the pool, and a grin spread across her face, as well as her heart. "Shut up! You weren't supposed to jump in here with me."

Jodi captured her hand and tugged her back against her chest. "I couldn't help it. You looked so cute acting all dominating, strutting like a mistress."

Madison smacked at Jodi's arms. "You were supposed to wait until I made you masturbate, while I watched."

Jodi kissed the tip of her nose. When Madison poked her bottom lip out, Jodi tapped it with her finger. "I'm sorry, sweetie. I'll try harder next time. Maybe you should think about keeping your clothes on until after that little scene?" Jodi grabbed her ass, and lifted her legs around her waist. "This luscious body makes me forget what role I'm playing."

Madison snorted and pushed Jodi's hands away. "Yeah, well, next time, don't forget."

"Are you two having sex and role-playing in the damn pool again? How am I ever supposed to get the thing clean if you won't get out long enough for me to vacuum?"

Madison and Jodi whipped around. Contessa, the real pool girl, stood with her arms crossed and glared at them.

Madison smiled. Jodi busted out laughing.

"Sorry, Contessa." Madison led Jodi across the shallow end then trudged up the steps. "It's just, um, we love you so much, and well, Jodi wants to be you! I tried to stop her!"

Jodi scoffed and turned humorous blue eyes on Madison before turning back to Contessa. She shrugged. "Contessa, she begged me to pretend I was you so she could dominate me." She wiggled her brow and lowered her voice. "I think she has a thing for you."

Madison grinned and batted her lashes, though Contessa didn't return the humor.

"Both of you get your strange asses in the house while I clean the pool. And for God's sake, stop fucking in the pool on the days I'm scheduled to work." She yanked the pole from the edge of the diving board where Jodi had left it. "You didn't do anything freaky with the pole, did you?" She shoved her hand in the air, fighting her laughter. "I don't wanna know! Both of you, go the hell away from me!"

Jodi grabbed Madison's hand and quickly led her across the pool deck. "We won't do it again, Contessa. Promise."

Naked, they both scurried inside while Contessa shook her head and continued scorning them with her dark brown eyes. A smile tugged at her lush lips when they ducked inside the house.

Once Jodi closed the glass door, Madison flashed a devilish grin. "Want to play doctor now?"

Jodi tilted her head to the side and quirked her brow. "That depends. Do I have to be the nurse?"

Madison winked. "Of course you do. What doctor do you know who seduces her patient?" She started up the winding staircase.

"Oh, doctor. I need your assistance in room number two," Jodi's sultry voice teased behind her.

Madison took the stairs two at a time.

Fair Play

Nicki Wachner

My bat crashed to the floor of the dugout. Sitting down, I ripped off my hat and flung it down as well. I buried my head in my hands. I was frustrated at striking out again. I knew I could hit off Trish; I had done it before. It must have been the nerves of the finals. I never did well under pressure. I tried to get her to play on my team, but she told me she played better when I was on the opposing team. I thought we had played well together in high school.

Standing to my full height of five foot six I knew that, while I was not tall, my well-toned body intimidated my opponents. But Trish was never intimidated. She was always cool, never allowing any other player to intimidate her. She knew the game and played it to perfection.

I attempted to get my head back in the game by putting on my catcher's gear. The pads acted like an anchor, centering me before I had to take the field.

Glancing at the scoreboard, the game remained tied at zero. The pitching on both teams was at its best. When someone made contact with the ball, it was easily cleaned up by the fielders. If our pitcher, Blair, could stay in the game, and strike out the next three hitters, we would go into extra innings.

I watched as Blair walked up to the plate. She was our last at bat and more importantly, our last hope of staying alive. I knew Trish loved to strike out the opposing pitcher in the last inning; she knew this would rattle them. Blair swung at, and missed, all three pitches. Trish struck her out, ending our at bat.

We had to shut them down.

I jogged onto the field with Blair's glove. Handing it to her, I tried to reassure her. "It's OK, we stop them down now, and we can go into extra innings. Don't let it get to you. It's been a hard game, but I know we can do it."

She gave a weak smile. I had a sinking feeling Trish had taken our pitcher out of the game.

"We can do this, ladies!" I shouted to the women jogging onto the field.

"Three up three down."

First up was Naomi. She was strong at shortstop being long and limber, but not one of their best hitters. Blair's first pitch caught her swinging. By the way the ball hit my glove, I knew that Blair had lost some of her game. The next pitch was a strike she let pass. The third pitch was tight inside, just catching the plate. "Two more, just like that!" I yelled as I threw the ball back to Blair.

Next up was Dolly. She was not a strong player. I heard a rumor that she was only on the team because she was dating the coach. Blair dispensed of Dolly in three pitches. I started to get anxious at the thought of extra innings. One more out was all we needed. "One more ladies, we can do this."

Trish was up; this didn't look good for us. I knew if Blair didn't get back in the game that Trish would pounce on her weakened state of mind. She was even more ruthless now than when we were in high school.

My eyes were glued to Trish as she sauntered up to the plate. She looked me up and down, giving me a sly wink before turning her attention to Blair. I sank down into my crouch.

I knew that there was nothing I could do now but hope. The first pitch was a strike that Trish let go without a glance. She was toying with Blair. The second pitch was wide to the side. Trish stood there, cool, in the sweltering ninety-eight degree heat. Sweat started dripping into my eyes as the next pitch came flying toward my waiting mitt. Before it reached my glove, I heard the distinctive crack of a wooden bat hitting a ball. I watched as Trish tore off toward first base. The ball looked like it was going to soar over the fence. At the last second, it dropped. It came to rest about ten feet away from our closest player. Brandy went full speed for the ball. Picking it up, she turned, throwing it to Fawn, the cut-off woman.

Trish was fast. She was already rounding third base, heading for home. I signaled for the ball, trying to cover the plate at the same time. Crouching down, I prepared for a collision, as Trish turned her shoulder into me. I felt the ball hit my glove. Turning toward Trish, I was going to get rocked. She knocked me wide of the base. I felt the ball release from my glove as I slammed the ground. With it went any chances for extra innings. I lay there knowing I had just lost the game. We were eliminated from the tournament.

Trish bent down and offered me her hand. I smacked her hand away, and sat up. I didn't need a hand from the woman who had run me over to win a game. She shrugged before bouncing off to the dugout full of her screaming teammates.

It was hard to whisper "good game" around the disappointment that lodged in my throat. I sat in the dugout as everybody filtered off the field.

The locker room was already empty when I finally made my way there, my catcher's gear still on. My teammates had already left for the local watering hole. I was still upset at losing the game, but more than that, I was upset that Trish had run me over. I walked across the hall to the opposing team's locker room. Except for the running showers, it was quiet. I knew Trish was in the shower—she always showered alone, with all the showers turned on to create steam.

Walking into the showers, I enjoyed the sight before me. Through the heated mist I could see Trish facing the wall. Her body was a fine-tuned machine. Her muscles rippled beneath her skin as she washed her hair. I had always admired her tight ass in her softball uniform, but I loved the way it looked with cascading soapy water on its way down her toned legs.

"What the fuck was that?" I yelled at her wet backside.

She didn't jump; she simply looked over her shoulder. "I believe it was a home run. I thought you knew that, Brenda," she said.

"You know what I'm talking about." The steam was making me hot.

"I can't hear you. Why don't you take your clothes off and come over here and talk to me," she said before going back to the task of rinsing her hair.

I stood there a moment, stunned that she would even suggest something like that. She turned toward me, tempting me to join her. I started to undress. I couldn't believe that I was going to get naked to talk to the woman who ran over me to win a game.

"Fine. Now that I'm here, why did you do that? You could have really hurt me," I said, facing her.

"While you're here, wash my back," she said, handing me a bottle of soap. "I was winning a game. I did what anybody would have done."

"And you think because you ran me over I should do anything for you?" I took the soap only because her back looked so good.

"No, I think you should, because you want to fuck me," she said, turning around.

I admired her backside, but I worshiped her front. Water flowed down, flowing between perfectly round breasts, over gently rippling abs, only to disappear in the valley between her legs and continued its journey down perfectly muscled legs. I wanted to follow the same trail with my tongue.

Looking in her eyes, the desire was evident. I tenderly tasted her lips. I tasted mint. I slid my hands around her slick body and pulled her close, feeling her taut nipples against my own hardening nipples. She moaned into my mouth as my tongue slipped past her lips.

I slid my leg between her thighs, eliciting a moan. She was hot, slick, and needy. Taking her hands, I held them above her head and placed them on the shower nozzle, stretching her so she had to stand on her toes. "Don't move," I said.

My hands slid down her arms. Feather-light touches caused thousand of goose bumps to appear on her smooth skin. I enjoyed seeing what my touches did to her body.

Kissing and licking her neck, I could feel her rapid pulse beneath the surface. I continued kissing down her body, eliciting moans of pleasure. When I came to the valley between her breasts, I made a detour to her right breast, taking her nipple between my lips. I twirled my tongue around her hardened nipple, and followed up with light strokes over the tip. She arched her back to my lips, urging me to take more. I nipped at her breast enjoying the sounds each nipple and flick elicited.

Trish's hips were riding my thigh, trying to relieve the pressure building at her growing clit. My hand played with the wet hair between her legs, only teasing the slick folds. I could feel the blood gather between her legs as I sucked and nipped at her left breast. Her hips continued to grind against my thigh making it slick with her juices. Flexing my leg, I teased her clit. She tried to ease as much pressure as she could while riding my leg.

Her soft whimpers begged for my touch. This was not about relief; it was about paying her back for beating me. The soft cries that came from her were driving me wild. I wanted to torture her for knocking me on my back. I could have left her there full of want and need, but my fingers itched with want to be inside her. I stepped back, hearing her gasp with the loss of contact. I watched her body heave with desire. Arms already weak from the game started to shake as she tried to remain on her toes. I removed her hands from the shower. Turning her around, I placed her hands against the wall and leaned into her.

"What do you want?" I whispered in her ear, tracing its edges with the tip of my tongue while my fingers snaked around to her wet folds. She pushed against me with her ass and I moaned at the contact.

"I want you," she moaned.

"What do you want me to do?" I asked before taking her lobe between my teeth.

She sucked in a sharp breath. "I want you to fuck me."

"How do you want me to fuck you?" I asked as my hands started caressing her clit.

"Hard, I want you to fuck me hard," she gasped.

I stepped away. "Turn off the water," I told her.

I turned and walked out of the showers. Looking back, I saw that she was still against the wall. I could see her body shaking from need. I knew she was going to follow.

I heard the showers turn off one at a time until the only sound that could be heard was her bare feet slapping against the wet tiles. "Where do you want me?" she whispered.

"Come here." I held out my hand and brought her to me. I led her to the massage table in the middle of the room. It was old and the leather was cracked. It did not look comfortable but was softer than the floor; still I laid a towel down for cushion.

"I want you begging for release," I said before covering her lips with mine. My tongue assaulted her like she battered me during the game. Her low moans only fueled my desire. I sat her on the rough table. I placed one of her legs on either side so I could look at her hot, wet pussy. Trish was flush with desire. Her nipples were hard with need; her sex was pink and open. I could see the wetness between her legs.

Climbing on the table, I lowered my head to the breasts being offered for my taking. I took her left nipple between my teeth, gently biting down. She arched her body off the table, holding herself up by placing a hand on each side. I continued suckling her breast while running my hands up her thighs. Her hips moved forward seeking the touch of my hand. I grazed her outer lips lightly with the tips of my fingers. I could smell her heady scent. Scooting back, I kissed down her body, forcing her to lie back on the bench. Crawling off the table I crouched down, coming eye level with her pussy.

I forced her legs farther apart. The scent coming from her cunt was intoxicating. My mouth watered with the need to taste her. Running my hands up to again tease her puffy red lips, I allowed one finger to slide into her slick folds. She gasped as I flicked my thumb over her sensitive clit. I continued to tease her, kissing my way down to where her need was the greatest. I slid two fingers inside her, curling them to reach the spot that she craved.

Her body arched, begging for my fingers to fill her. I watched her hips thrust down on my fingers. I removed my fingers so I could taste her. She tasted like the sweetest peaches. I slowly licked my fingers. Her hips continued to rock .I put the now clean fingers back inside her, and continued to stroke her while adding speed to match Trish's thrusting hips. Her hands were above her head, holding the bench as her body arched to take in more of my hand. My tongue continued to stroke her throbbing clit. I tried to keep pace as her hips continued to rock against my fingers and tongue. Suspended above the bench her body was tense with the onset of her orgasm, her breath was coming in short gasps. I wrapped my free arm around her hips, bringing her back down onto the bench. Her body was telling me that she was close. Her body was begging for release. I took her clit between my lips, sucking as she found her voice. She screamed out my name. The sound echoed through the empty locker room. Her hands wrapped around my neck, trapping my head between her muscular thighs. I lapped up every drop that escaped from her. She tasted good on my tongue.

Withdrawing my fingers, I slowly slid each finger into my mouth, sucking them dry. Her eyes gleamed as her body continued to shake with aftershocks. I stood up, wrapping her legs around my hips, taking her in my arms. I kissed her, allowing her to taste herself on my lips.

"That was for knocking me down," I said, withdrawing from her.

"Well, had I known that I would have knocked you down sooner," she said, nibbling on my neck, her body glistening with sweat.

"I think there is more hot water if you want to shower," I told her. I was already looking for my uniform.

"So what's for dinner?" Standing on shaky legs, she moved toward the shower.

"You, naked in our bed. See you at home," I told her as she walked back into the shower.

Laid Over

Tara Young

I fidgeted in my window seat, buckled up, and checked my watch, 6:47 a.m. My body vibrated with anticipation as we prepared for takeoff. I was on my way to New Orleans for a long weekend of partying with friends in the French Quarter. But, as excited as I was for the breasts and booze on Bourbon Street, I was even more excited to touch down at LAX.

When I booked this trip, I made sure to choose the flight that stopped in Los Angeles—the home of Jeanine Robinson, the hottie I'd been e-mailing for the past two months. She was silly and sweet and sexy as hell. I couldn't get enough of her.

It was ridiculous the way I'd look forward to every message, the way my stomach would flip at the slightest compliment from her. The way I couldn't stop smiling every time I thought about her.

Any suggestive comment drenched my panties. Jeanine loved to tell me in explicit detail what she would do to me when we met. How she would tongue my pussy until I came in her mouth. Over and over, all night long. And wake me up the next morning with her head between my legs to make me come again.

She drove me wild, and I knew I was falling for her. I could only hope that she felt the same way. When I told her I'd be in Los Angeles for a layover, I was overjoyed when she suggested that we meet at the airport.

I only had eighty-seven minutes, but I was determined to make it work. If I met her near baggage claim, I'd have to go back through security, wasting precious moments that we could be spending together.

But meeting at the gate would be no easy task since she would need a boarding pass. After much internal debate, I decided the latter would be the best option, and I ordered her a one-way ticket to nowhere.

The plane reached cruising altitude, and I opened a book and tried to focus on the words and not the mixture of desire and nerves that coursed through my veins. I had two hours to kill, but it felt like an eternity. The story did little to hold my attention; every page made me think of Jeanine.

She captured my attention from the beginning with her amiable charm and sense of humor. Our banter and flirting made my heart feel lighter than it had in months. My face looked like I swallowed a coat hanger from the huge grin plastered on my face whenever we talked.

Two people could not have been more different than she and I—we both grew up on the wrong side of the tracks, but we had taken varying paths to get to where we were. I was the good girl who always did the right thing. She was the teenage runaway who fought to survive. She had experienced hell on earth but lived to tell the tale. I admired her for that.

Despite our differences, the pull was undeniable. Of course, that could've been because she was absolutely gorgeous. And she turned me on like no one ever had. Every morning, I awoke hard and throbbing, wishing Jeanine was in my bed. I would slide my hand through my slick folds and rub my protruding clit while I fantasized about having my way with her. In the shower. On the beach. In my car. Anywhere and everywhere.

A few strokes across my rock hard bulge had me coming with such force that my body would lift off the bed. My whole being shook violently, and I fought for breath. When the trembling finally subsided, I was left with a sated grin and ready to face the day.

Thinking of that on the plane ride left me weak and wanting, and there was still an interminable wait until we landed. I was tempted to throw a blanket over myself and let my fingers do the walking right then and there, but I tried to exercise some self-control.

Finally, the wheels touched down on the tarmac, and I was

just minutes from seeing the object of my affection, my Jeanine. I checked my watch again as we taxied to the gate. 9:18 a.m. We arrived exactly on time.

My excitement quickly turned to frustration as I waited to get off the plane. *Why did I get a seat in the twenty-sixth row?* I cursed. *And why is everyone so slow? Get out of the way! I want to see Jeanine!*

I reached the Jetway and maneuvered through the crowd, trying to quell my irritation. I nearly ran to the waiting area, stopping briefly to check my next connection.

The flight to New Orleans was scheduled to take off on time at 10:45 from another terminal. I had already lost ten minutes getting off the plane, and the call for boarding would come about thirty minutes ahead of takeoff. Damn, our eighty-seven minutes together quickly dwindled to forty-seven, and we would lose more time getting to the next gate.

I scanned the area and noticed Jeanine standing to the side. She seemed to radiate light, making it easy to find her amid the throngs of people. My first glance into her eyes from a distance took my breath away, and I couldn't stop from grinning. She was even more beautiful in person than her pictures.

I tried to walk toward her, but my feet were rooted to the spot. I'm sure my jaw dropped as I took her in. She wore navy shorts and a gray tank top, exposing her flawless skin and her toned arms and legs. Her straight, dirty-blonde hair cascaded over her shoulders, and the corners of her perfect red lips tugged upward as she smiled back.

Thankfully, she took mercy on me and came to stand next to me. I still wasn't sure I could move.

"Hi, I'm Susan," I said unnecessarily, eliciting a chuckle.

"It's nice to meet you." Her green eyes twinkled.

She surprised me then by enveloping me in a hug. I was sure I had stopped breathing all together when our bodies touched all along their lengths. Then I surprised myself when I reached up to cup her face and pulled her in for a kiss. Our lips touched for the first time, sending a jolt of electricity through my entire body. I knew then that I had to have her.

I had intended only a brief peck, but the kiss deepened as I ran my tongue along her lips, begging for entrance. She opened her mouth to oblige, and my passion soared as she kissed me back.

For a moment, I was lost in the touch and taste of her, forgetting—or maybe not caring—where we were. It was only when we got jostled by a harried passenger hurrying to her next flight that I was brought back to reality. I figured we should look for a more private place.

I pulled her in for another tight embrace and whispered, "God, I want you so bad, baby. I want to make you come."

"Yes. Just do it," she replied, a little out of breath.

I looked around and smiled. "This is probably not the best place for that."

She took me by the hand then and guided me toward my next gate. "I know just the place." I would've followed her anywhere.

She led me through the horde of travelers, and we sidestepped rolling suitcases and swinging bags to get to our destination—the Hudson News souvenir shop. A section in the back was under construction and walled off by some plywood. We sneaked into a round alcove covered in newly applied paint and avoided the ladders and cement in the center of the space.

I had imagined our first time to be in a romantic locale. Perhaps a suite at the Four Seasons with flower petals on the bed and champagne and strawberries nearby. But that wasn't an option, and I couldn't wait. I looked at her expectantly.

"I sort of cased the joint while I waited for your flight to arrive," she admitted sheepishly. "No one came back here for at least a half hour. Hopefully, that'll continue."

She was obviously thinking ahead. Jeanine had already determined the gate for my connecting flight before I got there. The fact that she had given some thought to this made me want her even more.

I pulled her in for another kiss, and she gave herself willingly. Her lips scorched my soul, and I had an overwhelming desire to touch her everywhere. My hands had a mind of their own as they roamed over her tight ass, up her abdomen to her breasts, and around her shoulders.

I couldn't get enough of her. I pushed her flimsy tank top up and out of the way and broke the kiss. I sucked one nipple in my mouth and caressed the other with my hand.

"Oh, God, Susan, yes," she moaned as I continued my assault on her breasts. She let out a whimper as I pulled away, but she had to know I wasn't done yet.

I grabbed her by the arms and turned her around, pushing her up against the wall, her face shoved into the cool surface. I caught my first glimpse of the black panther tattoo on her left shoulder, its intense green eyes staring back at me. So much like hers. I purred like a jungle cat and kissed her body art, finding her even sexier than I had before.

I had forgotten there were people just on the other side of the wall who could walk in on us at any moment. I didn't care. Only Jeanine and I existed.

I held her hips and rubbed my crotch against her firm ass, reveling in the feel of her pressing into my clit. I let out a moan of appreciation and almost came from the contact. But I wanted to take care of her needs first. I placed her palms flat against the surface and held her wrists above her head.

"Don't move your hands," I admonished as I kissed her neck and rubbed my breasts against her back. "Understand?"

She nodded, and I slid my fingers down her arms and back to her breasts. She stayed as I commanded, and I rewarded her by pinching her hard nipples.

She gasped. "Please. I need more. Please, Susan. Fuck me! Please!"

God, I loved to hear her beg for it, and I was more than happy to oblige. I reached around her waist, unbuttoned her shorts, and slid down her zipper. I was tempted to tease her, but I didn't have time, and I didn't think I would survive much longer.

I pushed her panties aside and slid my right hand through her wet pussy. She was soaked, and my two fingers entered her easily. I moved my left hand back to play with her breasts. I pounded her cunt and stroked her tits in rhythm.

Her hips bucked and her cries grew more insistent, so I knew she was close to the edge. I removed my fingers from inside her and moved them to her hard clit. I rubbed my fingers in circles over her bulge until I felt her body stiffen.

"Yes, baby! Right there!" Jeanine screamed. I quickened my pace when she let out a long guttural moan.

"Let go, baby! Come for me! Come all over my hand!" I encouraged.

I felt her jerk before panting, "I'm coming! I'm coming! I'm coming!"

I caught her around the waist as her body shook and sagged against the wall.

"It's OK, baby," I cooed in her ear. "I've got you." I held her close until she floated back to earth.

Just then, a voice over the loudspeaker announced the boarding call for United Flight 1620 to New Orleans.

I looked at Jeanine with a mix of wonder and sadness. Making love to her was amazing, and I was loath to leave her. I fixed her shirt, zipped her shorts, and tried to make it look like she didn't just have her brains fucked out. But the silly grin on her face gave her away.

I kissed her long and slow before we walked to the gate hand in hand. I held her until the last call for boarding came, enjoying the feel of her in my arms. She fit so perfectly against me. I reluctantly let her go and walked to the Jetway, sneaking a peek over my shoulder at her and waving one last time before I disappeared from sight.

I got out my cell phone and tapped a text message as I made my way to my seat. "You know . . . my layover is longer on Tuesday when I fly back."

"Yes," she replied, "and next time, it's my turn to make you come."

The Parking Garage

Shanna Katz

We walked into the parking garage together, and I watched as she fumbled through her purse to find the money to pay for the ticket. As she fed the slightly crumbled dollar bills into the machine, I pushed the button for the elevator, leaning against the wall nonchalantly as I watched her. I'd been watching her all evening. She was gorgeous, incredibly sexy . . . not society's definition of sexy per se, but she just oozed it in a take-charge, fierce, femme fatale kind of way. It was only our first date, but I wanted to see her, the real her, to envelop her curves, and to discover what made an intriguing and beautiful woman like her tick. As cliché as it might be, I wondered what this goddess looked like underneath that perfectly coordinated outfit. I imagined waking up next to her, rolling over while wrapping my arm around her, and falling back asleep.

The ding of the elevator startled me out of my deliciously naughty thoughts, and I held the elevator door for her, placing my hand at the small of her back as I followed her in. The doors shut, and suddenly she was on me, her lips hungrily grasping for mine. I was trying to go the polite route and was being chivalrous, but if she was ready, then I sure as hell wasn't going to wait. I started kissing back, and in a few seconds I had her pinned against the wall. Clasping both of her hands, I pulled them about her head, pressing my body against her soft curves, my lips devouring hers. Her lips were delectable, and tasted as though they were created for me. My lips broke the kiss and wandered desperately up and down her neck, discovering new territory, pausing on her earlobe, delicately nibbling at first, and then more forcefully as I heard her moan into me. Her hands were on my back, her nails lightly scratching through my shirt.

Now my hands were running up and down her body, slowly working their way up her shirt, lifting it over her head. She wasn't pinned anymore, but I was pretty sure she wasn't going anywhere. Unhooking her bra, I let it slide to the floor and I grabbed one breast with each of my hands. As beautiful as the rest her body was, her breasts were her crowning glory. They were perfect, and fit perfectly in my palms—two huge globes of perfection. There was just nothing else to say about them, and I wanted them in my mouth.

The doors dinged open, the elevator having reached our destination. She swore, some intelligible words coming out of her lush and beautiful lips, and she reached over, hitting the "door close" button. Her taking charge like that turned me on so much—I wanted her badly, and intended to continue this tryst as long as she'd let me.

I began to move down her body, placing kisses and pecks down her collarbone and to her sternum. I kissed her breasts lightly all over, just avoiding her nipples. When her breathing became heavier, I let my tongue flick them, making them even harder than they already were. Lowering my mouth onto her right nipple, I started to alternate between sucking and gently biting. Her moans let me know she was enjoying it as much as I was, and I switched to her left nipple. I went back and forth between them, becoming rougher as I went. I didn't want to hurt her and thought about easing up, until her hand latched onto the back of my head, pressing my face closer into the beautiful expanse of breasts. I wasn't about to argue. I'd just discovered this flawless female was a little bit kinky, and to be honest, it just turned me on even more.

After a few minutes of this, she pulled my face up to hers and went after my lips. I felt her hands winding their way down my body, toward my waistband, wanting to see what I had to offer. Once I felt her hands on my fly, I growled and brushed them away, grabbing them and pinning her against the wall again. Tonight was going to be about her, and I was going to give her more pleasure than she could handle. I didn't need her distracting me. Pressing against her, I carefully forced my knee between her thighs as her head rolled back in delight. She had told me that she loved giving up control to someone she trusted, and I was honored she had given me that trust. My leg was between hers, and I could feel her start to grind her body against it. Perfect. She was hot and turned on, which was exactly how I wanted her. Her pelvis was creating a rhythm of its own, pressing against me, desperately trying to gain the friction she wanted so badly. I used my knee to open her legs even farther, so she couldn't get herself off the way she wanted. I wasn't ready for that yet. I wanted to see more of her, learn more about her, bring her to the edge of ecstasy over and over.

I thanked whatever deity there was that this gorgeous woman had seen fit to wear a knee-length skirt. Granted, the boots she had on were incredibly sexy, but they didn't give me the same easy access that her skirt did. Bending down, I ran my hands up and down her thighs, caressing her everywhere but where she wanted to be touched. She gyrated her hips into me, her eyes meeting mine, pleading. She reached down to encourage my hands inward, but I pushed them up. By now, she should have discovered that I was in charge here. This continued, my hands making their way over her entire body, pinching her nipples and tickling her thighs.

Her skin was smooth and she smelled faintly of lilacs. Chalk that up to one more reason I love femmes—they always smell perfectly, almost without even trying. Why the hell was I thinking about that now? I had this beautiful, sexy, and partially naked woman in front of me, and all I could think about was how she smelled like a lilac bush on a warm spring day after the rain. Shaking my head, I returned to the moment, and let my hands continue their determined path all over her flawless skin.

Finally, when I thought I might have teased her enough, I moved my hands to where she was dying for me to touch. I slid both of them around her and up under the edge of her skirt. Brushing them lightly over her, my insides jumped when I felt lace under my fingertips. I didn't need to lift her skirt up to know that they were lacey boy shorts. I lifted just the edge and saw the black lace; they made her already delicious ass look simply divine.

Her wearing them meant she had planned at least part of this, and I stopped to think whether I really was in control of the situation.

A slight gasp of pleasure coming from her brought me back to reality. My fingers gently danced over her underwear, enough to cause her to breathe faster, but not quite enough to give her the pressure she craved. I could be devious when I wanted to be. Surreptitiously, I slipped my fingers into the top of her waistband, allowing them to slowly creep down on their treasure hunt. She was dripping wet. Simply drenched. I almost groaned out loud. I wonder if she knew what she was doing to me. She was just as turned on as I was, and that's saying a lot. Just as my middle finger began to encircle her clit, the elevator doors dinged open again.

Screw this. She gasped as I yanked my hand from her underwear, grabbing her hand, shirt, and bra, and dragging her toward the corner of the lot where I'd parked only a few hours earlier, never guessing the night would end in this passionate display of discovering each other in such an intimate way. Again, thanking heaven that I'd chosen to park in a more deserted corner of the lot, I took her around to the front of the car, kissing her deeply, and then pushed her back on the hood. Sliding her underwear down until it was just hanging off one of the boots, I told her to lie down, and I spread her legs open. Dear god, I had been hoping for this all night.

As perfect as her breasts were, I lied. They weren't the best part of her. Her cunt was absolutely outstanding. It was truly perfect: the shape, her tiny inner lips, and her clit throbbing in the mildly chilly night air as it stood out from under its hood. I stood looking at it. Fuck, I was so goddamn lucky. I dove in, like a wild animal, desperate for a taste of her. Running my hands up the inside of her thighs, I spread her legs farther and gently blew on her clit. She gasped and her body tensed. I took her momentary surprise to go in, and I placed my mouth on her, sucking her plump lips into my mouth, biting just slightly. She pushed her cunt up into my mouth, and I wrapped my hands under her ass and pulled her closer into me as I felt her trembling in excitement.

As I carefully approach her clit with nibbles, licks, and sucking on her lips, I pulled back for a second. Taking my middle finger, I reached up and placed it in her mouth, letting her lick and suck it before I slowly pressed it into her. God, she was wet, and her tight cunt hugged my finger. Working it in and out of her slowly but with firm pressure, I once again lowered my mouth to her clit. My mouth along with my finger had her body writhing, and shortly, her hands were in my hair, her pelvis pressing up against me as she groaned and grunted and came hard, laid out on the hood of the car like some kind of naughty pin-up girl.

But I wasn't done with her yet. As soon as she was done climaxing, she began to sit up, still shuddering in pleasure as she came down from her high. I allowed her a quick kiss, and nudged her back down again, my middle finger still buried in her cunt, moving maddeningly slowly. Taking it out, I placed two fingers in my mouth, sucking off her delicious juices, wetting them both before slowly working them back into her. Feeling her cunt adjust to me inside her was just heavenly, and I just stayed there for a second, relishing the feeling. Then I began to push them in and out of her, working her as she moved with me, moaning and groaning. I sped up, fucking her harder and hard.

When I thought she was getting close, I slipped in a third finger, hearing her gasp deeply, and I continued to fuck her with all three. She pressed down on them, and as she started to orgasm, I felt her cunt contracting on my fingers. I pushed them as deep inside her as I could, my other hand resting on her pelvic bone with my thumbs working her clit. As she came, she bucked off the car, her hips riding me. I discovered that she is just so fucking beautiful when she comes. I mean, all women are, but she was absolutely unbelievable when she climaxed. I rode her orgasm with her, and when she was done, and was splayed out on the trunk of the car, I pulled her close to me, kissed her, and lay with her while she got her breath.

Once we were back to our normal states, and her clothing was back on, she looked at me with a twinkle in her eye. I raised an eyebrow as she suggested we get a monthly pass for this garage. Who would have ever guessed that a first date would turn into a night for passion, sex, and discovery?

Bowl Me Over

Allison Wonderland

"Strrrike!"

From my place behind the scorekeeper, I follow proper pouting protocol. Grousing, griping, grumbling.

Freddie saunters over, swiveling her hips, smacking her lips. "How many strikes is that now? Five? Six?"

My pupils propel darts at Freddie. My finger flicks the crooked nametag affixed to her navy polo shirt. "Seven," I mutter, rising to my feet.

En route to the ball return, Freddie gooses my denim-clad derriere. I whip around, jaw unhinged, eyes expansive in diameter. A cross between Betty Boop and a Pez dispenser. "Freddie!" I chide, feigning indignity. "You fondled my fanny!"

"I know," she affirms, pressing her crotch into my backside. "And now I'm gonna hump your rump."

I dissolve into giggles, pushing Freddie away as her pelvis begins to gyrate. "If you'll excuse me, I have a game to lose," I inform the rump humper, sliding my fingers into the electric blue sphere.

I approach the foul line. Release the ball. Hear it clunk against the artificial wood. Watch helplessly as it veers into the gutter.

"Sorry, sweetie," Freddie croons from her swiveling chair. "But I really don't think this game is up your alley."

She giggles.

I glower.

Her eyes survey the empty establishment. Just me and my gal. "Well, on the sunny side," Freddie muses, releasing her hair from the elastic band wound around her tresses, "at least there's no one here to watch you strike out."

I decide to indulge her, perpetuate the banal banter. "Speaking of which . . . you, Miss Manager, are striking out with me," I counter. "Have I told you lately how much I loathe you?"

Freddie rises from her chair. Shoulders drooping. Head tilting to one side. Lower lip protruding in a pout. "Have I told you lately that you really bowl me over?" she queries, gliding her palms along my arms.

Every nerve ending beneath my skin hums.

Every sensory receptor in my body stirs.

Our lips connect.

It is a kiss as delectable as a hot fudge sundae. Oozing with thick, gooey chocolate sauce. Smothered with whipped cream globs in the shape of cumulus clouds. Drizzled with sprinkles in colors spanning the entire spectrum. And, plopped on top, the crowning glory: a single maraschino cherry, plump and succulent.

This is why I fell for Freddie. This is what has sustained our relationship for nearly three years. One chaste kiss, one ethereal touch, one clichéd quip, and I smolder.

Her hand meanders to my backside, slips into the pocket of my blue jeans. I feel her tongue probing my lips, demanding entry. Two pink ovals cleave, commencing an oral exploration. I navigate the familiar orifice. Trace the ridges and grooves of the hollow interior. Savor the flavor of her mouth, a fusion of grape bubblegum and sour apple jellybeans.

We disconnect, giddy grins tugging at our lips. We lean forward, foreheads contiguous.

"I love you," Freddie murmurs, whispers of air caressing my skin.

She clasps my hands, the silver halo of her ring pressing into my flesh. It is the ring I gave her for our two-year anniversary. I finger the studded red hearts embedded in the circumference.

"I love you, too."

Silence descends. It is a cozy kind of silence, the kind that lovers lapse into when words become superfluous.

Warmth radiates from her gaze, heat emanates from her body. Seeps into my pores, surges through my veins.

"I'll meet you back here in ten," Freddie murmurs. The guttural tone of her voice galvanizes my arousal, and I tremble slightly.

Moments later, I am standing at the sink in the restroom,

cleansing my hands under the faucet, waiting for Freddie to finish closing up.

The door to the washroom opens. A figure advances toward me. I glance into the mirror above the sink, admiring Freddie's reflection.

The eyes, with their jade-green irises that sparkle like a crystal chandelier. The mane, with its cardinal curls that swish against her shoulders. The figure, with its honey-hued skin and Mae West curves.

"Lemme give you a hand," Freddie offers, joining me at the sink. She compresses her breasts against the groove of my spine, her arms forming a wreath around my waist.

"That's *two* hands," I tease, nudging her abdomen.

The four hands caress one another, producing a foamy, sudsy lather. I angle my head, enabling eye contact. Freddie plants a kiss at the corner of my mouth, fingers tracing the dip of my hip, dampening my shirt.

She pries my thighs apart with her knee. Moisture pools inside my panties, absorbed by the thin strip of cotton concealing my cunt.

My hand fumbling for the faucet handles, rotating them counterclockwise in an attempt to halt the flow of water. "I thought . . . I thought we were waiting . . . till we got home," I stammer.

Freddie's fingers seize the hemline of my raspberry turtleneck, slither beneath the fabric. "Don't be such a procrastinator," she chides, faux demure and all allure.

I watch as she glides the top along my torso. I raise my arms above my head, assisting her in the removal of the garment. My bra is the next casualty, as she unfastens the clasp, divesting me of the garment. My body shudders, the erect nipples further stimulated by the cool temperature of the room.

I turn in her arms, facing her. Our lips connect. I untuck her polo from the waistband of her slacks, maneuver the shirt along her abdomen. Our mouths sever briefly, allowing me to remove it. My hands reach around her, digits perusing her back, pausing at the band to detach the clasp.

In unison, two sets of hands unfasten the buttons binding two pairs of blue jeans.

I face the mirror again. "I feel like I'm being watched," I remark, bashful, blushing.

Freddie's lips stamp kisses along my shoulder. "Don't be shy," she coos, peeling my panties from my bottom, sliding her skivvies down her thighs.

She swivels her pelvis, rubs her pussy against my backside. "Time for the daily grind," Freddie murmurs, her wetness oozing onto my flesh. Smooth and creamy, like melted ice cream.

One hand caresses my breasts, kneading, needing.

One hand scales my thigh, in pursuit of my pussy.

"Here, kitty, kitty," Freddie croons, her pitch the purr of a frisky feline.

She submerges her fingers in my cunt. Instinctively, I clench my eyes shut, reveling in the sensation. Succumbing to temptation, my lids flutter open, and I watch as our movements become synchronized.

Freddie curls her digits into a J shape, connects with my G spot.

She withdraws, then returns. Withdraws, then returns. Withdraws, then doesn't return.

My head pivots sharply. I fasten my gaze to hers.

Expecting, anticipating, salivating.

"You left me high and dry," I mewl.

Freddie inspects her digits, drenched and dripping.

She smirks. I simper.

"Well, maybe not dry . . ." I amend.

I watch as she guides her fingers to my mouth, traces the curve of my cupid's bow.

"Open," she instructs, and I move my lips asunder to allow the entry of her finger. My tongue strokes her skin, silky slick and sticky sweet.

She retreats to the cavernous aperture, liquid arousal seeping, creeping down my inner thighs, her digits plunging further and farther inside. She grinds her palm into my mound, moving her hand in concentric circles, generating friction, eliciting moans.

I whisper her name when I come, almost imperceptible, but I know she hears me.

"My turn," Freddie announces, and before I can resuscitate, my body has made a ninety-degree turn, my hand has made contact with a cluster of curls and ripples. Freddie is nothing if not impatient.

The corners of my lips curve into a gluttonous grin, and I am more than happy to reciprocate. But I take my time. And, as antsy as she is, Freddie doesn't protest.

I begin at the patch of chestnut-colored coils, nestled directly beneath her navel. Tickling, petting, stroking. My hand ventures lower, traversing the cluster of shiny-slick folds, navigating the calla lily lips. The skin is supple and succulent and shifts beneath my digits, exposing her clit. Gingerly, I touch the pad of my finger to the engorged nub. I feel it pulsating, like an accelerated heartbeat.

I observe the gratifying effects of my touch, a visible shudder and an audible moan. My eyes flicker to Freddie's heaving chest, beads of perspiration cleaving to her flesh.

My fingers find her cleft, skim the perimeter, teasing, taunting. Will I? Won't I? I will. I slide inside. Discover a deluge of molten lava, as though I've just dipped my digits into a vat of caramel.

I withdraw, then return. Withdraw, then return. Withdraw, then don't return.

Freddie's eyes, once at half-mast, are now wide open, and she blinks at me, dumbfounded. How dare I delay her impending orgasm?

"Park it here," I instruct, patting the freshly scrubbed countertop.

Freddie complies, hoists herself up.

"Good girl."

I giggle. She glowers.

"Do I look like a four-legged canine that barks and sits on command?" Freddie demands, her twinkling pupils belying the harshness of her tone.

My eyes traipse up and down Freddie's body. I scrunch my

brows, pretending to mull over her inquiry. "No," I conclude. "You look like a two-legged sex kitten who's smitten with a lousy bowler."

"But a not-so-lousy lay," Freddie points out, stealing a smooch.

"Touché," I concur, and wink, sink to my knees. The loyal subject kneeling at the feet of her queen.

Freddie is the first woman I have ever had the pleasure of pleasuring orally. Always a taker, never a giver, I am a self-proclaimed pillow queen. Or I was, until I met Freddie. A tit-for-tat type of woman.

I stretch my neck, advance toward the target, aim for the bulls-eye. And miss.

Freddie slams her thighs shut, creating a barrier between her lips and my mouth.

How dare she delay her impending orgasm?

Open. Close. Open. Close.

Access denied.

"You're such a tease, my little accordion."

Open. Close. Open. Close.

Roadblock. Minor hurdle. Detour.

I reach up, tickle her belly button, eliciting shrieks and swats and kicks.

Open.

Access granted.

"Good girl."

Our lips meet. My mouth makes contact with the tender tissue. My tongue maneuvers the slippery satin ribbons. Burrows into the undulating furrows. In search of the prized pearl.

I know I've found it when Freddie hisses, twists my hair around her fingers.

My attention strays from the cunt I am devouring, eyes drifting upward, drinking in her expression.

I marvel at the sight. The lips, pursed and glistening. The eyes, hidden behind clenched lids. The nose, wrinkled like a crumpled paper ball.

Freddie lifts one lid, gazes down at me. But before she can

inquire as to why her pleasure is once again on hiatus, I resume the stimulation, descending upon her cunt, ravishing her.

Freddie infiltrates my senses.

Her cries penetrating my eardrums.

Her scent filtering through my nostrils.

Her taste trickling into my mouth.

Her orgasm no longer impending.

I dab daintily at the veneer of nectar clinging to my lips.

"Have I told you lately," I query, rising to my feet, "that you really bowl me over?"

Freddie's mouth cleaves to the pillar of my throat. Bereft of cognitive thought, she can only nod in response, gliding her palms along my arms.

She climbs down from the counter, takes her place behind me, arms enveloping my midsection.

In unison, two sets of eyes turn toward the mirror. We examine our reflections.

Our hair is rumpled. Our complexions are rosy. Our expressions convey euphoria and serenity.

Silence descends. It is a cozy kind of silence, the kind that lovers lapse into when words become superfluous.

Just me and my gal.

Me and Freddie.

My Freddie.

My Freddie, who pours gelatin into ice cube trays, and sulks when the misshapen molds will neither jiggle nor wiggle.

My Freddie, who sings songs she doesn't know the words to, and ponders pseudo-philosophical questions, like, If there are convenience stores, are there also *in* convenience stores?

A giddy grin tugs at my lips.

My Freddie.

My Freddie intervenes when I bend at the waist to pull up my jeans. Detaches my hands from the fabric, guides me back into an upright position.

I look at her. Her pupils penetrate mine, dilating rapidly, an indication of her renewed arousal. She inclines toward me. Her palm covers my hand. Her chin perches atop my shoulder. Her lips locate my ear.

Freddie whispers something, but I can't make it out.

"Come again?" I probe.

Her response is a smug, self-indulgent smile, with a hint of debauchery.

"Love to."

Silent Penetration

Kinoya

I awoke with the taste of my girlfriend in my mouth, and the sound of thunder in the distance. A cool breeze crept through my window. I inhaled deeply, smelling the scent of rain and the hint of sex in the room. My body still felt sore from the night before. I lay there, rubbing the stiffness from my inner thighs; my pussy felt tight but wet. I turned to face my sleeping lover. At this moment she looked so peaceful, so calm, but last night she was the complete opposite. She never rushed; she makes sure that you are always aware of everything she does. There's an erotic intensity to her, it's always there when she is making love or fucking you with her calm masculinity. Just thinking about her that way was making me want to repeat last night all over again. I craved to have her between my legs rubbing her clit against mine. I caressed her strong shoulders and back remembering last night, how she slid into me as she lifted and parted my legs, placing one on each shoulder. I remember laughing to myself saying, "is she going to do what I think she is going to do." It wasn't until she began fucking me with long, deep strokes that I realized this may be old school but it was working for me. At this age, I wasn't sure if my knees could reach my ears, but like I said, there's that erotic intensity and attentiveness. Put those things together and you got me coming and wondering what will be the next position she will put me in and how soon will it happen.

I sat up in bed carefully pulling away the blanket, revealing the rest of my lover's body and her musky scent. Her smell drives me crazy. I almost went in for the kill, but I didn't. Instead I watched as the sunlight climbed slowly through the window, casting a perfect shadow of her naked body against the wall. I kneeled on the bed next to her, slowly tracing her shadow with one finger, stopping when I got to her ass. I left my shadow fantasy to admire the contour of her round ass, fighting the urge to run my tongue between her cheeks.

My lover moved a little trying to find a comfortable spot on the bed. After a moment she finally settled on her back. I waited until she fell back into a deep sleep; I wanted this moment all to myself. After a few minutes, I continued my "foreplay" I leaned over and gently blew on her nipple. I watched as it hardened. It begged to be sucked, so I did, careful not to suck so hard, just enough for it to arouse my mouth with its salty sweetness.

I lay beside her remembering last night, when she whispered to me "open your legs, spread your lips, and show me your clit." She watched me as I followed her instructions; I spread myself wide for her, showing her my world. She kneeled in front of me between my legs, playing with her nipples, making them harder and harder. She leaned over and moved her nipple up and down over my clit reaaallll slow; this was a new and sweet sensation. I watched as she worked her nipple into the folds of my lips, paying close attention to my clit, my clit beginning to swell and throb. Then without warning, she pressed her nipple hard against my clit and moved slowly down between my lips into my wet pussy. Then she would put it inside my hole, bring it out again, and rub it up and down. I let every nerve in my body focus on her nipple until my mind and body went into frenzy at the idea of being nipple-fucked.

I moved closer to my lover and kissed her on those full soft lips. She still had my scent on her breath. I moved my nose closer to her face, smelling her mouth, nose, and chin all saturated with my scent. I couldn't help but think of the times when my lover would use her lips to make love to my pussy, when she'd kiss so gently, so softly, that it would drive me insane. Her tongue would never touch me, just her lips and kisses would tease me; she would do this until I would come so hard I could do nothing but grab her by her head and be silent. Then there were times where I would be reminded about that special gift she has between those lips—that tongue. It would move like a snake around my inner thighs, lips, and clit. A little flicker here, then another little flicker there. It would move this way for what would seem like an eternity, tormenting me, fucking me, one minute pretending to let me come, the next it would stop without warning, sliding between my lips to lick me inside in circular motions, catching my juice. Then all of a sudden she would grab me under my ass, pull me close, and eat me with all her might. Her tongue fucking me, her lips sucking me, and her nose just buried, she would devour me until I was done screaming "God" and ejaculate on her face. She'd raise her head and look at me, with this faraway, glazed look in her eyes, her lips, chin, nose completely covered with my wetness. She would then show me her hand and I knew what would be next. I just wanted to wake her up, sit on her face, and shove her head into my pussy, begging her to suck me senseless. But instead I got out of the bed with wobbly knees and a wet pussy and opened the window a little more.

I stood by the window, the wind sneaking between my wet thighs. I liked the way it felt so I stayed there, closed my eyes, and leaned my head against the cool glass, letting the wind tease me. I loved having this moment to myself to think about my lover while she sleeps. As I stared out the window completely naked, I thought about how much of a good fuck she is, touching myself, enjoying the smell of freshly cut grass and wet pussy. I wanted to stay by the window taking in the breeze and rain, my fingers gliding from the center of my wetness up into my clit. My mouth became dry and my heart was pounding. But my legs got weaker and it became harder to stand; my clit got hard and I wanted to come so badly.

I looked over to my girlfriend and noticed that she was still sleeping. I wondered if she woke up right now what would be the look on my face. I walked over to the bed and stood over her. I looked over every inch of my "man's" masculine curves. Her pussy is completely bald except for the one patch of hair she calls her Mohawk. I like the way she holds my head, moving it up and down when I am sucking her off, pushing herself into my mouth, letting her bittersweet taste flow easily onto my tongue.

Then there are her abs, hard under soft, smooth, mocha skin. I wrote my name on her abs last night, my pussy juice was the ink and my finger the pen. She liked that, she liked how the letters shined against her dark skin in the candlelight. She said that my come was good for her skin, so I sat on her stomach rubbing my pussy back and fourth. She would flex her muscles making them harder and softer, keeping in time with my strides. I felt like I did when I was a kid. Coming home from school when nobody was home, I would sit on the arm of the sofa and rub myself back and fourth, pressing down hard. I always stopped before the point of climax, never having the courage to finish. But last night, that little girl was gone; I came all over my girlfriend's abs, leaving a slick, opalescent trail from her belly button to her Mohawk.

I looked at her hands, those long and slender fingers. They always seemed to be in the right place at the right time. Like when I am being fucked from behind, she always reaches over and plays with my clit at the same time, all the while never missing a stroke. Or when we'd masturbate together, she'd kneel between my legs, touching herself, watching me touch myself; she'd like when I rubbed my clit real fast and penetrated myself. She would vibrate her clit up and down, never taking her eyes off my fingers or my pussy. While she came, she would rub her pussy against my hand. I also liked when we were out to dinner, I'd just hold her hands in mine admiring the strength and flexibility of her fingers, wondering when the next time would be when I would feel them inside of me. Would it be on the way home in the taxicab or on the park bench that sits in the shadows, or would she take me on some dark side street, pushing me up against the wall and plunging her fingers into me.

After my imagination took me to exploitive places, I quietly got back into the bed. I held her hand in mine looking at her fingers. On two of them there was still residue from last night. I closed my eyes and smelled her fingers. I put the two fingers with the residue into my mouth, slowly moving my mouth up and down. My mouth began to salivate as I licked between her fingers. I just needed a quick fix. All I wanted to do was put her fingers inside me; my mind was going wild with ideas. Finally, I decided to get out of the bed. I placed one knee on the bed and the other leg on the floor. I took her hand and put two of her fingers inside me. I closed my eyes and just started to move up and down real slow; just having her inside me felt sooo good. I love when she is finger-fucking me; her fingers take command of my pussy, charming their way into me deeper and deeper until she opens me so wide that I can take her entire fist. I don't know how she does it. I never felt like this before, but before I know it I'm wrist deep in ecstasy. The fisting feels so good; it makes me feel like a dirty bitch, it never feels like enough, you just want it more and deeper. It makes me talk dirty—my lover calls me her "sweet little dirty mouth"—and by the time I am done coming all over her fist, I want to be fucked every way imaginable, and she delivers from the front to the back.

It feels so good riding her fingers; I feel my wetness leaving my body and working its way down her fingers. The sound of gushing wetness echoes in the room. I'm going to move just a little faster, oh yeah . . . This feels sooo good. I am trying not to breathe heavy or make a sound, trying not to wake her, but I am sure you can imagine that just the thought of what I am doing is enough to drive me crazy; the penetration is just sending my body into miniconvulsions. I think I could come like this without her knowing, my legs are shaking, but I could do it. Ooh yeah just a few more. Her fingers feel so fucking good. When I come it would be a secret only me and her body would know; I could come quietly, softly. I'm close to climax, just one more finger . . . aaaahhh yeah oh yeah, mmmm that's good. These long and sweet fingers can easily reach my spot. I'll just push down a little deeper, move a little faster ahhhhh yeah ooh baby give it to me, give me everything. I bite my lip to hold back the scream when I finally put her thumb inside of me. Yes . . . that's it . . . oooooh that's it, ooooh. I ride her fist with the sound of thunder in the distance and the smell of sex in the room. All the while she never said a word.

The Sighing Sound,
The Lights around the Shore

Charlotte Finch

The moment I saw her I knew. She strolled into the bar and there was a sudden lightness in my soul. With casual grace she crossed to the table and stood before me, her smile quizzical, her gaze penetrating.

We looked at each other for some time without speaking. There was a glimmer of recognition in my mind, although this was our first meeting. I felt I had known her before.

Her eyes sparkled as she gazed at me, and the corners of her mouth betrayed the beginning of a smile.

I found it difficult to breathe.

Finally she spoke. "Do you mind if I sit?"

"Not at all," I replied, never breaking eye contact.

As she relaxed in the chair opposite, I took a moment to study her.

She had a lean, muscular frame and the alert posture of an athlete. Her smooth skin seemed to glisten in the moonlight and contrasted sharply with the pristine white of her shirt. She wore her dark hair very short and had meticulously teased it into a tousled array of spikes. Her handsome face was almost feline, with high cheekbones and a delicate mouth. And her hazel eyes were rich and inviting like warm caramel.

I was transfixed.

She returned my gaze with a self-assurance that was challenging, but at the same time exciting.

"Have you been waiting a long time?" she asked finally.

I couldn't help smiling. "You arrived just in time."

She was suddenly serious. "Is there anything in particular you would like to do?"

I considered the question. All at once, a thousand thoughts collided in my mind and I blushed. "Maybe a walk," I ventured.

She stood immediately and offered me a hand.

Hesitating before taking it, I breathed in deeply. It seemed a significant moment and I wanted to be sure I was paying attention. Finally, I summoned the courage and placed my hand in hers. Her skin was soft and warm and as her fingers closed around my own, I felt an unfamiliar surge of elation. My legs felt strange as I climbed to my feet and my heart raced painfully.

She guided me out of the bar and to the street. Tourists passed in a blur as we headed from the bright, main strip and away to the darker streets beyond.

When completely alone, she suddenly turned to face me. "Where shall we go?" she asked in little more than a whisper. She was flushed and a light sheen of perspiration had broken out on her brow. Although late, the evening was hot and humid. Before I could stop myself, I reached out and stroked her face, moved momentarily by her androgynous beauty. She blinked twice and stared at me, as if I were a puzzle she couldn't quite resolve.

"The beach would be nice," I murmured.

She exhaled loudly and smiled a knowing smile. I squeezed her hand.

With renewed purpose, she turned and pulled me gently toward the sea.

We didn't speak as we moved through the darkness, but our entwined fingers danced frantically, exploring each other's hands and wrists.

I stole a glance at her serious face. Her forehead was creased with anxiety. I wondered if she were afraid or troubled. We were moving quickly, but I didn't want to wait.

I stopped suddenly. The cobbled road to the beach was deserted, and in the relative silence I thought for a moment I could hear my own heart beat. "Is this OK?" I asked nervously.

She sidled close to me and I felt her warm breath on my cheek as she whispered in my ear. "It's OK. I like the beach."

With her so intimately close, the raw energy was overwhelm-

166

ing. I wanted her so much I ached and I felt the growing excitement seep into my pants.

I breathed in deeply. Her scent was intoxicating, a heady mix of exotic fragrances: mango, citrus, spice, and the unique smell of her body. I closed my eyes and kissed the damp skin of her neck, causing her to gasp. She pulled me tightly against her and my stomach somersaulted violently. "Let's go to the beach," she whispered.

I walked in a daze, only vaguely aware of where we were going, as she led me from the road and through the tamarisk trees lining the beach. She stopped in a clearing, her eyes twinkling in the ethereal light. "Here?" she asked, her breath coming in short, sharp gasps. I shook my head. "By the water," I said and guided her farther into the darkness.

Finally reaching the shoreline, I stopped. The ocean lapped rhythmically against the swollen mound created by its relentless, tidal advance. I turned to face her. I was suddenly afraid. The feelings she evoked were distantly familiar and in their presence I felt awed and tiny. She sensed my trepidation. "Are you alright?" she asked, moving closer.

"Yes," I said.

She tilted her head curiously to one side. "Have we met before?" she asked, studying me closely.

"I think perhaps we have."

She rested her hand on my waist, her touch light and electrifying. I started involuntarily at the contact and she smiled. "What do you want?" she asked.

I hesitated and looked into her eyes. "I want you to fuck me." Then she kissed me.

And everything stopped. We were fixed in an instant, beyond everything that is and was and ever would be. Together, as though we had no right to have ever been anywhere except joined in that moment.

Suddenly I was overcome with a passion I hadn't known before. It started in my chest and consumed me. In an instant, we were prostrate together on the cool sand, struggling free from our clothes.

And then she was on top of me, her naked flesh warm and smooth against my own.

I felt the firm skin of her nipples and as her pussy brushed my thigh, the hot fluid of her arousal trailed over my skin.

Her mouth fixed firmly on mine, her tongue probing and searching. I moaned as she sucked my lips and teased me, flicking her tongue and biting gently.

I dug my fingernails into her back and pulled her hard against me, willing her to feel the intensity of my desire.

She ground her hips, urging her pussy against my own; I felt the heat from her and gasped as my stomach spasmed violently. Sliding her hands around my back, she pressed against me slowly at first, then worked up to a smooth rhythm. I sighed as her clit connected with my own and a bolt like electricity trembled inside me. She moved on top of me, kissing my neck and breasts hungrily.

I felt the surge grow in my core and I arched against her aggressively. She knew I was close and moved away.

"Not yet," she said, kissing my throat, my shoulders, then moving down to my breasts.

Anticipation welled inside me as she took my nipples in her mouth, sucking gently and then massaging each in turn with her tongue. I groaned and ran my fingers through her hair, longing for her to fulfill the promise.

With agonizing care she moved down my stomach, kissing me slowly and tracing every inch of flesh with an expert tongue. Her hands glided over my body, down my legs, then back and forth inside my thighs.

I could think of nothing except her inside me and my pulse roared in my ears as I willed her onward. I felt the heat of her mouth as she brushed my groin with her lips and moved inevitably down.

As she finally fixed her mouth on my pussy, I grabbed her head with both hands. Her tongue slid down and entered me forcefully. The sensation was blissful and I arched back in ecstasy. She rocked my hips against her mouth, pushing farther and farther with her tongue. I wrapped my legs around her neck and ground against her. I could sense her growing excitement and she moaned and held me tightly.

She began to work my clit with her tongue. It was swollen and she enveloped it with her lips and sucked forcefully, releasing wave after wave of excruciating pleasure.

I heard a voice somewhere. "*Oh fuck me. Fuck me.*" I didn't realize at the time it was my own.

In one swift movement she slid two fingers inside me, reaching deep with an animalistic urgency.

And that was as much as I could stand.

The orgasm ripped through me like a blade. I arched backward and squeezed her to me with unintentional force. Hot liquid erupted from deep inside me.

I was lost, my mind black, consumed entirely by the incredible sensation of her love.

Tides of bliss swept over me as she continued to fuck me until I could take no more. Exhausted I fell back, my body spent.

She withdrew gently and knelt across me, watching in silence as I lay motionless and gasping for breath.

Tenderly, she took me in her arms and held me against her, whispering soothing words in my ear. I don't remember now what she said exactly, but I do recall feeling a joy and love at that moment that triggered a distant memory.

She lay beside me on the sand and stroked my hair. I opened my eyes and looked up at the immense night sky. A million stars blinked down at me and a benevolent moon threw out a kindly radiance. Beside us, the ocean continued its relentless dance with the shore and the sound of their tenuous embrace was musical.

I turned to face her and she smiled affectionately. The moonlight accentuated her beauty and I kissed her. Stroking her face gently, I sighed. "I want to make love to you."

She returned my kiss and pulled away. "There's no need. I am completely satisfied."

She looked at me for some time and again I got the impression she was trying to solve a riddle that had her temporarily perplexed. Finally, she stood and dressed quickly, so I did the same.

Taking me by the hand, she led me across the beach, through the tamarisk trees, and to the dark, cobbled streets beyond. In silence we moved back to the bright lights of the town and in no time at all, were dodging tourists on the busy streets of Scala

Erossou. We returned to the bar where we had met earlier that evening and I sat in the same chair. She stood before me and smiled a quizzical smile, her gaze penetrating.

Moonlight stole through the broken canopy overhead as it shifted in the wind, and pale light danced momentarily across her beautiful face.

Before I could stop myself, I spoke.

"Will I see you again?" I immediately regretted the words.

"I think it is inevitable," she whispered.

For a moment neither of us spoke. She held out a hand to me and I reached out, caressing her fingers with my own.

She was suddenly serious. "There is a poem by Rossetti. It is very beautiful:

'Has this been thus before?
And shall not thus time's eddying flight
Still with our lives our love restore . . .'"

I was puzzled, but nodded my agreement. "I know of it."

She sighed deeply. "I will see you again."

And with that she was gone.

Insanity

Dawn Jones

I could barely control myself with her hands on my skin, leaving invisible marks that I knew I would feel for days.

She begged me to stop, shook her head no, but she moved me with her hands and hips and pleaded for me to continue. Her body wrapped around mine, her hands in my hair, tangling it into knots around her clenching fists as she moaned into my ear tiny pleas of self-satisfied surrender. Her tongue flicked out against my neck, leaving a long wet line that sent shivers running up my spine.

"God, I want to fuck you so bad," she whispered into my ear, rolling me over as she took control, her hands slipping up under my shirt. Pinned beneath her I had no choice but to surrender as she deftly removed first my shirt and then my bra with hands that nearly shook in anticipation.

Her breath came out in hot, moist waves against my skin as she shivered above me. Her eyes roamed my bare torso, taking in all of me, before meeting my own eyes with a look that took my breath away.

That's when she leaned in to kiss me, covering my mouth with her own and stealing away more than my breath. She took my heart with her kiss, swallowing it down with the sweet sounds of my own gasps as her hands squeezed my breasts with enough force to bruise my pale skin. My body reacted to her in ways it had never done before, pulsing with an intensity I had never felt. Every touch, every kiss, every lick sent new shockwaves that left me feeling dizzy and aching with a need that I had never experienced with such force.

I knew in that moment that I couldn't have stopped us now if I had wanted to.

She took my nipple between her teeth and bit, pinching and sucking all at the same time. I would have cried out but she covered my mouth with her hand, hissing between her teeth as she gently reminded me that we didn't want to wake anyone else in the house.

The urge to laugh shook me silently and she grinned up wickedly from her place between my breasts, her eyes shining with a fire that burned deep within her soul, a fire that threatened to consume me.

Her fingertips followed invisible trails as they slid down my sides, making me squirm, before their path was blocked by the waistband of my jeans and the belt that held them securely in place. She growled, an angry frustrated sound, her eyes meeting mine from where she now rested between my legs. The look in them was feline and predatory. My heart began to race. She grabbed the crotch of my jeans, forcing them against me, and growled again.

"Take them off," she demanded in a hushed voice, a tiny, ravenous smile turning up the corners of her full lips.

With shaking hands I complied as she watched. Her eyes followed every movement of my fingers as I slowly undid the leather belt and the clasp of the jeans. Impatience gleamed in those eyes and before I had the jeans fully unzipped she was pulling them from my hips, lifting me off the bed with her momentum.

Her smile spoke volumes as she took in the sight of me lying beneath her. The corners of her lips twitched. Time seemed to slow and I felt awkward beneath her penetrating gaze. Her years of experience were starting to weigh on my mind and I began to wonder what she was thinking, worrying that I was suddenly not what she wanted.

Her eyes met mine again and the look on her face softened as she consumed my fear, taking it into herself and understanding. She leaned over me, the fabric of her cotton tank top rubbing against my already sensitive nipples. Her lips touched mine, softly, and she whispered against my mouth. And I was lost in another kiss.

I was emboldened by her lips, the passion in her kiss, the fact that I could taste her tongue ring in my mouth and smell her arousal on the air as it mingled and merged with my own. I let my hands travel the length of her body, smoothing down her tank top before changing course and stripping her of the article of clothing. The air hit her bare skin and she breathed deeply, straightening, as I took in the sight of her.

Her body was beautiful: full breasted, tanned; her shoulders strong, broad, and covered in dark freckles that ran down her arms. Her skin was smooth as silk beneath my hands. Each breath caused her full breasts to rise and fall as she tried to drink in the air. The candlelight reflected off of the tiny silver barbell in her navel. Momentary awe struck me and I understood what had caused her hesitation when she had seen me. My breath caught, a lump in my throat, and I knew that the love I felt for her was laid bare in my eyes. So short a time and already I knew how much I loved her. Already she filled my heart.

I sat up, as far as I could with her straddling my hips, and laid a tentative kiss on her lips before moving on to taste the rest of her. I let my fingertips play along her skin with one hand at the small of her back as she arched herself to give me better access. I took one of her breasts into my mouth as far as it would go then let it out, nipping her nipple with my teeth and causing her to gasp louder than she had allowed me earlier.

I grinned mischievously as she yanked back on my hair, hard, bowing my own back and pressing our naked flesh together. The feel of her skin against mine, the warmth of her, caused me to moan against the curve of her neck. She tightened her grip in my hair and I moaned again. The sound of her honeyed voice joined mine and I knew that she enjoyed every sound I made.

Her lips found my ear and her tongue flicked out, tickling, as she whispered more seductive words. Illicit fantasies that she wished to play out. Things she wanted to do to my body, wanted me to do to hers, and every word made my body tighten more. Every hushed whisper made me wetter, my breath coming out ragged as I flushed in anticipation.

My hands slid down the curve of her back, into the waistband of her shorts, to cup the fullness of her ass and pull her tighter against my body. With quivering hands she tore at the front of the shorts, undoing the tie string that held them in place, and they quickly joined my clothing somewhere on the floor.

I laid her back against the pillows, resuming control, and took in the entirety of her.

I traced her collarbone with my fingertips, letting them trail a line between her breasts and along the soft contours of her belly. The candlelight that filled the room made her tanned skin glow and my hands against her looked oddly ghostlike. My fingers, long and thin and small, leaving goose bumps along the paths they created as they worshiped her, memorized her. I took my time, wanting to absorb every inch of the woman before me. Her eyes burned, their color changing with her passion. She tried to sit up but I gently pushed her back down, forcing her to suffer in her impatience while I took my chance and burned the sight of her into my memory.

My fingers reached the apex of her thighs, her hips rising to meet me, and I could see that the cotton panties she wore were soaked through with her need for me. My body tightened again, the ache of my own need almost unbearable. My eyes locked with hers as I removed the thin cloth. Her breath was fast and shallow, her eyes wide. I knew what she wanted. It was the same thing I wanted from her, but she deserved to be worshipped. She deserved to know what it was like for someone to take the time and love her body the way she needed to be loved.

I let my fingertips draw invisible circles on her thighs and she whimpered, reaching for me. I took her hands and let her draw me down on top of her, my leg between her thighs, pressing gently against her hot wetness.

Our lips met briefly.

"Please baby," she begged, her voice a hushed whisper. "Please."

I pressed my thigh more solidly against her and she whimpered, her body beginning to quake beneath me. Holding her tightly, I slid my hand along the length of her body, shifting my weight as I slipped it between her thighs and finally let myself touch the sweet, wet warmth waiting for me there. Her breath caught and for a split second I thought her heart had stopped, but

I could feel it pulse beneath my fingertips as I slowly slid them over the sensitive spot above her inner lips. Her body convulsed with the sensations I had sent shooting through her and I couldn't hide my fascinated smile. I tested the spot again and again got the same reaction, only the second time she grabbed a thick handful of my hair and twisted it in her fist, painfully, pulling my face to hers.

Our lips met and the kiss was deep, intense.

Her free hand encircled my wrist, pushing me away from the spot I had been so fascinated with, guiding me to where she wanted me. I took her direction and slid two fingers into the hot center of her. Her body arched and I pressed deeper, forcing myself farther into her, dragging a ragged breath from her lungs.

She bit my lip in her attempt not to scream out.

I slowly removed my fingers and she whimpered into my mouth. Tears began to stream down her cheeks as she twisted her fist tighter in my hair, her tongue filling my mouth. I tightened my grip on her as I slid three fingers in and she gasped. I felt her nails rake down my back and I winced, but the stinging only excited me more. I kept my movements slow, deliberate. I wanted to ravish her but I continued to move in a steady rhythm that her body quickly picked up. Soon her hips were rising to meet my hand.

Her grip on my hair tightened again and she pulled my lips away from her neck, where they had wandered.

"Faster," she demanded, haltingly. "Harder."

I complied, happily bending with her will.

I followed the rhythm her body began to create: a fast, hard ride that forced my fingers as deep inside of her as they would go. Each thrust brought sounds from her lips that I tried to muffle but the closer she came the harder it was to stop the sounds she made. Her body tightened around me, her thighs tensing. Her free hand slid down my arm, the other still tangled in my hair, and I felt her fingers join my efforts, rubbing the sensitive spot she had distracted me from earlier.

Her voice came out rushed, hot, and breathy as she begged, pleaded, and let me know that she was coming. Her body shook and laughter joined her tears as she began to release, crashing over the precipice I had taken so long to bring her to. She tightened around my hand until I could no longer move and her breath stopped as her body let go, soaking my hand and arm with her juices.

She held tightly to me, untangling her hand from my hair, as she began to breathe again, still laughing, still crying. I returned her embrace, smoothing back her sweat-soaked hair and kissing the perspiration from her brow as she slowly came back down to earth. I listened to her racing heartbeat as it slowed, felt her begin to take larger breaths as her body relaxed.

Soon she lifted my face to hers, kissing me lightly on the lips, smiling.

"I love you," she whispered as the candles burned out. "My sweetface."

B & E, & B

Heather Towne

When Melissa slipped her key in the lock and opened the door, she instantly knew something was wrong.

Her nostrils flared, scenting the faint, foreign smell of tangerine. Her pupils narrowed, sighting the slightly open drawer in her cubbyhole desk against the wall. And her ears pricked, sensing the far-off squeak of something moving somewhere in the apartment. All that, and the fact that there was light streaming from underneath the cracked-open bedroom door, clued Melissa into the probability that there was an intruder in her home.

She thought about phoning for the police, then dismissed the idea. This was her house (since moving out of the parental home two months earlier), and if anyone other than the snoopy landlord thought they could violate the sanctuary of her home and get away with it, well, they had another thing coming. Shy by nature, independence had steeled the girl. And having her Smart car and mountain bike stolen in the course of the past two weeks, and her identity briefly thieved, had left her growling like a crime dog.

She eased the door shut, lowered her pink canvas gym bag to the carpet. Fresh from Tae Bo, she was still wearing her pink exercise shorts and lavender tank top, long, blonde hair pulled back and tied with a violet ribbon, lean body oiled with sweat, primed for action. She ducked into a fighting crouch, slitted blue eyes piercing the darkness, hairs on the back of her long neck standing up and taking notice as another squeak sounded—in the bedroom. Her bedroom.

She glided across the living room carpet, slid up against the wall next to the bedroom door. She considered a weapon—a bread knife, a pair of scissors, that Jesus-on-the-cross letter opener her mother had given her—then dismissed that idea, as well.

Her hands and body were her weapons. Far from lethal, but certainly slightly dangerous, at least. And who wants a weapon taken away and used against them?

More squeaking. Closer now, Melissa recognized the sound: a drawer in her childhood, bunny-decorated chest of drawers being pulled open. She kept her underwear in that particular stick of furniture, and other, even less-mentionable things.

Coiled body buzzing with high-tension adrenaline, she reached out a shaking hand and used four trembling fingers to sliver the bedroom door even farther open. Holding her breath, she peeked inside.

Someone, a small figure dressed entirely in black—black shirt, jeans, and toque—was rifling through Melissa's drawers. *You don't send a midget to do a man's job,* the blonde thought grimly to herself, mentally sizing up the break-and-enterer at five foot two to her five foot eight; ninety-five pounds to her one-twenty-five.

The sneak thief plucked a pair of tiger-striped panties out of the drawer and casually sniffed them. And that proved the trigger point for Melissa's pent-up rage. She burst the door wide open and barreled into the room, squalling, "Grab wall, dirtbag!"

She was all over the perp's back in an instant, shoving the undersized intruder up against the wall and spreading arms and legs, pushing face into the winking-moon-and-grinning-stars wallpaper. Putting her Citizen Awareness Day activities at the local police precinct to good use.

"Make love to that wall!" Melissa bawled. She kept the cat burglar kissing wallpaper with her left hand, as she yanked a pair of black stockings out of the open drawer with her right. She jerked the robber's arms down, quickly winding the stocking around tiny wrists and knotting them together. "There," she rasped a rodeo eight seconds later, spinning the one-in-custody around. "Let's get a good look at you, scumbag."

A woman's face greeted Melissa, shocking some of the toughness out of her. A pretty, fine-featured face featuring a pair of brown eyes and red-glossed lips, and a thin, haughty nose. The woman looked to be around thirty, and she grinned at the bewildered blonde, displaying teeth as white as Melissa's knuckles.

"Guess you got me," she commented, leaning back against the wall.

Melissa blinked her eyes, recovering some of her confrontation at the other's insolence. She yanked the toque off the woman's head. Midnight hair tumbled free, collecting in a shimmering curtain around the woman's small shoulders.

"You're going down, lady," Melissa stated firmly.

"If you're lucky, Melissa," the woman replied easily.

Melissa snapped her hands onto her hips. "Just how do you happen to know my name?"

The woman grinned some more, glancing at the animal-print panties crowning the bunny-dappled chest of drawers. "It's sewn into all your underwear. My name's Gabriela, by the way."

Melissa chewed her lip and sniffed, "Well, I don't want to lose anything. There's a lot of crime in this area."

"Copy down all your vibrator serial numbers, too, huh?"

Melissa's eyes dove down to the bottom drawer, her face flooding crimson. "I'll teach you to go digging around in other people's private things." She flung her head back and marched over to the SpongeBob SquarePants phone on the bedside nightstand, punched in 9-1-1.

She had her back turned to her prisoner for only a moment, just long enough to be put on hold by the overburdened police department, when she heard Gabriela say, "Maybe you should use these?"

Melissa whirled around. Gabriela was holding up a pair of fur-lined handcuffs, her wrists free and clear.

"Hey! How'd you get—"

"I'm really up to no good tonight," Gabriela teased.

Melissa dropped the yellow sponge receiver and grabbed onto Gabriela's shoulders, pushing her down into the padded chair in front of the bureau mirror. She hastily pulled the woman's wrists back and cuffed her. Then she snatched up a pair of sheer blue stockings and fastened Gabriela's slim ankles to the metal chair legs.

"Better tie me up around the waist, too," Gabriela suggested. "I'm pretty slippery—when wet."

Melissa *had* noticed that the otherwise cool and collected

woman was perspiring almost as much as she was. So she dug around some more in her dainties drawer and pulled out a pair of black nylon panty hose, kneeled back down in front of Gabriela.

"Pull my shirt out of my pants," the woman instructed, "so you can tie it tight around my bare skin—like you did with my ankles."

Melissa glanced up from the tangled hose. Gabriela's face was glowing, her bronze skin shining, moist, her red lips parted and liquid-brown eyes half-hooded by long, black lashes. Like she was excited, almost; anything but fearful. Melissa dropped the panty hose in Gabriela's lap and anxiously cinched the stockings around the woman's ankles even tighter.

And as she did so, Gabriela moaned. Her eyes fluttered shut and she bit into her plush lower lip. Melissa quickly reached behind the hard-breathing woman to check on the boudoir handcuffs. Their faces almost touching, Gabriela's eyes suddenly popped open. And she kissed Melissa, soft and wet and urgent, right on the lips.

Melissa recoiled, stunned, staring into Gabriela's sparkling eyes. She wondered if the woman had just committed another chargeable offense; wondering just what she was up to; wondering, as well, if the soft, sweet impression left on her tingling lips would ever go away.

Her hands moved on their own, pulling Gabriela's shirt out of her jeans. Gabriela shuddered, full body jumping against her restraints when Melissa's fingers brushed her bare stomach. "Tie me up—tight!" the raven-haired beauty hissed.

Melissa rapidly threaded the legs of the panty hose around Gabriela's tiny waist, the woman gasping encouragement, her breath coming hot and humid in Melissa's burning face. Melissa knotted the panty hose legs together and cinched them tight around Gabriela's middle, the silky fabric digging into the caramel-colored skin.

Gabriela groaned, then desperately sought out the other woman's lips and found them, pressing her mouth against Melissa's mouth. Melissa just kneeled there and took it, her whole body flaming as hot as her face now, Gabriela's wet lips moving against her lips, tangerine-scented body spray clouding her mind, flooding her good senses, the woman's intoxicating lips and fiery heat setting Melissa's head to spinning.

"Tie up my chest," Gabriela breathed, the one controlling the situation, now and maybe from the beginning. She painted Melissa's lips with her wet, pink tongue.

Melissa rushed to dig yet another silk stocking out of the drawer, to obey the bound woman's command. She grabbed a white one this time, then fell to her knees and began wrapping the fine-woven leg garment around Gabriela's T-shirted chest, but she noticed Gabriela shaking her head. Melissa gazed up into the glistening pools of the woman's eyes, confused. Until another kiss exploded against her lips, and she knew what to do.

She hurriedly rolled up Gabriela's tight shirt, up and over the twin swells of her breasts. She stared at the golden apples, the pointing, chocolate nipples, hypnotized by the rapidly rising and falling beauty.

"Tie up my tits," Gabriela said.

Melissa sashed the stocking around the woman's bare chest, Gabriela gasping, groaning as the sensuous material covered and caressed her little breasts, draped her jutting nipples. Melissa knotted the stocking behind Gabriela, her arms encircling the woman's body and their mouths meeting, tongues flashing together. Melissa pulled back and was bedazzled by the stunning contrast between the soft, snow-white fabric of the stocking and the burnt-sugar rigidity of Gabriela's nipples.

"Suck my tits," Gabriela ordered.

Melissa bobbed her blonde head down and captured a silken bud in her mouth, sucked on it. Gabriela arched against her bonds, pretty head tilted back in exquisite despair. Melissa looked up at the straining woman, baby-blue eyes wide, earnestly sucking and sucking on a rubbery, stocking-sheathed nipple. Then she released the one shiny nipple and moved over to the other, engulfing it with her warm, wet mouth.

Gabriela's yelp of joy reverberated all through Melissa, the two women connecting on a level Melissa had never experienced, never even really considered before. She cupped Gabriela's wrapped breasts and licked the stiff, gauzed nipples, tugged on them with her lips, soaking them and the woman and clotting the stocking with her ardor. And when she sunk her teeth into a buzzing bud, she felt Gabriela shiver with pleasure, felt the woman's fingers dig into her blonde locks.

Melissa jerked her head back. "Hey! How'd you . . ."

Gabriela smiled, wagging her once-again free hands in front of the girl's astonished face. Then she said, "I'll show you how to really tie up a woman." She easily unknotted the panty hose that bound her stomach, the stockings that secured her ankles. Then, leaving the saliva-slick stocking around her chest, she jumped up and grabbed Melissa's hand.

"Um, I'm not really sure I want to be . . . tied up," Melissa hesitated, the spell temporarily broken like Gabriela's bonds. "Because, well, um, I don't, you know, really know you . . . that well."

"Think I'm going to steal the place clean while you're tied up, huh?" Gabriela wasn't smiling anymore.

"No, I—"

Gabriela yanked Melissa to her feet, jerked the girl to her toes in a half nelson. She steered the protesting blonde into the bathroom that ran off the bedroom. She racked the ducky-spotted shower curtain to one side and shoved Melissa into the tub.

Melissa stumbled over the lip, and Gabriela spun her around and lashed her wrists to the shower curtain rod with the same stockings Melissa had used to tie her down. Only the knots were much tighter, and became tighter still with struggle. And in the blink of an eye and bead of a pussy, Melissa was bound to the curtain railing, arms outstretched wide apart over her head.

Melissa fought against the bonds, rattling the rod, until Gabriela jumped up onto the enamel edge of the tub, grabbed the girl, and kissed her, mashing her mouth against Melissa's mouth, drowning out any further objections. She tore Melissa's tank top down the center, fully exposing the girl's chest.

Melissa hung her head, cowed by Gabriela's strength, her flashing eyes, and fearsome sexual hunger. Gabriela licked her lips and unhooked Melissa's bra, leaving the bound girl's pale, pink-tipped breasts hanging out and heaving in the open. She touched the soft, smooth flesh of a rounded breast and Melissa gasped, the shower curtain rod shaking in rhythm to the rest of her.

Gabriela jumped down off the tub and stripped off her own clothes, everything, except for the Melissa-wetted stocking around her breasts. Her body blazed bronze under the bright lights, pussy shaven clean, lips shining pouty and dewy. She leaped back up onto the tub and clasped Melissa's creamy-white body against her own brown body, melding their heated breasts together, her tongue swimming inside Melissa's mouth and thrashing about.

Melissa excitedly entangled her tongue with Gabriela's, desperately tried to wrap her arms around the woman's pulsing body. But couldn't. She rattled the rod in frustration.

Gabriela pulled her head and one arm back and touched a finger to Melissa's vulnerable rib cage. Melissa shuddered, the fingertip traveling light and infuriating over her electrified skin, up and into her open armpit, teasing and tickling. The finger looped back down again, over Melissa's tingling breast. She closed her eyes and savored the sensation, the raw, sensual feel of the soft, balled fingertip brushing her brimming breast. Then she flat out vibrated when the finger began tracing quick, fiery circles around her puffy aureole.

There were two fingers on Melissa's breasts now, tantalizing her, circling and circling her anguished nipples, tripping over the achingly erect buds. The fingers trailed down her breasts, her stomach, traveling into her dampened shorts and panties, and meeting at last at the blonde fur apex of her trembling legs.

Melissa opened her wet eyes and stared into Gabriela's eyes, hot tears rolling down her cheeks, her breasts and pussy burning like never before. Gabriela licked up the girl's salty emotion, then yanked her shorts and panties down in one fell swoop. She ran her fingers into Melissa's moistened fur, over the girl's slick, swollen pussy lips. Melissa fought with the railing, but it was no good. And oh so very good.

Gabriela slid two of her fingers into Melissa's dripping sex, Melissa hanging her head and whimpering and watching, feeling all through her body and soul Gabriela dig the two slender digits deep into her needful cunt. "Oh, God!" she moaned.

Gabriela kissed Melissa, frenched Melissa, pumped Melissa, cupping her own brazen pussy and rubbing, polishing her puffed-up button as she finger-fucked the tied-up blonde. "I can walk and chew bubblegum at the same time, too," she hissed, face contorted with lust.

Melissa quivered with delight, Gabriela's flying fingers swelling her with sexual electricity, pumping and pumping her full of white-hot joy. Gabriela glared at Melissa, bit into Melissa's lip, her own body shaking, fingers frantically buffing her tingling clit, the pressure building and building and building.

"Yes! Oh God, yes!" Melissa shrieked, the pussy-pistoning and trussed-up eroticism sending her sailing far beyond her bonds.

Gabriela screamed back, blistered by her own orgasm, fever-ishly fingering the both of them to gushing ecstasy.

When the last spasm had finally sounded, Gabriela slowly extracted her sticky fingers from the pair of smoldering pussies. Then she unleashed the violet ribbon from Melissa's hair and looped it around her own wrist, as a reminder, perhaps. She left the gasping girl hanging, quickly dressing and exiting the apartment.

Melissa popped the shower curtain rod out of its bracket at one end and easily slipped her hands off. She smiled—a satisfied, satiated smile—confident that the pussy burglar would one night return to the scene of the crime.

Incense

Geneva Nixon

I'm spellbound. Quite frankly, I'm unable to look away, breathe, or mutter one word. My eyes are fixed on her standing there, bathed in candlelight, grinning at me with her mouth half opened. Beautifully poised in her red satin night garments, the ends fluttering a bit with the movement of a moment's breeze. And now she stares back, speaking a million words a minute with her eyes alone, calling my name with so many words that my ears fall deaf but my skin hears. And hairs stand up now, tickling along my neck, goose bumps arise as well sending cold chills down my spine. It's enough to make me exhale deeply, fall to the floor, and lie there. Lie there and pretend that I am asleep and this is all a dream, for such a reality could never exist.

But she captures me again, hooks my eyes, and focuses my thoughts right back to her. Obviously she's reading them, she knows exactly what I'm thinking cuz suddenly she approaches me. Her feet hit the floor with the utmost amount of grace, more like floating over the surface. And with every step her breasts push their way against her garment, piercing it with her nipples, which only distract me more. Two feet away I pick up her scent, liquefying my brain on contact, rushing though my entire nerve system, commanding my heart to beat harder. One foot away my swallowing becomes hard, still unable to look away from her. Then here at last, face to face, she leans against me, placing her head under my chin to lay against my collar, pulling my arms around her. And I hold her because in such a moment she is God and I have no choice but to obey her every whim.

Slowly her hand rises to the side of my face, tracing along the edges of my lips as she lifts her head, smiling at me so slyly. My heart thunders now, and of course she knows this because two seconds later she kisses me, and such a kiss she gives is meant for one thing only: to ignite me. Spark my interest in making love to her, surrendering over to her laid plans. I kiss her back in the same fashion, now falling prey to her; holding her closer in my arms as I press my lips into hers, enjoying the movement of her tongue in my mouth. Then she lets go of my lips, kissing at my neck and collar, seducing me even more in her provocative game, sucking gently at both, breathing softly in between her kisses. Unable to restrain myself I spin her body and place her back against my chest, kissing her terrific skin along her neck as my hands pull up the front of her gown. "Yes," she mutters in her half breath, half moaning voice, wrapping her arm to the back of my head, pushing me down more into my own kisses. Pulling her gown higher and higher, now feeling the softness of her thighs, then higher still, until her gown is gripped in my left hand around her waist. Quiet now as my right hand slides up her inner thigh, feeling her own excitement rise as I watch her chest heave and fall. Watching her nipples cry for release from her gown. Upward my hand continues to go, feeling her wetness trickle down her inner thigh, igniting me more as she has probably foreseen. "Please," she asks of me, still using that moaning tone, as she breathes harder, pumping her chest now. How am I to deny such a being? Even now as my head lies on the back of her shoulder, smelling sweet perfume caught in her hair, I've set my course.

Now arriving at her sex, I slide two of my fingers into her, breathing heavily on her neck as I kiss at her skin, listening to her with my eyes closed, as she moans sweetly for me. And everything else was a blur . . . this is all I can remember. However, I do not blame it on her lack of fulfillment. No, she was wonderful at that. I blame the incense that took over the air the moment I knew what I was doing. The moment I knew that she had won, and checkmate was hers once again.

About the Contributors

MORGAN AINE has been penning poetry, short stories, and erotica for many years. Her imagination has fired her passion for erotica. She is an active member of the Erotic Readers Association. Her emphasis is on BDSM-themed erotica with some lesbian, vampire, and vanilla sex tossed in for good measure. Her erotic writing has been showcased at various Web sites, such as ERA, AmoretOnline, Adult Story Corner, and Emerald Collection. She lives beside a large lake in the South with four cats and one very annoyed large dog. Her boyfriend provides scenes for her BDSM and vanilla themes while her lesbian roommate offers great input for those fem-to-fem themes.

Author RAVEN BLACK still prowls the streets of the French Quarter with lover, Charlotte Whyte. She constantly seeks that first kiss of autumn that inspired her as a child in her hometown, New Orleans.

Canadian-born JOSEPHINE BOXER began her writing career in 1986 as a music journalist. She's worked in print, radio, and television, including directing a couple of music videos. Previous lesbian erotica pieces have been published in *The Good Parts* (2005) and *Tales of Travelrotica for Lesbians, Volume 2* (2007). Currently, she and her writing partner are shopping around a two-hour feature film script, which she describes as "a lesbian love traumedy."

RACHEL KRAMER BUSSEL (www.rachelkramerbussel.com) is an author, editor, blogger, and reading series host. Her books include the Lambda Literary Award finalists *Up All Night* and *Glamour Girls: Femme/Femme Erotica; First-Timers: True Stories of Lesbian Awakening; Naughty Spanking Stories from A to Z 1* and 2; *Spanked: Red-Cheeked Erotica; Yes, Sir; Yes, Ma'am; He's on*

Top; She's on Top; Caught Looking; Hide and Seek; Crossdressing; Soles; Ultimate Undies; Secret Slaves: Erotic Stories of Bondage; Dirty Girls; Rubber Sex; and the nonfiction anthology *Best Sex Writing 2008.* Her writing has been published in over one hundred anthologies, including *Best American Erotica 2004* and *2006; Best Lesbian Erotica 2001, 2004, 2005, 2007,* and *2008; Single State of the Union; Desire: Women Write About Wanting;* and *Everything You Know About Sex Is Wrong.* She's contributed to *AVN, Bust, Cosmo UK,* Fresh Yarn, Gothamist, Huffington Post, Mediabistro, *New York Post, Penthouse, Playgirl, San Francisco Chronicle, Time Out New York,* and other publications. She serves as senior editor at *Penthouse Variations,* hosts and curates In the Flesh Erotic Reading Series, and wrote the popular Lusty Lady column for the *Village Voice.* Her first novel, *Everything But . . . ,* will be published by Bantam in 2008.

CHARLOTTE DARE's fiction has appeared in several online publications, and in print in *Travelrotica for Lesbians 2* and *Ultimate Lesbian Erotica 2008.*

CHARLOTTE FINCH has worked in education for ten years and currently works as a deputy head teacher in a school for young people with special needs. She is a prolific writer in her spare time, concentrating on short stories, poetry, and plays. She has recently completed her first novel. She lives in Lancashire in the northwest of England and enjoys long-distance running and hill walking.

SHANNA GERMAIN is a poet by nature, a short-story writer by the skin of her teeth, and a novelist-in-training. Her work, erotic and otherwise, has been widely published in places like *Absinthe Literary Review, Best American Erotica 2007, Best Bondage Erotica 2, Best Lesbian Erotica 2008,* and *Salon.* Visit her online at www.shannagermain.com.

DAWN JONES is pleased to have her first published story as part of *Wetter.*

ABOUT THE CONTRIBUTORS

SHANNA KATZ is a sex-positive, kinky queer feminist with a love for all things related to sexuality. Currently, she's working on her master's of human sexuality education at Widener University, and hopes to continue in the field of sexuality. Originally from Colorado, she currently lives in Pennsylvania with her cats, Kinsey and Athena, and is constantly exploring her own sexuality as well as the concepts of sex, gender, orientations, and sexuality in general. Her Web site is www.essin-em.com.

RANE KETCHER was born in Washington, D.C., but her hometown is Annandale, Virginia. She has lived in Massachusetts, Florida, Wyoming, and now Pennsylvania, where she has settled down with her partner, Diana. She has poetry and short stories published, and is currently working on a novel to center around a historic lesbian romance.

KINOYA is an African-American lesbian originally from Brooklyn, New York, currently residing in Atlanta, Georgia, with her fiancé and their two children. She writes lesbian poetry and erotic short stories, and is currently working on an erotic book containing poetry, short stories, and a poetic memoir.

SHERI LIVINGSTON lives in South Carolina, and after twelve years, her partner is Still the One. Writing erotic stories wasn't a dream, it just became the dream . . . and she hasn't woken up yet. Please see her print and e-books at www.sherilivingston.com.

LORA McCALL is recently retired (thirty-one years as a professor, fifteen years as a department chair—and thirty-five years as a lesbian) and has published in the academic world. She is now doing freelance work. Her story, based on a real-life trip to Maui, is her first attempt at erotica.

SHANNON McDONNELL, a freelance writer and photographer, is the author of thirty stories (and counting) published in *Penthouse Variations*. Her erotic fiction has also appeared in the Alyson anthology *Body Check: Erotic Lesbian Sports Stories* and

189

in the magazine 18 formerly *BabyFace*). McDonnell lives in Arizona.

GENEVA NIXON is a twenty-two-year-old college student living in Bayou City, also known as Houston, Texas. She's always been amazed by the chemistry between two women—the split seconds that are exchanged between them as arousal climbs. It's her goal to capture that essence within everything she writes. That way, those who aren't sure what pure ecstasy feels like will be able to experience a taste of it from her written words.

SAPPHYRE REIGN is an entrepreneur and native of Texas. Addicted to the language of literature, Sapphyre read extensively as a child and penned short stories and poetry for fun, but it eventually became imperative to her existence. As an adult, writing allows her to breathe and express all the hidden places she dares to take others. And creative passions, such as photography, spoken word, and motivational speaking, allow her to share pieces of herself and the art of creativity. She loves to inhale the beauty of words and exhale the experiences she discovers on every journey she invents, walks, or lives.

KR SILKENVOICE has been writing and recording erotic stories since 2005. She writes in an attempt to reach others, to help them rediscover the sensual immediacy of life, and to provide erotic material that women and couples can enjoy. She attended one of the Seven Sisters colleges, where a roommate gave masturbation workshops and occasionally borrowed her "toy" collection for demonstration purposes. This story arises from her experiences there.

DIANE THIBAULT is a queer writer and translator who lives in Toronto, Canada. She enjoys pushing the boundaries of dyke sex in her writing and in her life. Her work has appeared in *S.M.U.T.* magazine, *Hot Lesbian Erotica 2005*, and *Sexiest Soles: Erotic Stories About Feet and Shoes*.

JULES TORTI's work and devilish thoughts have appeared in

ABOUT THE CONTRIBUTORS

Karin Tulchinsky's *Hot & Bothered* series (1, 2, and 3); Maxim Jakubowski's *Mammoth Book of New Erotica;* Alyson Books' *Beginnings, Early Embraces 2, My Lover, My Friend, Awakening the Virgin,* and Nicole Foster's *Ultimate Lesbian Erotica 2007.* Jules finally scratched out her own epic novel, *Accidental Love and Death,* which will one day soon move from her laptop to your hands. She lives on the west coast of Canada with her perfect partner and a golden retriever, working as a massage therapist by day, and dreamy writer by night.

HEATHER TOWNE's writing credits include *Hustler Fantasies, Leg Sex, Newcummers, 18, FRM, Forum, Abby's Realm, Scarlet,* and stories in the anthologies *Skin Deep 2, Mammoth Book of Women's Erotic Fantasies, Show & Tell, The Good Parts, Tales of Travelrotica for Lesbians 2,* and *Ultimate Lesbian Erotica 2005.*

RAKELLE VALENCIA has coedited several fascinating erotic titles and has written for some of the sexiest anthologies on the shelves today, including several from editor Nicole Foster at Alyson Books.

NICKI WACHNER lives in Arizona with her wife and two dogs. When not working her daily job with tech support she can be found reading or writing. She started writing when she was seventeen. She thanks her large group of friends and family for their support.

YEVA WIEST loves writing erotica and comedy, and tries as often as possible to merge the two. Her work appears in *Tales of Travelrotica for Lesbians 1* and *2, Fantasies 3,* and will be released in the upcoming anthologies *Best Lesbian Love Stories: Summer Flings* and *Ultimate Lesbian Erotica 2008.* Her e-books include *Paybacks Are Hell* and a forthcoming novella *Apache Eyes,* an erotic lesbian western. Yeva's MySpace URL is www.myspace.com/yevawiest.

ALLISON WONDERLAND has a BA in women's studies, a weakness for lollipops, and a fondness for rubber ducks. Her favorite sound is Fran Drescher's voice, and her cocktail of choice is a Shirley Temple. Allison's first venture into erotica, "Quite Contrary," received an Honorable Mention in For the Girls' 4th Birthday Fiction Competition. In addition to erotica, Allison pens plays and flash fiction, and is also a mixed-media artist.

TARA YOUNG moved from Pennsylvania to Oregon in search of a fresh start and a new life. By night, she edits articles for a newspaper, and later at night, she edits manuscripts for a lesbian publishing company. Her first short story will appear in *Ultimate Lesbian Erotica 2008* from Alyson Books.